King of the Gypsies

Advance Praise for *The King of the Gypsies*

Lenore Myka is a skilled craftswoman, sketching stories so exquisite and sincere that their power is unexpected and often fierce. She imbues each tale with candor and nuance, letting her characters thunder forth on their own, unprotected from life's realities yet carried by the dream of how things could be. The result is a portrait of Romania painted by its disenfranchised, its émigrés, and its foreigners, that shakes off stereotypes—or digs down to their roots—and hones in on the hopes and the vulnerabilities that dwell in the human soul. Rarely have I felt so quickly drawn in to a collection of short stories. Rarely have I wanted to begin again as soon as I reached the end.

—Sarah Erdman, *Nine Hills to Nambonkaha: Two Years in the Heart of an African Village*

The stories in Lenore Myka's *King of the Gypsies* do what we want great fiction to do—illuminate the world for us with fresh lighting. Under Myka's unblinking gaze, the world illuminated is both harrowing and heart-wrenching—Romanian orphans and street kids fighting for survival, the trafficking of teen prostitutes by their "husbands"/pimps, American aid workers (and American parents of adopted Romanian orphans), feeling out of their depth while trying to help. These are stories complex and relentless, their characters unsparingly yet empathetically observed, the moments of quiet connection rich and startling. Lenore Myka's triumph is that she illuminates not just with fresh lighting, but with lightning.

—CJ Hribal, *The Company Car* and *The Clouds in Memphis*

Lenore Myka's collection of short stories, *King of the Gypsies,* heralds the debut of an extraordinary writer. With compassion, insight, breadth of knowledge, black humor, and an exquisite use of language, Myka crosses from Romania to the United States and back again, telling tales of characters cruelly haunted by having lived under totalitarian rule. Each story is brimming with wisdom about the human condition; this is an author I would trust and follow anywhere.

—Marnie Mueller, *Green Fires, The Climate of the Country,* and *My Mother's Island*

King of the Gypsies

Stories

Lenore Myka

winner of
the G. S. Sharat Chandra Prize for Short Fiction
selected by Lorraine M. López

BkMk Press
University of Missouri-Kansas City

BkMk Press
University of Missouri-Kansas City
5101 Rockhill Road
Kansas City, Missouri 64110
www.umkc.edu/bkmk

Financial assistance for this project has been provided by
the Missouri Arts Council, a state agency.

Executive Editor: Robert Stewart
Managing Editor: Ben Furnish
Assistant Managing Editor: Cynthia Beard
Author photo: Dennis P. Callahan
Romanian language consultant: Dr. Bogdan Suceavă

BkMk Press wishes to thank Betsy Beasley,
Ashley Wann, Siara Berry, Paul Tosh, Alexandra Wendt.
Special thanks to Zoë Polando.

The G. S. Sharat Chandra Prize for Short Fiction wishes to thank
Valerie Fioravanti, Laura Maylene Walter, Leslie Koffler, Linda Rodriguez.

Library of Congress Cataloging-in-Publication Data

Myka, Lenore
[Short stories. Selections]
King of the gypsies : stories / by Lenore Myka.
pages cm
"Winner of the G. S. Sharat Chandra Prize for Short Fiction, selected by Lorraine M. Lopez."
ISBN 978-1-886157-99-6 (alk. paper)
1. Romanians--United States--Fiction. 2. Americans--Romania--Fiction. 3. Romanian Americans--Fiction. 4. Romania--Fiction. I. Title.
PS3613.Y52A6 2015
813'.6--dc23

2015028303

ISBN 978-1-886157-99-6

Printed in the United States of America.

Acknowledgments

Grateful acknowledgment is made to the following journals where these stories first appeared: "Day of Lasts," *Iowa Review*; "Wood Houses," *West Branch*; "National Cherry Blossom Day," *Alaska Quarterly Review*; "Lessons in Romanian" and "King of the Gypsies," *The Massachusetts Review*; "Real Family," *Booth Journal* (Winner of the 2013 Short Story Contest); "Palace Girls," *H.O.W. Journal*; and "Rol Dobos," *Upstreet Magazine*.

I owe tremendous thanks to the many people whose help and encouragement sustained me through the process of writing this book: Kevin McIlvoy, Dominic Smith, C.J. Hribal, Stacey D'Erasmo, and the community of friends I discovered at Warren Wilson College's MFA Program for Writers; Emma Patterson, agent and friend; Memory Blake Peebles and Lisa Van Orman Hadley, whose careful reading of the stories here was essential to its completion; and Sean Cotter and Bogdan Suceavă for assisting me with Romanian language usage. Extra special thanks goes to Jennifer Wisner Kelly who read and edited the book as if it were her own. The Writers' Room of Boston provided the gift of space and Somerville Arts Council financial gifts; many of these stories were written there. Thanks to my parents, siblings and extended family for being the most enthusiastic cheerleading squad ever. I'm indebted to Jason Bassilakis for his patience, generosity and love, and for never once suggesting that I might find a more useful and lucrative way to spend the time I otherwise spent writing, believing always that my artistic pursuits were of the utmost value.

Finally, this book would not exist were it not for the wonderful and inspirational friends I made in Romania and in the Peace Corps who took care of and embraced me while I lived there. Special thanks to Livia Marinescu. Your love and support made this book possible.

For Jason

Contents

Foreword

In *King of the Gypsies,* Lenore Myka's characters release uncountable fibers, connecting them to one another in the linked narratives, binding them to the harshly beguiling Romania they inhabit and that inhabits them even after departure, and extending to us as readers. From the first page, such sympathetic threads fasten us to these bold beings whose actions flow forth as causes before returning as inexorable and often harrowing effects.

—Lorraine M. López
Final judge, G. S. Sharat Chandra Prize for Short Fiction

King of the Gypsies

In the park behind the orphanage, Dragoș clambers up onto one of the few remaining stone busts of Ceaușescu, perching like an oversized pigeon on the crown of the former dictator's head. In the hubbub following the revolution, that statue was forgotten; when it was rediscovered the locals just shrugged their shoulders. *Ce să facem?* they muttered to each other, but no one had a reasonable answer. They were all too exhausted by events of recent history to bother knocking it down. And so it remains, converted without needing to be redesigned into a jungle gym for Dragoș and the other children like him.

Dragoș takes a moment to scan the burnt-out patch of grass surrounding him. The other children play tag and hide-and-seek, their bodies made runt-like from the angle at which he observes them. The roses that line the perimeter of the park, like everything else living here, have been left to grow as they wish. They entangle each other's thorns, their heavy buds browning at the edges, the scent of their nectar souring in the relentless sun. In the far corner is a dense cluster of trees and bushes. Dragoș has seen men go one by one into that thicket of overgrowth before, only half-hidden, satisfying themselves. Indeed, he has accidentally stumbled upon them on more than one occasion, chasing after a loose soccer ball that finds its way towards that particular corner of the park. Although their looks terrify him, their eyes strangely wild or squeezed shut, their mouths frozen in a grimace, he knows without anyone having to explain it to him that they cannot harm him. Somehow, in that moment, they are more vulnerable than he.

Dragoș brushes his thick, shaggy hair from his forehead, puffs up his chest. "I am King of the Gypsies!" he declares.

The only child to pay him any attention is Răzvan. Răzvan is missing his left hand, and he brandishes his stub at Dragoș. Dragoș has always thought the end of Răzvan's stub resembles the dried prunes his mother would force him to eat whenever his stomach felt bloated.

"The Gypsies did this to me," Răzvan snarls before another child tags him, calling out: "You're it!" The possibility of conversation, of fierce argument, is left behind. Răzvan is off, chasing a girl who runs with her arms held up, birdlike, the folds of her skirt catching between her thighs.

Dragoș has heard stories like this before. Children, homeless children living on the street or taken from the state facilities, are used by adults. They beg for money all day long, and in the evening the adults come for them, scooping up every last cent, giving the children a bite of bread, perhaps some salami if they're good. Sometimes, so the rumors go, they sever limbs to make the children more pitiful and thus, more lucrative.

But it is not the Gypsies who do this. Dragoș knows better. The day before his mother brought him to the orphanage she gave him a bit of advice. "Whatever you do," she urged, "don't believe everything people tell you about us." As if he already had made this mistake, she cuffed him gently on the back of his head.

It's an organized system, Dragoș knows, an intricate ring, like the Mafia. The business of begging.

"Not *Gypsies*," corrects Dragoș, even though Răzvan is no longer listening, "*Italians*. Italians!" He pounds his fists against his chest, letting out a howl that echoes across the park. The other children stop and stare up at him, mouths unhinged, a line of dark, fleshy holes. He has the rest of the world's attention. For now.

The dog is one of the two dozen or so that lie at night in the yard of the middle school and terrorize the children up and down the street when they go from the *casa de copii*—the children's house, the orphanage—to school every day. He is the single black mutt in a pack of dirt-colored mongrels.

The other children have named the dog Țigan. "He's a special dog just for you, Dragoș," they laugh, giving Dragoș a shove in the direction of the snarling animal, who barks out one ferocious warning, a stream of milky saliva dangling from his jaws. The dog lurches, but Dragoș isn't afraid. Without pause, he kicks the animal in the ribs the same way he kicks a soccer ball during recess. It yelps and cowers, trying to seek solace in the pack of other dogs that growl and crouch in the shadows of the crumbling block apartments, the laundry hung out from windows, listless in the still Bucharest heat.

Dragoș hates these dogs. Especially that black one. When he first began living at the orphanage, he was too small to defend himself against the dog. Once it chased Dragoș five blocks from school, all the way across Piața Amzei, past the rows of eggplant and tomatoes, the melons and loaves of bread. People were everywhere but no one seemed to notice the terrified boy, the raging and frothy-mouthed dog. Țigan caught him at the back of his ankle just as Dragoș attempted to climb the single tree that grew despite the city scene surrounding it. Dragoș could feel the dog's teeth sink into his Achilles and pinched his eyes tight, the pain so severe he lost all ability to cry out. But then it was the dog that was crying out, yelping in such anguish that for a moment Dragoș took pity on him. A man from a nearby vegetable stand had left his potatoes and onions behind and was beating the dog off of Dragoș, grabbing the animal's jaws and wrenching them open. "*Du-te dracu!*" he cried, waving the end of a broomstick at the dog, which, limping and dragging itself, ran away.

The man scooped Dragoș up in his arms. It reminded him of the way his father used to carry him, one strong arm tucked under Dragoș's knees, the other bracing his thin back.

The man gave Dragoș an onion, peeling it for him. He ate it as if it were an apple, the juice cutting crooked paths in his dirtied skin. The man checked his wound, patching it up with a bunch of napkins from a nearby coffee shop, securing them with twine.

"Do you live at the *casa*?" the man asked Dragoș. Somehow they always knew.

Dragoș nodded even though he'd always thought it a misnomer: home of children. The *casa* resembled nothing of the single-bedroom apartment he'd known to be home for the first five years of his life. It was nothing like the houses in the old and outlying areas of the city, where people grew grapevines across cool patios, had enormous bedrooms and kitchen tables where you could sit and watch your mother or grandmother prepare stuffed cabbage on a Sunday afternoon. Instead, it was hollowed and damp, with bars covering the windows, a fence crowned with barbed wire. There was no place to hide but the single cot each child was assigned in rooms where a dozen or more of them slept at night.

"Alright then, I'll take you back," the man said. "But first: what would you like?" He waved his hand across the *piața*. He wore a wool cap that was frayed at the brim and his skin was as dark as Dragoș's but from outdoors, not from birth. Dragoș could see the white pinpricks of a beard appearing on his chin.

"Cherries," he whispered. "I'd like cherries."

The man carried Dragoș all the way to the *casa*, handing him off to the director at the front door, never crossing the threshold. He suggested to her that she might want to have a doctor look at the wound; the dog had been wild, after all. Later, sitting on his bed in the dormitories, waiting for the doctor to arrive, Dragoș dug into the brown bag of cherries, selected one, and peeled it open with his fingernails.

"You must check for worms," his mother had warned him, holding up an example. "See?" He saw just in time the white tail end, the creature burrowing deeper, hiding from the open air, the world outside.

Tonight there were no worms, just the deep red color of the fruit's pulp. Dragoș smiled as his popped the cherry into his mouth, sucking the pit clean.

Now Dragoș is bigger; he no longer fears the dogs. He carries stones in his pockets to fend the dogs off, hurtling them whenever the animals threaten to come closer. He likes to save a few extra ones just for the black one, Țigan.

The girl is thirteen, a year older than Dragoș, but she is so thin and malnourished she looks eight. She is dressed in a long floral patterned skirt and an oversized t-shirt emblazoned with "New York Bulls" and "#1," and wears a silk scarf tied across her head. The gold coins woven into her braids were never removed; they clatter against each other when she walks down the hall to the dormitories.

"Her older sisters brought her here," the director of the *casa* explains to Dragoș, running her long fingernails through her curly, purple-hued head. "They snuck her out of her parents' home the night before her wedding."

Dragoș waits through the story, wondering what any of it has to do with him. When the director moves around her desk so that she might sit closer to him, her perfume surprises him, traveling through his opened mouth, the smell of jasmine catching at the back of his throat.

Dragoș coughs and squeezes out a questioning "Yes?" brushing tears from his eyes.

"Cover your mouth, Dragoș," the director scolds, frowning in a way that suggests she doesn't expect any better from him.

"We want you to watch out for her," she continues, gesturing toward the closed office door. "Not to take care of her but to help her out. To be her *buddy*. " The director uses the English word. It's been bandied about a lot at the *casa*, ever since those British social workers came last summer to train the orphanage staff in "more modern" childcare techniques. He remembers one of those Brits, a young man who laughed at everything people said to him, even if it wasn't a joke, his face straining from the weight of a persistent grin. He played soccer for hours with all of the boys at the *casa*. Dragoș had liked to sit next to him and touch the downy blond hair on his arms. His name was Peter, but they all called him the Romanian equivalent, Petre.

Before he left, Petre promised to send Dragoș a postcard from Bristol. After nine months, Dragoș is still waiting.

"Do you understand, Dragoș?" the director asks now. Without waiting for a response, she leads him to the door of her office, giving him a gentle shove through it. "Go see that she's found her bed, would you? Her name's Irina."

Dragoș finds Irina in the last room of the eastern wing, the wing where all the girls sleep. His face goes hot as he passes the open doors of the rooms, feeling the eyes of the girls on him, scowling, whispering to each other and occasionally to him. "You're not allowed here, Dragoș," they say, not bothering to disguise their hatred. He does not look beyond the toes of his sneakers, his chin tucked to his chest.

Irina is alone in the room, sitting on the bed closest to the window, the one that has been claimed by a particularly popular girl at the *casa* named Luminița. Irina is holding one of Luminița's dolls in her hands, singing and laughing to herself.

She does not look up when Dragoș enters the room, but says: "This bed is mine now. These dolls are mine." She hugs the one in her hands, as if this will magically make it so.

"You can't sleep there," Dragoș says. "That's not your bed. This one here is." He points to the only empty cot in the room. It is unmade, a wool blanket, white sheet, and pillow stacked on top of the stained mattress.

Irina sneers and fixes Dragoș with her eyes. Her hair is dark like his, as is her skin, but her eyes are blue with shards of gray cutting through them, like Petre's. "I'm not sleeping there," she says and turns back to singing and telling herself stories no one else must understand.

The other children start referring to her as Dragoș's sister. "Tell your sister she's late for breakfast," they say, or "Your sister cheats at checkers." Irina doesn't seem to notice, or at least she does a good job of ignoring them. Instead, when the others begin to tease her, she pulls the scarf from her hair and waves it around her, singing a song in a language they cannot understand, perplexing them, laughing and grinning like she has a secret none of them will ever know, jutting her bony hips at them.

Sometimes she spits at their feet so they run, screeching in all directions around the schoolyard. "Humpf," she declares, hands on hips, when they have all gone away. "Humpf."

Irina does not know how to read. "It's useless," she says, "why bother?" She says that her father and uncles wouldn't let any of the women learn how to read; they would beat them with magazines and books if they found them hidden in the house. "It's not a woman's place," she explains, a dull expression settling on her face.

In class, the teacher matches Dragoș and Irina together and tells him to help her. But the minute the teacher turns her back, Irina rolls her eyes and mutters under her breath, imitating the teacher, giggling wildly, unabashedly when she reprimands her. Once, she throws Dragoș's book at the window. It hits a vase of freesia another student had brought for the teacher that had been sitting on the windowsill, spilling water and shattering glass. Irina stands, defiant. "I don't want to be here," she shouts, and as if it were that simple, marches out the door.

"Why does she do that, Dragoș?" the other children ask.

It infuriates him that they ask incessantly, more so that he does not have an adequate enough answer to satisfy them.

One morning Dragoș goes to the cafeteria for breakfast. The room vibrates with the nervous chatter of children, the clattering of spoons and plates. He takes a seat next to Răzvan who whispers, his eyes going wide, "Irina is gone."

Her husband-to-be, he says, discovered where her sisters had hidden her. He stole her back in the night, creeping into the dorm room so quietly that none of the other girls awoke, not even when the gold coins still woven through her braids jangled warnings.

"They're probably already married," Răzvan says, his voice tinged with envy. "I bet they live in one of those houses, the ones past the airport."

Dragoș knows the houses he's talking about; he saw them once from a bus he took out to the country with his mother. He'd heard they had dozens of rooms in them, but not a single piece of furniture; just rugs covering the cement floors. Enormous houses, he remembers, like castles, with spires of copper, roofs made of shiny tin. He imagines Irina's face staring out from a third story window of one of those houses, looking down on him with her crystalline eyes, her lips pursed in a secret grin.

When Dragoș's father left for Germany, he said that he would be back in a year to get Dragoș and his mother. After two years had passed, his mother said that she was leaving as well, to look for him.

"You'll be fed in the *casa*," she'd said. "You'll go to school."

"What if someone takes me?" Dragoș was trying to be brave, but his lower lip trembled when he asked. After all, other families had done the same thing and were never reunited. There had been his neighborhood friend, Constantine, whose parents had placed him in the *casa* when they'd been run out of their apartment and had to live on the streets. One weekend, when they went to visit him, he was gone. A couple in America, they'd been told, had taken him back to their home in a place called "Boy-zee."

"They won't," Dragoș's mother replied, fixing his shirt collar, licking the pad of her thumb and wiping the corners of his mouth, neatening her son up before she left him behind.

"But what if they do?"

She kneeled before him and grabbed his small shoulders in her hands. "They won't, Dragoș. No one will take you."

The way she said it, her jaw set, angry almost, he knew she was right and that the reason, the secret to her knowing, was some deficiency inside of him, something so horrible that no matter how hard he might try, he'd never be able to change.

That was seven years ago. Dragoș waits for that time when he will be eighteen and old enough to go find his mother and father himself. He does not have a passport but he has befriended one of the men who stand outside the post office, muttering to people as they pass, *marcs, forints, dolar,* all day trying to trade money for money, tricking more out of people than they realize. Once, when Dragoș told the man that he was going to go to Germany when he was eighteen, the man said: "Let me know. I'll get you a good deal on a passport." When Dragoș asked how, the man smirked. "Just like that," he replied, snapping his fingers.

Every evening, after lights out, Dragoș lies flat on his back and practices the art of remembering. He grows stronger and taller but it seems, to him, his mind grows weaker. Sometimes he cannot recall his mother's face; his father's has left him completely but for the pinched corner of his mouth squeezing a hand-rolled cigarette between cracked lips. He would prefer to recall with vividness the important moments—the day trip they all took to Lake Snagov when Bucharest was in the midst of a heat wave and the water had been shut off for weeks, the last birthday he spent with his mother; how it felt to be held in her arms. Instead all it seems he can remember is the food prepared in the kitchen of their old apartment on the thirteenth floor of the block building next to the National Stadium—eggplant salad smeared on warm bread, stuffed grape leaves and polenta with sour cream, crêpes rolled with cherry preserves, the shots of *palincă* served as nonchalantly as orange juice at breakfast. Sometimes the only part of her body he can recall is her hands floating over and around him, serving him plates and bowls of food—fried eggs bathing in a puddle of sunflower oil, sour tripe soup. "Eat," she would say, "eat, my king of the Gypsies."

Always he obliged her. Even the tripe soup.

There is news of more foreign visitors to the *casa*. Someone says they are from France and will be bringing trucks filled with donations.

"Great," Dragoș overhears one of the cafeteria cooks yawning one morning as she slops cream of wheat onto plastic trays, "ten more tons of butter. Just what the children need."

It's true, the donations are sometimes disappointing. Once the clothes that arrived were for adults; not a single thing fit any of the seventy-eight children housed at the *casa*. Another time a van-load of books came from Israel—all in Hebrew. Most painful was the dozen televisions and stereos from a church in New York—without a single electrical converter so that they might be plugged in. They still sit today in their crisp cardboard boxes, collecting dust in the *casa* basement.

But regardless of past disappointments, the children are optimistic, especially Dragoș. Days after the first whiff of news passes through the cold halls of the orphanage, he has learned that the trucks carrying goods won't be coming from France after all, but from Germany. He is convinced it is a sign. His mother, maybe even his father, is coming back finally to get him. He cannot contain his joy, his absolute conviction, and when the other children tease him in the schoolyard one afternoon shortly before the scheduled arrival date of the donations, Dragoș hurts them in the best way he knows how.

"My mother and father are coming to get me," he boasts. "They'll be on that truck from Germany. When are *your* mothers and fathers coming to get *you*?"

Some of the smaller girls' eyes fill up like buckets. But the boys scuff their shoes against the gravel, kicking up silvery clouds, muttering to each other, *Lies, Dragoș lies.*

Răzvan eyes Dragoș suspiciously. "How do you know they're coming for you?"

"They're coming on the truck," Dragoș replies, stepping close to Răzvan, as if his question is a threat, even though he knows Răzvan is no match for him and could never be, not with only one hand.

"That's not what I asked." Răzvan's tone is cool. "I asked *how* do you *know* they're coming for you?"

"I just do," Dragoș replies, suddenly flustered.

"Did you look in your crystal ball? Or your coffee grinds?"

This gets a chuckle from the other boys, who echo Răzvan—*yeah, you look in your crystal ball 'er somethin'? Coffee grinds! That's funny.*

"You're just jealous," Dragoș whines, turning his back on the crowd of children that has gathered, heading toward the doors of the *casa*. "You'll see. They're coming like they always said they would."

A week later, the trucks arrive, pulling up to the front door of the *casa*. There are three of them total. The *casa* staff members and children crowd on the front steps, applauding as the engines of the trucks are cut, shouting *Bine ați venit!* The cabs of the vehicles are high up above them so that no one can see inside; they all stand on tiptoe, craning their necks, as if this might help them get a better look.

Dragoș squeezes his way through the bodies of the other children, vying for a spot at the front of the crowd. As the doors swing open he searches the faces of the visitors, studying their expressions and mannerisms for a familiar smile, a shrug of the shoulders; he's not sure how much his parents have changed since he last saw them and is afraid that he won't recognize them. Two men from the first truck step down. They are tall and wear heavy work boots. Dragoș watches on as one of them approaches the director and shakes her hand. This man is too tall to be his father. Dragoș peers past him to get a look at the face of the other following close behind, but sees that this man is too old. His heart flutters against his ribcage, seeking an escape. He makes his way to the second truck and stands still, staring up at the cab, waiting. A man that looks no different to Dragoș than the first two steps down and grins, ruffling the top of Dragoș's head, unaware of the agonized look the child has given him.

Dragoș runs to the rear of the line. This cab is empty; he follows the sounds of voices coming from behind the trailer and takes in the last two guests. There is nothing remotely familiar about these men, nothing in the tenor of their voices or the way they move—as if they are in a hurry to get back to Germany—that is comforting. And there are no women—not a single one—among them.

Dragoș seats himself on the ground under a tree, just a few yards distant from the trucks, pulling his knees up to his chest, covering his face with his arms. "Where's Dragoș?" he hears one of the children—perhaps Răzvan—asking. "I want to ask him which of these guys is his dad!" There is a crackle of laughter; another voice saying: "He's probably looting the trucks!" This comment is followed by the muffled reprimand of a teacher and then the director, clapping her hands to get the children's attention, barking orders to other staff members to better manage the crowd.

The men begin unloading used clothes and toys and furniture from the trailers, occasionally passing the lighter boxes of donations to the children who, despite the warnings of *casa* staff to *Step back! Let the men through!* cannot be contained. There is so much excitement—so much rifling through goods, trying on clothing, squealing over stuffed toys, snacking on candy the men hand out—no one notices when Dragoș scurries behind the building and across the playground, wriggling on his belly through a hole at the bottom of the fence, stepping out into the street beyond.

He wanders the city, cursing his failing memory, trying hard to remember the streets that will take him there, a place he hasn't been to in years. If he had any money, it would be an easy trip, just the number 36 trolley, all the way to where the line ends, at the back gate of the stadium. But he has nothing in his pockets and so he walks, trying to recall landmarks. There is the small square with the dried, crumbling fountain, unused for years; when he comes upon this, he is encouraged to continue. It starts to come back to him. Just beyond this square should be the American and French consulates, and the Belgian and Greek embassies, their wrought-iron fences opening only for dark-colored Mercedes sedans with foreign license plates, their sidewalks swept and hosed daily. But the city is dark; there is only the infrequent streetlight to help him, and he cannot see anything clearly unless a passing car flashes its dim headlights across his path. He continues anyway, following an instinct, a tickling in his gut that tells him this is the right way. And after hours of walking, his feet sore, blisters rubbing his heels raw, he comes to the place.

The gates of the stadium are closed and locked, the shortcut made inaccessible. He will need to take the long walk around the traffic circle, down seven more blocks. His legs ache and his head pounds; he hasn't had anything to eat or drink for hours, the excitement of the donation trucks' arrival having made him lose his appetite. But he manages the seven more blocks, knowing that at the end there will be rewards he hasn't allowed himself to imagine for years.

He nearly runs into the street sign, his eyes following the pole of it upward so that he can read: *Strada Pescărușului*. He turns right onto his street and heads into the apartment complex, a gray, giant-sized Lego-like creation; stack upon stack of cinderblock buildings rising precariously high, defying modern engineering, gravity.

The parking lots surrounding the block apartments are flooded up to the front walks. A main pipe must have broken again; somewhere off in the distance is the sound of running water. The sidewalks are invisible under the black sheen of water and so Dragoș must walk through it to get to the far side of the apartment complex. His steps break the perfect stillness, sending ripples that travel out beyond his scope of vision. The liquid is cool and oily and rises up mid-calf on his legs, so that he must roll his trousers above his knees.

Around him, the hundreds of apartment windows are black but some glow blue and flicker with the ever-changing scenes on televisions. Here and there a smattering of women shake out the last of the laundry, hanging it from lines fastened outside their bedroom windows or, if they live in one of the nicer apartments on the twenty-third and twenty-forth floors, from balconies five feet long, three feet across. Dragoș can see the red dots of cigarette butts above him, occasionally making out the outline of the face doing the smoking. One man hisses at him from some unseen spot above his head. *"Ce faci acolo?"* he asks, somehow aware that Dragoș isn't doing what he should be doing, isn't in the place he should be in at this time of night.

The entryways of each apartment building are lit with a single, yellow light. Dragoș reads the numbers and letters. *Block D, Staircase 12. Block E, Staircase 14.* He wonders for a moment if he missed it and stops, confused.

"What are you looking for?" a voice asks out from the darkness surrounding him.

Dragoș pauses, looking for the source of the question.

"Over here."

Off to the right, slightly behind him, an old woman pulls weeds from the patch of dirt that frames the apartment building, careful not to harm the tomato plants she is growing there.

"It's too hot for sleep," she explains, as if Dragoș had asked her why she was gardening at such a time of night. "So: what are you looking for?"

"Block F." Dragoș murmurs so quietly she asks him to repeat himself. "Block F. Stairwell 10."

The woman brushes her hands on her skirt and points toward the letters and numbers fading above the door. "This is it."

The elevator doesn't work. But then it never did. His body used to be familiar with climbing the thirteen flights of stairs but by the fifth floor Dragoș is gasping for air. Moths beat themselves against the exposed light bulbs on the ceiling of each landing; the air inside is heavy and hot.

The apartment is just across from the elevator; Apartment 13D. "D for Dragoș," his mother used to say to him. "We picked this apartment just for you."

The sound of radios and televisions echo out in the hallway; somewhere near the end a door closes. Dragoș stands in front of the door to his old apartment, straining his ears to hear something from inside—his mother's voice maybe, his father whistling a melancholic tune. But there is just silence. He raises his fist to knock but then sees the black buzzer next to him. It wasn't there before; it's something new. He presses it with his thumb and waits; presses again and waits. No one answers. He starts to do it rhythmically, counting the time: buzz, one-two-three; buzz, one-two-three.

"Just a goddamn second!" a voice from inside suddenly roars. "Who the fuck is it?"

Dragoș steps back from the thin door just as it swings open. The man is wearing boxer shorts and nothing more, he smells of vodka and sweat. Dragoș turns and runs, racing back down the stairs, skipping the last four steps, jumping hard on each landing.

"You think it's fucking funny waking strangers up in the middle of the night?" Dragoș hears the man yell after him. "Some fucking practical joke! You worthless piece of shit!" Out of the corner of his eyes Dragoș sees the blurred faces of people peeking out from their apartment doors as he races by. They are all waiting, watching for him.

Dragoș is within range of the *casa* when the sun begins to rise; a thin, horizontal sliver of gold against the blue-gray sky. His legs have passed the point of being tired, his stomach from being hungry. He is too exhausted to cry and too distracted to notice the cluster of people standing outside a bar as he heads toward it. It isn't until he is about to pass them that he overhears their conversation. They are talking about him.

"Hey! You!"

Dragoș looks up and through bleary eyes sees Irina before him. She is the only girl surrounded by a group of men. She is wearing the same clothing as before but the gold coins have been removed from her braids and her face is painted up in a clownish fashion with make-up, lipstick running from her mouth, mascara dotting the deep crescents under her eyes. A man who looks to be twenty years older than her has his arm draped over her shoulders.

"Do you want a piece?" he asks Dragoș, pointing at Irina with his free hand. "Fresh Gypsy pussy. Virgin pussy. We can make a deal."

Irina laughs, burying her face in her companion's chest, holding the folds of cloth from his shirt in tight fists. But when she sees that Dragoș has continued to walk on, she extricates herself from the man's hold and stands out on the sidewalk, defiant.

"Hey! You! Dragoș!" she yells. Dragoș turns at the utterance of his name; she's never used it before now. When she sees she has his attention, she claps her hands as if she is privy to a tune no one else can hear, and starts to dance, shaking her hips left and right. The man who held her before now begins to sing; one of his buddies taps a rhythm on his thigh, the others whistle and yelp. Irina laughs, tossing her head back, her face pointed toward the gradually lighting sky. She raises her arms up above her head, rotating her wrists in slow circles, humming along to the song the man is singing. It is as if these men have hypnotized her with their song; she is at its whim. Irina is twirling and spinning now, faster and faster, so that the tail of the scarf in her hair becomes a multicolored halo encircling her head.

At the steps of the *casa*, Dragoș sees that Țigan is waiting for him, his tail tucked between his legs, his eyes bloodshot with exhaustion. The beast rises to his feet when he sees the boy approach, letting out a growl, but Dragoș is ready for him, realizes that he has been expecting the dog to be here. He reaches his hand inside his pocket and runs his fingers over the sharp edges of the rock, feeling the density of its matter. Pulling it out, Dragoș raises the rock, tossing it once or twice in his hand. Looking the dog straight in its eyes, he draws his hand back past his head and takes aim.

Lessons in Romanian

I.

Apple is *măr*. Peach is *piersică*. Watermelon is *pepene verde*. The banana is *banana* or plural, *bananele*. Tomato is *roșie* and yes, it is a *fruct*—fruit. Cherry is *cireașă* or *vișină*, depending on whether it is sweet or sour. Lemon is *lămâie*, but *fii atent!*—if you mispronounce this word, you will be asking for something quite different from a lemon.

What? she asked.

What *what*? asked her language tutor.

What will I be asking for?

Her tutor went *sfeclă*—beet—red. We don't discuss that here.

For the entire three years she lived there, she never bought a single lemon, because to buy one required asking, and to ask risked her asking for (so she'd learned from Andrei) a blow job.

II.

Left-handed is *stângace*.

The first day of class, she wrote her name on the board and the students burst into shouts of *stângace, stângace*! They were so loud that the teacher in the next room came over to see what all the noise was about.

After order had been restored, Ovidiu raised his hand.

Yes, Ovidiu?

Why are you left-handed?

It's just the hand I use.

My father was left-handed, said Iona, but his teacher forced him to use his right, slapping his knuckles—she demonstrated with her ruler, rapping it on the desk—each time he tried to switch.

Bill Clinton is left-handed, said Ștefan.

So was Jimi Hendrix, said Lavinia. He played his guitar like this—she pretended to strum with her left hand—and the bass strings were on the bottom. My brother told me that.

I want to be left-handed, said Rodica.

III.

I love you is *te iubesc.*

Andrei said *te vreau*—I want you—and she wondered if it was like the Spanish she'd learned as an exchange student in Salamanca her junior year of college: *te quiero*—literally translated as I want you—meant the same thing as *te amo,* I love you. But no, the French teacher at her school and her closest friend Dana said. No. It doesn't mean the same thing. It means he wants you.

Sometimes he said *am nevoie de tine*—I need you—and she nearly believed it.

He's using you, said Dana. He thinks you're rich and can take him to America.

She hadn't said that maybe she might be using Andrei too. Just *puțin*—a little bit.

Sometimes (more often than she liked) he asked her: How hard is it to get a visa to the United States of America? Those were the only words he knew in English: *United States of America* and *cool* and *fuck* and *shit,* which he pronounced *sheet.*

Hard, she said, her fingers making figure eights around the small areolas of his nipples.

Can you help me?

He didn't understand; she was just a volunteer, she got paid two hundred dollars a month to live and teach there, she wasn't even allowed to enter the embassy.

I can ask, she lied.

Satisfied with her answer, Andrei smiled and disappeared under the sheet.

IV.

Homesick is *dor de casă*.

The first question people invariably asked her was: *Nu ți-e dor de casă*? Don't you miss home?

Bineînțeles, she said. Of course.

The second question they asked her was: What do you buy at the market? Followed by: What do you cook for food?

Pasta, she answered. Rice. Chicken. Vegetables.

Still, people were always knocking on her door and offering her elaborately prepared meals covered with linen napkins and presented on chipped china plates. They peered past her, trying to see what was in her kitchen, looking for evidence of the pasta, rice, chicken, and vegetables.

Thank you, she said, taking the plates but failing to invite them inside. It's very kind of you but really not necessary. I can make my own food.

But sometimes, after spending an entire weekend alone or not receiving a single letter for days or being unable to put a telephone call through to home, she'd sit at her kitchen table and gaze out the window across the courtyard to the wall of ivy that undulated and shivered in the wind. Then she'd make herself a meal of the insides of a loaf of bread, a box of concentrated fruit juice, and cigarettes.

V.

Sometimes her mother sent her packages from home. These included mixed cassette tapes, women's magazines, her favorite chocolates, peanut butter. Sometimes her mother sent her clothing because hand-washing stretched everything out, or because the soap turned all her whites gray, or because she was too tall or too broad, her breasts too large or her hips too wide, her ass too big, to fit into anything here.

Once, her mother sent her bras.

In addition to waiting for its arrival for a month and a half, when it arrived in order to get the package she had to take first one and then another tram to a satellite postal office on the far outskirts of town. She had to stand in line for nearly two hours. Finally, she had to wait for the women who worked there to inspect the package.

Take a look at this, said one postal employee to another when they saw the bras.

Ce fine sunt! Where are they from?

Din State, bineînțeles.

Can I see? said a woman standing in line.

Yes, please, said another. Hold them up!

My, my, all the women in the post office clucked. Look at those colors! Look at that lace! Such fine material!

The men gawked but remained silent.

As a general rule, she did not like to bribe. She did not like to feel that they were taking advantage of her simply because she was from America; she was proud that people sometimes mistook her for a native Romanian or, at the very least, Hungarian. But in this instance, she felt it was worth it, just to get the hell out of there. Please, she said, slipping the women a five thousand lei note. May I take my package now?

VI.

Water is *apă*, and sometimes, there wasn't any. Not in the bathtub, not in the kitchen sink, not in the toilet.

When will I have water again? she asked her landlord.

In a week, he said. The whole district's water has been turned off.

A week passed, and then another. She knocked on her landlord's door. I still don't have any water.

He shrugged. Neither do I. Or your neighbors. Or your neighbors' neighbors. He gestured in the general direction of the nearest shop. Buy some bottled water for the time being.

But when will it return?

How should I know?

Sometimes, she wrote home, I just hate it here.

VII.

Mişto is a *ţigan*—Gypsy—word, her neighbor told her, tossing a clump of weeds from her flower garden. I don't recommend you use that word.

Her neighbor was growing snapdragons, daisies, lilies, black-eyed Susans—words she'd never learn to say in Romanian.

Doesn't it mean *cool*? she asked. What's wrong with saying *cool*?

Her neighbor looked at her. You know *ţigan?*

She didn't answer; she felt unskilled at such conversations. But if she had answered, she might have told her neighbor that the flower garden reminded her of the skirts of the Roma women who sold *anti-baby* in the open air markets every weekend.

All of her students used *mişto* though. They told her that English was *mişto*, MTV was *mişto*, Indians and cowboys were *mişto*. They told her that Beverly Hills was *mişto*, and so was Texas.

They said baseball was *mişto*: would she teach them how to play? She didn't know much about it beyond the pick-up games she played as a child, but the volunteer agency provided her with bats, balls, and gloves. She taught them vocabulary: *first*, *second*, and *third base*; *home plate*; *single*, *double*, and *triple*; *homerun*, *foul ball*, *outfield*, *infield*, *umpire*, *pitcher*, *catcher*. The word *shortstop* was their favorite; they chanted it as they rambled out of her class and on to French each afternoon. *Shortstop, shortstop, shortstop*!

What is this shortstop? said Dana. They're driving me crazy with this shortstop.

She took them to the park down the block from the school; they used plastic shopping bags with pictures of naked women on them for bases. Her teaching amounted to the one thing she recalled her father telling her when she was first learning to hit: Keep your eyes on the ball. She'd forgotten how hard it was to learn this, hitting a ball with a bat. The students swung and spun, swung and spun. She gauged the atmosphere for mounting frustration. But they were undeterred. Each time someone hit the ball all the students applauded, including those on the opposing team, who threw off their gloves, tossing them as high as they could into the air.

They told her her accent was *mişto*, they wanted it—an American accent, *her* American accent. This made her laugh because for years her college roommates had made fun of her nasal As and hard Rs. She'd worked so hard to lose it. But her students shouted, No! *E foarte mişto!* It's very cool!

Much better, said Violeta, who rarely ever spoke up in class, than a British accent.

VIII.

Mişto and *shortstop* were words she loved because her students loved them. *Şmecher* was another word she loved, a word her language tutor taught her how to use but told her was difficult to translate. Dana said Andrei was *şmecher;* her neighbor said Gypsies were.

Sly, her tutor said, is the closest. But it's more than that. It's also clever and cunning and a little bit bad.

IX.

I've heard, said Andrei, that it's easy to get a visa. Really, she said. She dared not ask how, but he read her mind anyway. Yes, he said. You just have to get married and—he snapped his fingers—it's settled.

I'm hungry, she said, rolling out of bed.

She knew two words for cheese: *caşcaval* for hard and yellow; *telemea* for soft and white. In her refrigerator, there was only a bland *telemea*, not salty enough for her tastes, and no *caşcaval* at all. She pretended not to hear him when, from the other room, Andrei suggested they get married. Instead, she sliced the remaining bread and cheese and returned to the bedroom with a plate.

Hungry? she asked.

When he finally stopped trying and left for good, she didn't cry because she wasn't sad. She just remembered how it had been before Andrei, that whole first year, single and alone. She had been only twenty-three; when she'd first begun teaching, the guards mistook her for a student and prevented her from entering the teachers' lounge. Her closest friend was more than a decade her senior; no one could comprehend why a girl her age would want to come here alone, why her parents would let her.

X.

When toasting, you raise your glasses and say *noroc*! Or *sănătate*! Or even, sometimes, *salut*! If you are ethnically Hungarian, you do not clink your beer glasses, only your wine glasses. If you are ethnically Romanian or German, you clink all glasses, as long as they are full.

She stood with Dana and the biology instructor in the teachers' lounge, waiting for the faculty meeting to begin. The secretaries—the same two fuchsia-haired women who frequently asked her if she was C.I.A. in the same manner they asked for the time or the weather—arranged food and beverages. There were plates of salami and cheese, cucumbers and tomatoes, homemade cakes and meatballs dripping fat.

The biology teacher poured her some țuica and held his glass up. How do you say *noroc* in English? he asked.

Cheers, she said and swallowed her shot down. The biology instructor immediately refilled it.

Easy, said Dana. They don't have faculty meetings like this in the United States.

Is that true? the biology teacher asked her.

She nodded. There's not even food, much less liquor.

What a pity, he said, filling her glass again. Cheers! he said, and again: Cheers!

XI.

Goodbye is *la revedere* or *pa* or *ciao*.

I studied French at university, Dana said, folding blouses, placing them like delicate, breakable things into her suitcase. Brâncuși fled to Paris too.

Is that what you're doing? Fleeing?

It's easy for you to judge, Dana said. You'll be leaving soon enough. You've always had that luxury. You don't know what it's like, knowing you may always have to stay.

XII.

Christmas is *Crăciun*.

Her students liked to learn songs in English, particularly holiday songs, and so she taught them as many as she could: "Jingle Bells," "Here Comes Santa Claus," "Walking in a Winter Wonderland," "White Christmas," which it inevitably was. She taught them her favorite: "I'll Be Home for Christmas."

Every year, they held a school assembly. Her third and final year, her students appeared on stage, explained that their American teacher would be leaving shortly after the school year ended, and they were dedicating this song to her.

I'll be home for Christmas, they sang, *you can plan on me.*

XIII.

Floarea soarelui is sunflower.

When she returned home, people rarely asked her about her time there. When they did, they wanted to know about Dracula, the orphanages. But once, at a dinner party, a woman seated next to her asked her what her best memory was. It was just the sort of question she yearned to be asked but in that moment hadn't expected. Her mind faltered. Then it bloomed. Sunflowers, she said. Met with an uncertain smile, she explained: They were everywhere in the late summer.

It had been her favorite part of the train journey back from wherever she'd traveled—Hungary, Turkey, Greece, Italy, the Czech Republic—the part where the mountains fell away and the land flattened out and for miles and miles all there was to look at were fields of these flowers.

Years later, as she stood impatiently in line at the post office or passed by kids playing stickball on her street or selected fruit from a glowing but unscented pyramid of lemons, memories were triggered, triggered still more memories, a memory—*the* memory—and the flowers bloomed before her, nature's compass, guiding her, saying: Here is the sun. Look! Over here!

Real Family

While she waits for the new psychiatrist to arrive, Ginger distracts herself with thoughts of a dinner she imagines would make that smug-smiling *Cook's Illustrated* editor gnash his teeth and tear at his bow tie. Whatever people might say about her as a parent, no one can accuse Ginger of a poorly fed family. Butter-roasted chicken stuffed with garlic, lemon and fresh thyme. Cream cheese and chive mashed potatoes seasoned with imported Hungarian paprika. Sautéed green beans and slivered almonds, chocolate mousse. Or perhaps something lighter. Heirloom-tomato gazpacho; spinach, avocado, and grapefruit salad. Lately, she cannot get enough of her kitchen. The mountain-like assurance of the granite countertops, the welcoming mouth of her convection oven, the gentle rumbling hum of the refrigerator, some steady, distant train.

Beside her Ethan scratches his scalp, sighs. Morning sunlight bleaches the office of color, catching dust particles that sparkle like snow, creating a golden screen Ginger imagines hurtling through, disappearing. File folders are piled atop a laptop computer; diplomas, certifications, and licensures hang willy-nilly on the opposite wall. Clasping her hands, Ginger resists the urge to tidy things up.

The only personal touch in the office is a single, framed photograph. It faces outward from the desk, directly across from Ginger so that she cannot escape its image: a spontaneous moment, slightly blurred, of father, mother, and daughter laughing and embracing, a puzzle of arms and elbows, fingers and hands.

Reading her mind, Ethan waves at the photo, mutters: "Imagine getting Robert to sit on your lap like that?"

"He has."

Ethan laughs. "Oh really? And when exactly was that?"

"Why is it facing toward us anyway? Doesn't she want to look at her own daughter?"

Ginger flips the photo around. Boston cream pie, she thinks. Blueberry muffins.

The psychiatrist's name is Rita Blum. Looking at her, Ginger is reminded of posters a college roommate of hers had favored: toddlers dressed up as adults, doing adult things—handing each other roses, kissing under dimly lit streetlamps, wearing neckties and fedoras, feather boas; stethoscope, lab coat. When she offers her hand to Ginger it is soft and smooth, the skin not yet nuanced with age. Her bangs are pinned back close to her hairline with a flowered bobby pin. A dab of something, a remainder of breakfast, clings to her cheek.

Upon Dr. Blum's arrival Ethan had changed his position and now sits tall with both feet planted on the floor, elbows on chair arms, his mouth twisted as if he's on the verge of saying something clever. He gives Ginger a tight smile intended to be encouraging but that only makes her emotions bubble and belch against her insides. If only he were on board, she thinks, they wouldn't be wasting time in this place. But Ethan is insistent. Every day when he comes home from work it seems he has added another business card of some doctor to the refrigerator; they cover the freezer door like quilt squares. She does not ask him where he's gotten them from because the answer will only confirm her worst suspicions: he's been talking to people about Robert. Ethan preaches to her of treatment, therapy, medication. "It's all as American as apple pie," quips Ginger when she's feeling rebellious, running her fingers over those sharp rectangles of paper, tossing one or two of them away when Ethan isn't looking.

"Blame it on Robert!" she cries when she's feeling desperate. "Blame it on our *child*!"

But inside she's beginning to feel defenseless against her husband. He's been lining up reasons like soldiers and has organized an impressive army. Blum is soon to become one member of the infantry; Ginger can just feel it in the space between her husband and the doctor, their collegial smiles and head nods, much like the ones Ethan shared with their pediatrician and the social worker and the teachers at two of Robert's former schools.

Ethan doesn't seem to notice that she is the only one maintaining order, protecting her family from the chaos that would inevitably ensue if she weren't there. Ginger lives what she considers to be a normal life, cares for what she believes is a normal family. There's no need to jump to conclusions, she tells an infuriated Ethan. Children go through stages. And it is her official position that this is what Robert is going through. He's done nothing wrong. Not really. Not in Ginger's opinion at least.

Dr. Blum has opened up a thin file, begun to read. Ginger tilts forward in her seat, squints to get a look at it but is too far away. She glances at Ethan's watch. Nine thirty-five. They've wasted twenty minutes waiting for Dr. Blum to arrive and fifteen before that, sitting in reception. Ethan needs to get to work; Ginger needs to get back home, back to Robert.

"Doctor? I don't mean to be rude, but I'm anxious to get on with my day."

Ethan pinches the bridge of his nose. *"Ginger."*

"Just a moment more . . . " says Dr. Blum, her eyes still moving back and forth, reading. She never bothers to look up from the file.

The second specialist said the same thing as the first. When the first specialist had said it, Ginger was mute, disbelieving, her vision going fuzzy so that for a moment she thought the electricity in his office had gone out. With the second specialist, she said: "So that's really the term the medical establishment is using these days?" But it was, in fact, her official diagnosis. Bad eggs.

When she heard the words she could not help imagining her eggs as she had when she was a teenager in health class, watching a black and white animated movie titled *The Miracle of Life*, except that in her mind the eggs had faces, were rogue-like bullies with muscled, tattooed arms and leather jackets, punching the clean-cut cardigan-wearing spermatozoa out of her fallopian tubes. In the doctor's office, while Ethan had covered his trembling lower lip, cast his watery gaze at his empty lap, Ginger had laughed. Ethan and the doctor exchanged glances. Bad eggs, indeed.

"So what you're saying is this is my fault?"

"No one's fault," the specialist insisted. "Just bad luck."

Ginger stared at the palm of her left hand and with her index finger traced the shape of her love-line. She couldn't shake the feeling that he was lying to her.

Ethan reached out, squeezed her hand. "We'll figure it out, Gin. We'll find a way."

She thought this might be code; Ethan had on more than one occasion suggested they could live a childfree life. But Ginger had never believed two married adults constituted a family, at least not a real one.

They considered their savings, their retirement accounts. They sat late into the evening translating the fine print of healthcare plans and finally settled on a clinic. Ginger began treatments. The more time passed, the louder the rooms of their house vibrated with silence. When they spoke, their voices echoed out as if in a canyon. "The house is too big," she told Ethan. He'd walked in on her trying to drag a sofa across the length of the living room. "It's too much for me to manage." But there was nothing she could do to change it, no matter how much she moved the furniture around.

Another appointment; more disappointing news. On the ride home from the doctor's office one afternoon, Ginger stopped at a bookstore and bought both volumes of *Mastering the Art of French Cooking.* She'd envisioned family dinners together, something she'd never had growing up, both of her parents absent, one in body, one in mind. She didn't like to get into the details of it, didn't like to think about her childhood too much, the future always a better option than the past. She wanted not pasta and sauce from a jar but good, old-fashioned, homemade cooking, meals that required hard labor. A table set with polished silverware, cloth napkins, candles. A table made resplendent with shiny perspiring turkeys, midnight hued plums, tomatoes bursting from their seams. Succulence! Succulence! Maybe it was all a matter of the power of persuasion, thought Ginger as she carried the encased tome in the crook of her arm to the cash register. Cook it and they will fertilize.

But hours later pots bubbled over and burned up the stove, black smoke trickled out from a crack in the oven. "Good thing the fire alarms aren't installed," Ethan joked when he found Ginger curled up on the bed, her head buried beneath a pillow. "You'll get better. Maybe beef bourguignon is a little ambitious. How about scrambling an egg first?" He tugged at the pillow until Ginger finally let go.

She lay still while Ethan stroked her hair, closing her eyes when she couldn't bear to look at him any longer. "What if," he began, but Ginger knew what he was going to say and snatched the pillow back, covering her face, closing the fabric over her ears.

"Ginger. *Sweetheart*."

Ethan yanked at the pillow but she refused to let go this time. She inhaled deeply. It smelled of sharp human scents and fabric softener and aging down.

"Can't we be honest about this?"

She buried her face further into the fabric. Her voice came as if from the past. *"No."*

The adoption agency they finally settled on was headquartered in Michigan; the children were primarily Eastern European and Russian. It took nearly two years and lots of false starts, but eventually they found him in an orphanage in Bucharest, Romania. Ginger signed up for a cooking class, squeezed in three more before his scheduled arrival. He was nine months old, his name was Robert and—Ginger said when she first laid eyes on his picture—he was perfect.

Dr. Blum takes a notebook from the side drawer of her desk, picks up a pen. "Tell me more about Robert."

Ginger rolls her eyes, gestures at the file. "Didn't that tell you enough?"

Ethan places his hand on her forearm. "Do you want me to start?"

"Be my guest."

While Ethan speaks, Ginger turns toward the windows and gazes at the large parking lot outside. Heat rises off the asphalt, making anything that passes through its waves wobbly and uncertain. A woman pushes an extravagantly-designed stroller with wheels like giant chocolate donuts; people hustle to and from cars, the scraping sounds of their footsteps on the ground ringing dully in Ginger's ears.

Ethan and Dr. Blum think she isn't paying attention but she is. For each example Ethan gives, in her mind Ginger is stacking up counter-examples from her own childhood to refute his. Her brother went through a biting phase. She once got caught pinching candy bars from a corner store. She had difficulty making friends. She had a habit of getting lost, following distractions. Even now she can recall her mother's face whenever they were reunited, usually at information booths and checkout counters, her complexion white, not from fear but from guilt at allowing it to happen yet again.

Ginger presses her hand to her chest. The air in the office feels thin. A soup with all those extra potatoes, she thinks. A dessert bread using the over ripe bananas in the bowl on the kitchen table.

" . . . And then this past week . . . " she hears Ethan saying and instinctively she knows it is her cue.

"When we were kids my brother stabbed me," she blurts.

Ethan and Dr. Blum blink at her.

"Once—with a fork. It broke skin. Here." She begins to roll up the sleeve of her blouse.

"That was different," Ethan says. He's heard this story before. "Not that your childhood was any model of normalcy, but it *was* an accident. Joe didn't *purposefully* stab you."

"And you think Robert did?"

Ethan doesn't answer her.

"You weren't there," she says. "Maybe if you had been it wouldn't have happened . . . " She trails off, feeling his eyes moving downward to her lap. One hand over the other, she hides the spot that is covered with gauze and medical tape, the stitches still new. The spot on her hand seems to pulsate, like the nagging at the back of her mind, something about the past six years that shakes loose her certainty.

"What about ADD?" ventures Ginger. "Learning disabilities? I've read there are higher rates of it among adopted children."

Dr. Blum looks disappointed by this suggestion. "Certainly developmental and learning delays can be symptoms of something more serious. But right now there's nothing to indicate he might be challenged developmentally. His speech was delayed when he was younger, but that's not unusual for a child coming from his circumstances."

"But you should have seen the orphanage," presses Ginger. "It was a terrible place. They tied babies to their cribs."

Dr. Blum snaps the button on her pen, slips it into the chest pocket on her lab coat. There are three others just like it, their ends poking out like bullets on a holster.

"The teachers at his last school said that he lacked remorse," Ethan offers. "When he hurt other kids."

"He was protecting himself!" cries Ginger. "The other children teased him. One of the teachers even told me so." And yet it was Robert—not the other children—that had been removed from school. The teachers had sat Ginger and Ethan down in the art room at the kiddy-sized tables to tell them the news. Their knees kept knocking against the furniture while the teachers stood over them, looking down on Ginger, their faces failing to hide the obvious accusation: Bad mother. "You can't tell me the other children weren't at fault."

"It wasn't just the one time . . . "

"Why is it so hard for you to defend your own son? Is it because he's adopted?"

Ethan laughs ruefully. "You're not a cheap person, Ginger. Don't start acting like one now."

Ginger wraps her arms around herself, licks her lips. Hot chocolate with whipped cream from a can. Oil-popped popcorn smothered in butter. "He's a very good eater." She can hear how she sounds—defensive, desperate—but cannot stop. "Broccoli. Even brussels sprouts."

Dr. Blum places her elbows on her desk. "Fortunately, we're addressing Robert's situation at an early age. Hopefully we can get to work so that he's ready for some controlled classes. He won't be ready for mainstream school just yet, but in time."

School. Only yesterday Robert had thrown a tantrum over the Spiderman backpack he'd seen another boy wearing at the playground; it took all the strength Ginger had to haul him off to the car. It was wrong of her, she thought, to have strong-armed him from the playground; she'd handled it all wrong. She sensed too that other parents thought she had, she could feel their silent judgment even after she'd turned her back on them. If only she'd been more patient, hung in for a few minutes longer, tried to reason with him. Maybe that's the problem. Patience, her lack of it. When she thinks about it now she knows it was her fault. She'd driven him to it and then been forced to bribe him—lie to him—promising him she'd buy him his own backpack in order to calm him down. She'd told him she'd get him one for school, knowing full well Robert wasn't going back anytime soon.

"I'd like to see what the three of us can do together first, but I also want to assure you that there are other resources . . . "

Ginger had never thought of these things happening to Ethan and her. In her mind they happened to people who lived in rural trailer parks in Arkansas or West Virginia, people who left their children in rooms with uncovered electrical outlets and fed them food that had a shelf life of a decade and didn't bother strapping them into car seats. People with troubled histories, faces ringed like tree stumps with years of failing. People who never thought about whether they wanted children or not, instead leaving family to fate.

"We've done everything right," says Ginger.

"No one's suggesting that you haven't." Dr. Blum catches Ethan's eye, points at the box of tissues in front of him. Ethan pulls one out then shoves the entire box into Ginger's lap where it dangles for a moment before falling and landing between her feet.

Ginger stares at the box. It's so light she cannot feel its weight through her shoes. She realizes she'd taken it for granted, being a parent. She'd always assumed it would be easy; she'd believed she had an innate talent for it. "We're not supposed to be here."

Dr. Blum checks her watch. "I'd like to schedule some time with Robert and the two of you over the next several weeks. Fortunately, there are more options today than there were thirty years ago."

"Well thank god it's not nineteen sixty-two," mutters Ginger and gives the tissue box a kick.

As Ethan drives Ginger home, she reconsiders dinner.

"Cupcakes," she says. "Maybe I'll make cupcakes."

Ethan drums his fingers on the steering wheel. "I think Dr. Blum can really help us."

"Did I take the chicken out of the freezer this morning?" Ginger pulls a pencil and small notepad from her purse, taps the eraser end against her lips. "I just can't remember." She waits for the car to ease to a stop before she writes. *Yogurt. Half & Half.*

"Why don't we just order pizza tonight?"

"Pizza?" *Sea salt. Crushed red pepper.* "I bought chicken. But I could make pizza instead, if that's what you want."

"Not *make* it. Buy it. I thought that maybe you might want a break from cooking for once. We could get a movie, chill out together."

"I bought chicken."

Ethan reaches across the car, his fingers fumbling under Ginger's thick hair. He begins to massage the back of her neck, something he hasn't done in a while. She groans. "Things don't need to be perfect all the time."

Ginger stiffens, shakes off Ethan's hand. If he weren't working so much. If he were around more. If he'd try it her way for once. "It's not about being perfect. I *like* to cook. And if I left the chicken out—"

"—Fine." Ethan slaps his hand back on the steering wheel. "It was just a suggestion. Forget it."

For several minutes they ride in silence, Ethan shifting the gears roughly, the car bucking, suspending Ginger forward, thrusting her back. The seatbelt she is wearing locks, catching across her collarbone, pinning her in place. The next time Ethan shifts only her head moves back and forth with the jerking motion, the rest of her forced to remain still.

They pass by brightly colored Victorians, a community garden, the playground from which she'd earlier had to drag her screaming child. Ginger turns toward Ethan. His appearance stops her short. Fine hairs have begun to sprout from his ears; the skin around his jowls sags slightly, resisting the inevitable tug of gravity. Ginger reaches out and begins to stroke his cheek with the back of a finger.

"You look tired."

"No. Not tired."

Before Robert, it had been their Friday night ritual. They alternated topping and movie selections; one week his, the next hers. She used to fall asleep with her head in his lap, the movie flickering blue against the backs of her eyelids. You're missing the best part, he'd whisper, teasing, his warm hand resting on her belly bursting with pizza and beer.

"Okay," she concedes. "We can order out. Pizza *is* Robert's favorite."

Ethan glances at her. A smooth downshift. "You sure?"

"You're right," Ginger says. "I could use a break. We both could."

"Great. I'll get beer on the way home." At the next stoplight, Ethan leans over and pecks Ginger on the cheek.

While they wait for the pizza to be delivered, Ginger shows Robert how to frost cupcakes. When he'd come home from work, Ethan had stared at the plate cooling on the kitchen table for several minutes, his briefcase and sports jacket dangling at his sides. Then he shook his head. "We still need dessert," Ginger rationalized, the hand mixer she was holding poised over a bowl of frosting. "Tell me they're made from a box," Ethan said. She didn't mention she'd spent the afternoon organizing the refrigerator and freezer, marinating meat and chopping vegetables in anticipation of the next four days' meals.

Ginger finishes mixing the frosting while behind her Robert waits, kneeling on a chair at the kitchen table, his fist gripping a butter knife. She is sometimes asked by strangers if Robert is from Guatemala or Mexico. She knows it is obvious to everyone else that he is not her biological child; Ginger is the physical embodiment of her namesake. But she doesn't mind; she thinks Robert beautiful and covets his thick dark hair, the waves in it, his doe lashes.

She sets the bowl in front of her son. Robert dips his knife into it and roughly smothers first one and then another cupcake with frosting. Ginger pauses before leaning over him so that her chest presses against his back. When he does not flinch, she bends still further, puts her face to his head, closes her eyes, breathes in his scent of bubblegum and sweat and sour milk. She runs a hand along his arm. Recently he has begun to reject her affection, shoving her off of him, batting at her hands. But tonight Robert doesn't seem to notice her touch, so engrossed is he with piling more frosting on the cupcakes, his tongue taut, pushed against one corner of his open mouth. She smiles, relieved, and remains standing so that her body drapes over her son's.

"Here," she says. "Let me show you."

"I can do it," insists Robert. But he doesn't push her away.

Through his shirt she can feel his breath and heart. It always surprises her, the quickness, the rapid flutter. At seven he is still a child, still her baby. At seven he is still only a fraction of who he will be one day; his opinions and ideas, his personality even, not yet fully formed.

"I know you can," assures Ginger even as she takes a cupcake from Robert's hands.

Maybe people are always works in progress, she thinks. She swirls the frosting around so that it creates a pink mountain peak. Her son squeals, dazzled. Maybe she and Ethan—everyone, really—are only shadows of what they will be in two weeks, two years, two decades.

"It's my turn," Robert growls, pushing Ginger's arm away. "*Ma*-ma. It's. My. Turn."

"Relax, monkey. Here, let me help." She places her hand over his. "Relax your arm. That's right." She begins to guide him around so that the frosting swirls just the way she wants it to. "See? Isn't that better?"

But Robert's eyes have shifted away from their task and now watch the hand that envelopes his own. He presses the tip of his index finger to the white bandage she wears. "I did that." His tone is flat; it is a statement of fact.

Ginger looks into his eyes even though he refuses to look back. "Yes. But it's okay. It was a mistake."

"Does it hurt?"

Ginger wrinkles her nose. "Not really," she lies. What had surprised her was the sensation not—as she'd expected—of her skin ripping, but of it cracking open, like the shell of an egg. But that was hardly as shocking as what came next: she'd slapped Robert with the back of her hand hard across his cheek. It was in self-defense, she'd told herself afterward. But this only made her feel worse.

Robert eyes the dab of frosting on the edge of his knife and places the tip into his mouth.

"Don't do that, sweetheart. It's dangerous."

The knife slips from Robert's lips; his dark eyes meet hers. She thinks he is about to say something, but then she thinks his look says it all. She runs her fingers over the bandage covering her hand.

"You didn't mean to do it."

Robert shrugs, dips the knife once more into the bowl of frosting, licks the tip.

The doorbell rings.

Ginger kisses the crown of her son's head, rises from the table. "Finish frosting."

As she walks to the front door, she feels the lightness in her arms, the cool wood floor against the bottoms of her bare feet. The water pipes thrum; Ethan's still in the shower. "Pizza's here!" she calls up the stairwell.

When she opens the door she is surprised by how light it still is outside. Somehow she has missed this, the gradual passing of spring. For too long she has been stepping out the door with her head down, trying to make it through this phase of life. She squints into the setting sun, grins at the delivery boy, tips him generously.

Robert's head is still bent over his work when she returns.

"Time to wash up for dinner." She uncaps two bottles of beer, pours them into glasses she's left to frost in the freezer. "Do you want milk or juice?" She picks up the glasses, one in each hand, and swings around.

The first thing she notices is the color of the frosting on the cupcake in his hand, how deep a shade of pink it is, deeper than she recalls having made it. He just keeps circling around and around the top of the cupcake, as if he's dissatisfied with his workmanship, wanting to get the knife strokes perfect.

"Robbie? It's time for dinner."

The water pipes go silent. Upstairs, Ethan is whistling.

The kitchen fills with the humid scent of pizza, making Ginger's mouth water. "Robert." Her voice is stern but cautious. "It's time to put that away."

He continues to ignore her, his back hunched, obstructing her view so that all she can see is the tip of his knife poised over the cupcake. He holds the knife tip just over the dessert, as if he is waiting for something.

Ginger sighs. "Okay. That's it."

Drip. Drip. Two red drops fall onto the table drawing her eyes towards a puddle that has suddenly appeared there. The dye, Ginger thinks, but when she looks across to the kitchen countertop the bottle of red food coloring is where she left it, cap on, lined up next to the others of blue, green, and yellow, a row of oversized tears. Robert swipes at the hair that has fallen into his eyes and Ginger sees what has created the liquid puddle.

The sound of the glasses shattering against the tile floor jolts Robert. He drops the knife, twists in his seat. The hand he has injured—the left, just like Ginger's own damaged hand—grips the back of the chair, the cuts jagged and uneven, the skin sawed through with something blunt—the butter knife he's been using. The pain he must have endured to do the damage he has done to himself. Blood crawls between his fingers; his hand leaves messy smears on the wood of the chair. Ginger's view of the table is unobstructed now; it stuns her how easy it is to identify the cupcakes her son has frosted, the rage and sadness of them.

From above, footsteps pound against the hallway floorboards. Ethan calls out: "Everything alright down there?"

Ginger pushes her toe forward, hears the crackling of glass. Just step over it, she tells herself. That's all you need to do. But she is paralyzed, unable to move toward her son to help him, even though she knows that sooner or later she must.

"Mama?" Robert's face is contorted, preparing for the next trick of emotion. He lifts his arms up, reaches out to Ginger. *"Mama?"*

"What's going on?" Ethan is standing in the doorway.

Ginger grabs a dishtowel from the countertop, rushes to Robert before Ethan can. She feels the glass puncture the bottoms of her feet, the pain exploding inside her head. As she steps the slivers of glass sink deeper into her flesh. She throws the dishtowel over Robert's hand.

"What happened?" Ethan cries.

Robert sobs, his mouth drawn wide, gasping; he cannot get enough air. He pushes at Ginger, tearing at the towel she's forced over his hand.

"Nothing!" shrieks Ginger, wrapping her arms around her resisting child, stroking his head even as she feels the violent waves, protesting shudders of his body beneath hers. "Hush, Robbie. Hush up now," she murmurs but it only provokes him more. He struggles, digs his fingers into her locked arms, but she will not let go; she will never let go. She looks up at Ethan but cannot hold his gaze which is, in that moment, telling the story of their lives.

"It's just a scratch," she tries and nearly laughs at the absurdity of the words. She doesn't know what else to say; her mind won't work beyond tightening her grip around the fierce, vibrating body of her son. *My son*, she thinks and wants to declare out loud so that he understands: *You are my son*. But the words won't yet come.

Rol Doboș

She can smell their fur coats that carry the scent of chicken fat and rosemary, perfume and cologne. Saliva pools up in the caverns of her mouth. A few yards behind her, the guests of the Intercontinental Hotel push through the revolving doors of the front entrance, releasing blasts of hot air and piano music, the jingle of keys, laughter.

Irina's American is late.

She swallows hard. In front of her, great piles of snow have covered the cracked cement park, hiding its crumbling stairs and shrubs that in the summertime catch loose pages of newspapers and food wrappers in lifeless branches. It is below freezing, and there is more snow than Irina has ever seen. The wind blows it up and over curbs and collapsing benches, against the walls of buildings so that it creates tunnels of light down narrow back streets. Irina watches cars and people navigate the brown rivers of icy slush in Piața Universitații; a hunched figure dusts snow off the row of wooden memorial crosses displayed in the center of Magheru Boulevard, uncovering the date scratched onto all of them: December 22, 1989. It was only five years ago but feels to Irina like a century; she had been eight then.

A gust of wind dips up and under her knotted skirts, nips at her legs. She pulls her coat to her still-childlike chest, adjusts the string she uses to keep it closed; sucks on the tips of her bare, throbbing fingers. If she weren't afraid of the consequences, she'd curse her American. At least she has her boots. She'd discovered them only this morning. They are several sizes too big, the soles are worn flat, but the wool lining is still good and saves her small feet.

Irina has developed a routine over the past few months, as much as she has ever had one since escaping the brothel. In the early morning hours, after the last metro stop has closed and she has nowhere to keep warm, she kills time by moving. She searches dumpsters and sneaks into yards where someone might store sacks of potatoes and onions, jars of canned pickles and peppers, or might hang laundry outside in the cold air, as stiff as salted animal hides. Five times a week, en route to work, the woman pauses in the middle of her commute to take Irina to a café. Even now, with her face directly in the sharp wind, Irina can taste the cup of hot cocoa and the slice of *doboș*—the only thing she ever orders—and hear the heavy tongue of her American negotiating in Romanian for extra whipped cream.

Across the street, the church bell tower chimes nine o'clock. Irina squints into the gray winter light and listens to the slightly off-key bells that seem not to pay tribute to the heavens but to warble helplessly after them, reminding her of the mutterings of dying pigeons that line the city's building ledges and scramble under park benches, pecking at each other's eyes, fighting over a breadcrumb. It's been over an hour. Irina's stomach grumbles. She sucks harder on her fingers but they continue to throb. A sound like heaving emanates from above. The sky finally relents; once again it begins to snow.

The shoes are what tipped Irina off to her American. They are unlike any Irina had seen in Romania: bright purple clogs. "They're like a clown's," she'd once told her, but the woman didn't recognize the word, shook her head and laughed, repeating in her labored Romanian: "I don't understand. What is *clovn*?"

The first time Irina had seen them she had slapped her knee, delighted, and raced after the quick-stepping shoes. She knew it was pure luck, like the time she'd discovered the gold coins of her dowry, the ones that had been woven into her braids on her wedding day, hidden among her new husband's things. Irina lurched through the crowds, sidled up next to the woman, and latched onto the shoulder strap of her backpack, forcing her to stop.

"Te rog frumos, domnişoară: dă-mi bani."

The woman walked, not looking in Irina's direction. *"Îmi-pare rău. Nu am bani."* She tugged at the strap Irina still held. *"Lăsa-mă în pace."* The words were forceful but she'd smiled—warmly even—when she'd spoken them.

Irina let go of the strap but continued after the woman. After a while, she began to hum the tune of "America the Beautiful." *"Ah-MER-i-CA, Ah-MER-i-CA, dum-dum-dum . . . "*

The woman stopped. "How did you know that?"

Irina shrugged, glanced down at the woman's shoes. "Now can you give me some money? I haven't eaten in days. Dollars, please." Irina knew the woman had them tucked away in a wallet she believed was securely hidden. If the woman continued to resist, Irina would pickpocket her, directing the woman's attention to some distraction only a foreigner might care about—the kiosk that sold vodka in single-serving drink boxes, the bullet marks in the façade of some old building—and silently cut the cloth of her bag or the lining of her coat with her pocket knife, the wallet sliding out as easy as kidneys from a chicken.

Irina pressed her palms out. The woman seemed to consider them but then stepped backward, drawing her backpack in front of her, wrapping her arms around it. Irina moved with her. The woman stepped again, this time to the side, and again Irina followed, forcing the woman to engage in an awkward two-step, each time narrowing the gap between them.

"I don't have any money," the woman said finally.

"Your Romanian isn't half-bad, but you're a terrible liar."

The woman glanced down the street to the ashen backdrop of the city, as if she were expecting someone to come and intervene on her behalf. Then she looked back at Irina, and something in her face shifted. "I admire your persistence. But you know I can't give you money."

"Why not?"

"I don't know how you'll use it."

"For food, of course! What do you think?"

"I wasn't born yesterday."

"You don't trust me?"

"Not particularly."

Irina laughed hard, digging her fingers into her empty belly. "You're smarter than you look."

"I'll buy you something to eat, but I'm not giving you any money."

Irina stiffened. The suggestion made her want to spit on those bright purple shoes, that splotch of color. Who did this stupid bitch think she was? She wanted—had *demanded*—money. She opened her mouth, ready to yell, make a scene, badger the woman into compliance. But the woman had drawn herself up, adjusted the strap of her bag more securely on her shoulder, smoothing out her skirt, crossing her arms over her chest. "Well?"

Irina realized she'd underestimated this woman, had played the situation all wrong. "Fine. But *I'll* tell you what *I* want."

The woman raised her eyebrows. "Well, I was thinking you might want a pastry. From the café down the street."

Irina knew exactly which café the American spoke of, having smudged its windows with her breath on more than one occasion, before the ugly cows that worked there chased her away, coming outside to splash water or toss the butts of lit cigarettes at her, once even chasing her with a broom, sweeping at the ground around her feet.

"I'll go to the café," Irina said. "But on two conditions. One: I order for myself. You don't order for me."

"And two?"

"We sit and eat inside."

"Kel-ly."

Irina sings out the name, as if her American might materialize out of the morning rush hour, coming to her like a well-trained dog. "Where are you, Kelly?"

It is not her American's real name but one Irina has given her, something she stole from a television show all the kids had watched at an orphanage where Irina lived for a short time. Her sisters hid her there but it didn't last; eventually she was discovered and brought to the brothel. *Kelly Beverly Hills*. The name comes from Irina's favorite character on that television show, a girl with blond hair just like her American's and the same smile, too—straight white teeth so large they fill up her face.

Snow has begun to collect on Irina's head, the moisture seeping through her scarf, frigid water sinking into her scalp. She shivers more now, her teeth rattling when she relaxes her jaw. Recently her American has come later and later, and each time Irina resists thinking what this might mean. What if Kelly doesn't come at all today? The thought makes her want to scream and rage about the street, knocking over magazine displays, smashing the spotless windows of expensive restaurants, perfumeries, electronics stores that fill up the blocks of the boulevard. Instead, Irina works her stiff fingers over her scarf, trying to pull it more tightly to her throat, and approaches two boys on the other side of the park. They're standing over a fire they've built, burning trash in a steel drum that sends up souring plumes of yellow smoke.

"Nice fire." She comes close enough to feel its heat on her cheeks and briefly closes her eyes.

"Go away," the boys say.

When she doesn't move, the larger of the two steps toward her. "I said go away." He wears a cap of rabbit fur and has tied the earflaps so that they cover the sides of his face. Irina imagines how the fur must feel against his skin, how warm it must keep his face and head throughout the day, and wonders how it might be possible for her to slip this hat from the boy's head. She imagines nestling down to sleep with it on her head and tucking her fingers between soft fur and warm cheek.

"My hands are going black." She holds out her hands to show them she isn't lying. Black spots have begun to appear around her dirtied nails; her small fingers have swollen at the joints, red as blood sausages. "*Te rog frumos*. Can't I stand here just for a minute?"

"For a loaf of bread," the other boy says, casting an indifferent glance at her hands. "Not for free." He has an enormous gash on his cheek that is green with infection; under heavy-hanging lids his red eyes are gelatinous from glue snorting.

"A loaf of bread? Impossible!"

"Not entirely," says the glue-snorter's partner. "You think someone is going to give a loaf of bread to us? You'll have better luck than we will."

Irina knows he's right. They are still underage but they are boys and look too old to evoke the sympathies she might receive. For this reason she eats when she is able but never too much so that she can keep herself skinny and childlike. She knows it will not be this way forever. Even now Irina feels the eyes of the boys roaming over her body in the same way as the men from the brothel. One of the boys licks his lips. Irina tries to make a fist.

It is as if she's closed her fingers over a thousand pins. She squeezes her eyes against the pain, then rushes the barrel. The boys shove her back.

"Get the fuck out of here! Gypsy whore!"

She dashes at the boy closest to her, grabbing his hand, chomping down on it before he has a chance to pull away. His howling echoes after her as she flees, picking her feet up high in those oversized boots, working her legs as if she were riding a bicycle. Still, she moves expertly, swiftly, slipping into the crowds that overflow the sidewalks, racing down Magheru Boulevard.

Then Irina glimpses her American's shoes. She stops to catch her breath, keeping her eyes to the ground as they dart from these high-heel boots, those rubber galoshes. There it is again! Several yards ahead of her, a beacon of color flashing, then obscured behind a tangle of gray, black and brown pant legs. Irina leaps up onto the curb, speeding now, not bothering to avoid puddles and slush, running into briefcases and book bags, knocking the straps off shoulders, ignoring the comments thrown her way. She nearly passes her American by, shoving into her, hearing the faint *oof!* the woman makes. Irina skids to a halt. Wheels around. *Finally.*

"Kel-ly Be-ver-ly He-ills!"

The woman is not surprised to see her and—Irina cannot be sure—may not be pleased. "How are you, Irina?"

Irina throws herself upon the woman, clasping her around her waist, pressing her face into the American's side. With her nose pushed against wool, she inhales slowly, the scent filling her head, making her unsteady on her feet. Irina wants to burrow past the layers of clothing so that she might find the spot underneath where it is dark, silent, hidden. She wriggles her aching fingers through the folds of the woman's coat, trying to find a way inside. The woman accepts her embrace, even returns it, but the coat is buttoned up, impossible to penetrate.

"Okay, *dragă*," the woman eventually says. "*Lasă-mă*." Irina feels her working at her arms, prying them away.

She steps back but, unwilling to let the contact end there, grabs the woman's gloved hand. Heat radiates through the soft leather, warms her own palm so that it begins to itch. She cranes her neck back to get a good look at her American. "I haven't eaten since yesterday morning. You're late today. I nearly missed finding you." Irina waits for the woman to provide an explanation, but she offers nothing. "You'll take me to the café now, *nu*?" She tugs at Kelly's arm, trying to draw her forward. "I want two slices of *doboș* today."

Kelly laughs but there's something in it, a pitch Irina detects. "You *must* take me."

"I can't take you now. I'm late already. Later. Maybe tomorrow."

"Tomorrow's *Saturday*," Irina wails and presses herself hard against the woman, the force of her small body catching Kelly off guard, sending them against the window of a nearby shop. "*Te rog frumos*, I'm starving."

The woman holds her shoulders, steadying them both. "Okay. *Okay*. Quiet down now, Irina. I'll take you but only for a short while. They're expecting me at the orphanage."

Irina squeals, jumps, slaps her hands together. Pain like an electric shock shoots through them but she doesn't care and marches forward, singing in mock-baritone, *Doboș! Doboș! Doboș! Two slices now!*

But as they approach the café, Irina peers through the windows and catches the eye of one of the women who work behind the counter. The expression on the woman's face makes her cheeks prickle just under the skin. She slows her pace. Kelly has asked her something but Irina is following the woman as she catches the attention of her colleagues, waving them toward her. "Irina? Did you hear what I just asked you?" The women move in close to each other, occasionally glancing out the window, nodding and frowning. Irina pauses just outside the café door. "What? Have you changed your mind?" She feels Kelly pressing her forward, but she is concentrating on their orange, red, and plum-colored lips. *Americanca. Americanca. Ţiganca.* One of the women, speaking rapidly, shoves a basket of bread she's been carrying onto the shelf, the loaves jarring against each other. Irina fumbles for Kelly's sleeve, grasps her hand.

"What's gotten into you?"

As the door swings open, the women cease talking and rise from their slouching positions, pulling shoulders back, cocking chins. They stand side-by-side, arms crossed over heavy chests, their black and red tinted hair contained in nets: a line of neatly trimmed, impenetrable shrubs. One of them murmurs *"Bună"* to Kelly; they ignore Irina. The air is warm, vanilla-scented, swaddling. Spoons clink against espresso cups; the milk steamer gurgles. The pastry case is at Irina's eye level, beckoning her, and what had held her back only moments before dissolves inside. Her muscles relax, her bones settle.

There are turnovers sprinkled with crystals of sugar that catch light like diamonds, the liquid from the apple center oozing out of the folds of pastry. There are sleek, smooth-skinned chocolate bombs like a new mother's full, dark breast, sweaty and glistening. There are multi-layered fruit cakes festooned with flourishes of cream cheese frosting and bright slices of kiwi and pineapple and strawberry.

The empty spot in Irina's stomach flips over on itself, once, twice. She moves closer but does not touch the glass of the case.

There are elephant ears and delicate croissants that shed buttery flakes. There are éclairs with shiny brown coats, cream puffs she imagines pressing her face into, coming away with a white dollop of frosting on the tip of her nose. There is *doboş*, a full log sliced carefully, just as she'd imagined, each piece of magic collapsing backward against the one behind it. Irina moves in closer.

"I guess you know what you want," Kelly says.

Rol doboş. It is the cake she's imagined all morning, cut so as to reveal the dark and light spirals of its interior. The chocolate is swirled so carefully inside the fine yellow cake, the two parts—one spongy and resilient, one thick and malleable—hugging and supporting, moving and rolling, never squeezing too tightly, never suffocating, only sustaining. They are held together by a hard, caramelized shell, a protective orange shield that encases the entire confection and is Irina's favorite part.

Irina nods. "Two pieces. And hot cocoa," she directs the women behind the counter. "Extra whipped cream."

"Do you have money?" asks a woman with a large mole sprouting wiry hairs on her chin.

Kelly reaches into her bag. "I've got it. But just one piece of *doboş*. And a cappuccino."

"I want two pieces."

"I don't have enough, Irina." She speaks softly but firmly. "Only one."

Irina narrows her eyes. "Bring it to me when it's ready. I'm going to sit down." As she passes through the café, she feels the other customers eyeing her, can see their mouths twisted in disapproval, disgust. She cannot seem to control her legs—maybe it is because of the sudden warmth. They move stiffly, causing her to drag her feet so that the boots make loud scuffing noises across the floor. Through her coat she can feel her nipples go hard from the change in temperature, and wraps her arms across her chest.

An old man mutters something as she passes him; her face goes hot.

"*Târfa*," the man repeats, his lip curling as he takes another drag on his cigarette.

With a swift motion, Irina flips the man's espresso cup, splashing its contents on his shirt. Now suddenly emboldened, she glares at the others, but they all turn away.

The booth closest to the window is available. She eases herself onto the velvet seat as if it were a bath, and opens up her skirts so that they hang over the vent on the floor below, directing the warm air right up her legs. Goosebumps rise and then recede on her bare thighs, the heat moving further still, warming her everywhere. She shudders and smiles. Outside, snow is coming down more heavily now, sticking to heads and cars, the ground. Her fingers have still not recovered from the cold but she manages to open packet after packet of sugar, pouring it into her mouth, closing her eyes as the crystals dissolve on her tongue.

A popular disco song plays over and over again on a tape recorder behind the front counter, the volume turned up so loudly it distorts the sound. Irina sings along, banging her feet in time to its heavy drum beat. *Be my lover! Would you be my lover!* She likes this music; sometimes in the summertime she goes to Piața Unirii and hangs around the stands where people sell CDs and tape cassettes, memorizing the words, making up dances. Blood rushes back into her toes, ears, nose; the skin on her legs and arms burns pleasantly.

She watches Kelly waiting at the counter for their order and wonders how she could ever miss her American as she nearly did today. It's not just her silly shoes, those oddly colored, oddly shaped things she goes to work (to work!) in every day, or even her shock of blond hair that is a rarity in Bucharest. It is true that when they entered the café just now, everyone paused to look in their direction—in part, because of Irina—but more because of her American. It's more than her tallness, her broadness, hovering over most women and even some men. There is a mystery in her carriage, the secret to which is found in the way she swings her arms, the way she walks in long, elegant strides. She meets people's gazes and smiles when she shouldn't. Despite her jeans and heavy wool sweaters, her lack of makeup that embarrasses Irina, she smells of extravagant comfort. Irina shoves her pulsing, frostbitten fingers in her mouth.

Kelly pulls bills from her small purse. Behind the counter, all of the employees seem to be attending to her order. One woman fixes the hot cocoa and cappuccino, another the slice of cake. Another rings up the order, all the while speaking. At first, Irina thinks she is talking to the other employees but then hears the distinct notes of Kelly's voice. Irina pretends not to notice when the woman points in her direction, snatches bills from the cash register. Instead, she turns her face toward the street, working hard to ignore them.

Outside, the two boys who'd chased her from their fire appear, gawking at her through the window.

Irina waves to them, giggling uncontrollably. They bang their fists against the glass, making other customers startle in their chairs.

"How'd you get in?" the boy with the rabbit-fur cap asks.

I have a friend, Irina thinks. She points at Kelly.

"See?" One of the employees says to Kelly, gesturing toward the windows, the boys outside, Irina. "Do you see what I'm talking about?" She takes off her apron, throwing it on the counter, and crosses to the door, yanking it open. "Get the hell out of here or I'll call the police! You hear me?" She waves at them, as if this is all it takes.

The boys mock her, making faces, dancing on the sidewalk in front of the shop, grabbing at their crotches. The glue-sniffer licks the window, slowly, lasciviously in front of the young couple sitting closest to him, his saliva leaving pale, frozen streaks. The other boy presses his face hard against the glass, opening his mouth and blowing so that his cheeks puff out, distorting his features, making a little girl shriek.

"Hey! *Țiganco*!" They yell through the glass at Irina. "You owe us a loaf of bread!" They slip off down the street, disappearing into the crowds.

"They're only children," Kelly argues.

"Easy for you to say," another woman mutters, setting the drinks before her so they rattle in their saucers.

Kelly carries Irina's slice of *doboș* to the table, gives her a comforting wink, returns to the counter for the drinks. Irina knows she should wait but cannot; the *doboș* is sitting there, in front of her. She picks up the entire piece, managing with some difficulty to balance it on her fingers.

She chomps at the dessert, not swallowing in time for the next bite. Chocolate lines the outside of her mouth and colors her lips, cake fills up her cheeks.

Eventually, she can't fit anymore and pauses to make room, glancing up at the counter to see what is taking Kelly so long. Whatever conflict her American may have been having with the women, it seems to have subsided. They are smiling and nodding at her, all of them crowding around the space at the counter while Kelly speaks, her hands painting invisible pictures, her expression lively. When they all laugh it is shocking, an explosive burst of sound that rattles inside Irina's brain. She swallows hard, getting the rest of the cake down her narrowing throat, then shouts: "Hey! Kelly! Sit here with me."

Kelly slides into the booth and sweeps into a neat pile the empty paper packets covering the table. "Clean up after yourself, Irina. You're not an animal." She stirs her cappuccino but doesn't drink from it. "You should use a fork to eat cake."

Irina ignores her and picks up the caramelized shell, gnawing on it as if it were a bone. Done, she licks the plate clean and sucks the last remnants of sugar from her tender fingers. She moves on to her hot cocoa, shoveling whipped cream into her mouth, some of it dribbling from her lips. "I wanted more whipped cream. Can you get me more?"

"Not today, Irina."

Kelly continues to stir her cappuccino around and around. Irina feels the woman's eyes on her face and wonders if she sees what Irina saw last time she was in the bathroom at the Gara de Nord: a hollowing of her cheeks, curves forming under layers of clothing. She brings her arms in closer to her body, shrinks down into her seat so that she is half-hidden by the table. Irina realizes what it is about her American's expression that makes her edgy: she is regarding her in the same way she regarded those cows working behind the counter. The same way she would another adult.

"What?" Irina barks through slurps of cocoa. Kelly shakes her head.

When they first began to come to the café together, Irina had felt obliged to offer something in return for the food Kelly bought her. She decided to give Kelly language lessons, things she knew the American wouldn't learn from a proper tutor or in an organized classroom. Even though it's been months since the last language lesson they'd had together, something about the way Kelly's eyes fix on Irina as she drinks compels her to put her cup of cocoa down and raise herself up on her knees. "Time for some *limba română*," she says, pressing her index finger to her lower lip. "Repeat after me."

"Not today."

"*Du-te dracului.*"

"Irina."

"*Pupă-mă-n cur.*"

The man sitting next to them glances in their direction.

"That's enough."

"Repeat. *Mânca-mi-ai căcatu.*"

The man mutters something, gets up and leaves. Kelly glances over her shoulder at the counter where the employees shake their heads. "Stop it, Irina."

"*Futu-te-n gură.*"

Kelly puts her hand firmly on Irina's. "I said stop it. Now hurry up. I'm already late for work and they won't let you stay here alone."

As if to emphasize this point Kelly checks her watch. It is silver and gold and so shiny that Irina reaches out to touch it. Kelly obliges, moves her arm closer so that Irina can see. She presses her finger across the clean glass face, smudging it with her fingerprint.

"Can I have it?"

When they first knew each other, Irina had shocked Kelly. But it seems she's become accustomed to the requests—pens and pads, money, clothing. Irina has rifled through her bag with Kelly watching on in amazement, telling her she is *şmechera,* tapping her finger to her cheek. Once, Irina discovered a single earring not unlike the ones she'd seen sparkling from the delicate lobes of her beloved television actress. It was the one thing she'd stolen from her, pocketing it when Kelly wasn't looking, later taking it to a consignment shop. *We only sell pairs*, the man at the store had said, but then took a closer look at the stud when she tossed it onto the counter. *Where'd you get this?* Irina wouldn't say. *I'll give you twenty thousand for it, but that's it.* So much money. But later she couldn't shrug off the feeling that she'd been duped.

"No, you can't have it," Kelly says, pulling her wrist away. "Are you ready to go?"

Irina has licked the plate clean but she isn't ready. She squeezes her hands under her thighs, thinking this might help, but they feel too hot, as if she's held them inside the bluest part of a flame. She points at Kelly's unfinished cup of cappuccino. "Aren't you going to finish that?"

"I already had some this morning."

Irina arches her back. "I'll finish it."

Kelly laughs but her eyes strain with impatience. "Fine. But when I get back from the rest room, I'm leaving. That's it." She places her hand on Irina's head, ruffles her hair. "Got it?"

Irina slurps the coffee down, but it still isn't enough. She stares across the café at the pastry case. There are mincemeat pies, triangles of quiche, small steaming rolls.

Kelly has taken her bag with her but has left her coat. Irina wraps the sleeves around her waist, slips her small hands into the breast pockets, digs them deep into the side pockets. The lining is made of cotton or felt. She sinks her hands in deeper still. Something stiff, like paper. A bundle. There is not just one piece but several, folded over on top of each other. Irina pulls it out. Bills—ten, eleven—fresh from the bank.

She can't read the numbers but she can tell by the colors how much is there. It is enough money to last her two months, maybe longer if she is frugal, certainly enough for her to eat every day for a long while. She pinches her arms at the unexpected good fortune. She can start here and now, buy another piece of cake, one of those éclairs her American has urged her to try, maybe a whole loaf of bread. She considers whether or not to ask for the money. Surely she has plenty. She remembers how Kelly had told her she could not buy her two pieces of *doboș* because she didn't have enough. Irina runs her thumb along the edge of the bills, feels them gently scrape her skin. She slips the money down the front of her shirt.

She pulls her scarf over her ears, fastens her coat, slides from the booth. But when she stands up, her American is there, blocking Irina's way to the door.

"What are you doing?" Kelly's face is composed, her tone soft; she doesn't look angry. And yet. She puts out her hand. "Give me the money, Irina."

"I don't know what you're talking about."

"Don't lie."

"Me lie? You're the liar."

"It doesn't belong to you, Irina. Hand it over."

"Fuck off!"

Irina moves toward the door, but Kelly grabs her arm. "Give me my money back." She speaks calmly but her voice has grown louder.

Irina claws at the woman's hand, trying to release herself.

"I'll let you go when you give my money back."

Irina digs her nails into Kelly's wrist, just under the watch. The band breaks from the force of her fingers, slips from Kelly's arm. Instinctively, Irina scrambles across the floor, scooping it up.

The café is quiet but for the booming disco music. *Wanna be my lover! Wanna be my lover?* Kelly's cheeks are flaming, her nose running, hair flying loose about her face. Her eyes harden. Behind her, rows of faces stare at Irina, waiting.

Irina reaches into her shirt. "Here's the fucking money." She tosses the bills and they fly up in crooked arcs before rocking downward to settle at her feet. "Are you happy now?"

Kelly takes a breath, her chest rising. "Did you take my earring?"

Once, when she was very small, Irina and her family had visited the Black Sea, camping out on the beach, melting lard over an open fire, spreading it on chunks of bread, singing songs. Her mother had whispered a poem in her ear, lulling her to sleep, and it was so beautiful, Irina didn't know where the words her mother spoke ended and the sound of the sea began. The next day, she could not be kept from the water. The sea was the color of shadows mixed with the white chop of waves. She spent her entire time in the water, eventually growing exhausted. But she was too far from the shore to make her way back on her own, and her father had to drag her out. She remembers his dark head making its way toward her, his face contorted with fear and exertion, the figures of her mother and sisters on the shore, their voices rising over the water. She can hear their calls distincly now as she looks into Kelly's face: *Get out. Come back. Get out.*

"Did you take my earring or not?"

Irina inches backward on her palms, the weight of her body and the hard floor making her aware of how tender, how sore her hands still are. She drags her legs, her skirts fanning out across them, sweeping the floor as she continues to slide back closer to the door. Some of the money catches on their hems, making scraping sounds against the linoleum. Her palms are surely bruising through to bone, and her body feels heavy with the café's terrible heat, but she knows she must get up. She readies herself; her muscles twitch.

"Wait—Irina—"

Her American reaches out just as Irina scrambles up onto her feet, but Irina is faster, her life having trained her for such moments. She knocks over a basket of baguettes someone has just set out, still warm from the oven, spilling them across the dirty floor. She dashes out the door and into the street, running for blocks, past the shiny electronics stores and perfumeries, past the Intercontinental and the park and the boys with their stinking fire and demands for bread, past the crosses displayed in Piața Universitații, past the rows of kiosks and flocks of pigeons that surround them, running almost as far as Unirii, far enough so that she is sure she is far away from the café and the cows who work there and their unblinking, staring faces, far, far away from her American.

A week later, enough time has passed that Irina feels ready to return. She waits at her usual spot on the corner; waits again the next day.

Days go by, then weeks. Months.

She spends more time in Cișmigiu Park, cooling herself in the shade of the trees, wading into the shallow lake where the rowboats circle around and around, creating spirals of light and dark on the surface of the water. She collects change from people sitting in the beer garden, enough to buy ice cream and bottles of cola from street vendors, but she's grown a bit more and the handouts are less frequent. Children in the playground, there with their parents, glance at her sideways when she takes a turn on the swings or tries to strike up conversation over the seesaws. She wraps her chest in rags underneath her shirt, trying to hide the breasts that have begun to take shape, but she can feel them pushing against the cloth. They are so tender that sometimes at night she lies on them wrong and wakes to their pulsing soreness. There hasn't been a drop of rain in several weeks and people sprinkle water from plastic bottles on the dusty cement, trying to keep it from blowing up into their eyes and down their throats. Irina pays no attention to the dust. It clings to her face and her neck, to her bare arms; it settles at the roots of her hair. It coats her body in a thin, dry armor.

Sometimes, a man who works one of the kiosks gives her a package of wafer cookies or a candy bar. She accepts the gifts, tearing them open with her teeth, spitting the wrappers on the ground. There are no chairs for her, so she perches herself on stacks of magazines and papers that cover the counter of the kiosk. They stick to the backs of her legs, leaving smudges of ink on her skin. She munches mechanically on the cookies and candy, never tasting them, her eyes glazing over at some unfocused point in the distance, while the man watches her, reaching his hand under her skirt, his fingers crawling up her bare thigh. She closes her eyes then, and thinks of the safety of a warm place, a warm person, a velvet booth, a slice of *rol doboș*.

She lounges on the grass near the main entrance of the park, hidden by a dense, untended row of rose bushes, underneath the statue of a famous poet. Sometimes when the sun is too much to take, she sneaks into the university library to cool off. Paintings of this same poet are on the walls of the library, standing with books tucked under his arm, wearing shirts with ruffled collars and kneesocks, his thick hair combed back in luxurious waves. She cannot read but knows this must be a measure of his fame, his greatness, and the love others feel for him.

At the spot by the overgrown roses and the statue, Irina sees her American one afternoon. Her hair has been cut short and she is free of her heavy coat, wearing instead a tank top and a loose skirt that comes to her knees. On her feet are the same purple clogs.

Irina springs to her feet, popping up from behind the roses. "Kelly!" She runs after her, unable to contain her excitement. "Kelly! Wait up!"

Her American keeps walking, talking to another woman who is with her, occasionally raising a hand to tuck her hair behind her ear. Surely they've heard her calling?

Irina catches up, only a few feet behind the two women. "Look here, Kelly Beverly Hills. How about you take me to the café?"

Although she does not turn and acknowledge her, Irina can tell Kelly has registered her, bristling, her back stiffening, her shoulders rising up. Irina steps closer, trying to insert herself between the two women, but the woman walking with Kelly moves so that she fills up the gap.

Irina kicks at the back of the woman's calf.

"Move out of the way, cow! Kelly. Where've you been? I waited and waited but you never showed. I thought you went back to America."

Still the women continue on, ignoring her. Irina saunters after them, singing to herself, *Be my lover! Would you be my lover!*

She can play this game; she is nothing if not patient. They pass through the park, circling around the lake and the playground.

Past the rose garden and memorial, along the corridor lined with oak trees. Old men play chess, women sell bags of sunflower seeds, children ride a miniature train that circles, going nowhere. Irina catches stones between her toes; she's tossed the boots, running about in bare feet.

Several minutes later they reach the other side of the park and head toward the exit. She wants to stay here; she's not interested in being out on the open streets.

"Wait," she cries out to the women.

The scent of dogwood is lifted on a warm breeze.

"Kelly."

They continue to walk, increasing their pace.

"Americanca mea."

Kelly wheels around. "What did you say?"

Irina smiles, rushes forward, grabs Kelly's hand, limp in her own. "*Americanca mea.*" She tries the English. "My American."

Kelly frees her hand from Irina's. "I'm not your American."

"Take me to the café. I want my *doboş*."

The other woman snorts. Irina takes a good look at her: she is one of the women who had worked behind the counter at the café. Irina folds her fingers in on her palms, trying to make fists, but they've swollen in the heat and are impossible to close.

Kelly reaches into her purse. "Do you want money? Is that what you're looking for?"

The Romanian woman says, "You've wasted enough on her"—then, addressing Irina: "You should be ashamed."

Kelly offers Irina several crisp bills. "Here. Is this what you're looking for? Take it."

Irina flexes her fingers, trying to break through the blood. She feels blinded by the sight of Kelly and this woman together and it stirs something inside her, something dormant in the months since she's been to the café. Slowly it comes to life, lit by a fire. "I don't want your money. I want *doboş*."

Kelly sighs, shifts her weight. "Well, I don't care how you spend it. Go buy your *doboş* yourself if you want it."

The other woman presses a hand on Kelly's arm. "We've got to go."

"No. Kelly is taking me to the café." Irina looks between the two women. "Aren't you, Kelly?"

"I'm not going to the café with you, Irina." Kelly's voice is the voice of a teacher who thinks she knows better. "I'm done with taking you to the café." She leans slightly forward so that she can look at Irina more directly. "Take this. And leave me alone."

Irina can barely see her American's face as she snatches the money from her grip. She cannot see Kelly's eyes as the light in them dances and refracts. She cannot see her pupils shrink, startled when Irina holds the bills up toward the sky. It is too bad, Irina thinks. She wishes she could see her American's expression as she refuses her final act of charity and tears the money up. She wants to see her American's mouth drop open when the pieces finally fall through her fingers, lifted away on the wind. As she works on them, grunting with the effort, twisting them this way and that, she smiles just thinking of it. But the bills do not do as she commands them to. They slip between her fingertips, strangely unrelenting.

Irina's hands are burning, her fingers cramping up. Sweat trickles down her forehead, across the bridge of her nose. Her palms grow moist; the money becomes damp and somehow even more indestructible. She shrieks with rage, frustration. Rip! Rip! But the money will not give.

Manna from Heaven

Lately, she's been afraid to get out of bed in the morning. It's not just the cockroaches, the way she senses them fleeing to the darkest corners of the apartment when her feet meet floor. It's also this nagging sense of failure, an unsettling fog in the brain she cannot rid herself of. Not just for her job at the orphanage (Her only prior work experience had been at a summer camp and in women's clothing retail. What did she know of caring for orphans? Why in God's name would they hire her for such a responsibility?), but for everything here. She is certain she is failing at everything.

A week before, Magda had asked her: What would make you feel better?

What would she do without Magda?

Breakfast cereal, she answered. Breakfast cereal would make me feel better.

Magda smiled. Such patience. She gazed at Stella's kitchen table, saw the pile of unanswered letters there (How could she write home, admit her mistake in thinking that she was strong enough to manage this job, this place?), her mother's chicken-noodle soup recipe on the top. The drawing of a smiley face. *I love you, my beautiful girl!* Just like the notes she used to slip into Stella's lunchbox when she was a child. It humiliated her, knowing that Magda saw it. But she didn't stop her friend from picking it up, reading it over.

Won't this make you feel better? asked Magda, waving the recipe. Why don't we make this?

But now Stella suspects it's a test. Magda has assigned her to pick up the chicken. Only the chicken.

Saturday morning, the telephone forces her from bed.

Don't wimp out on me, says Magda.

Stella smiles into the receiver. I won't. Some days Magda is the only reason she can think of to stay in Romania. She does not deserve such a friend.

Cheek-en. Magda persists. A. Big. Fat. Live. *Cheek*-en.

Okay.

You remembered the sack I gave to you?

Of course, says Stella and picks up the phone, stretching the cord as far as it will go into the kitchen, swiping the burlap sack off the table. She gazes out the window. Across the courtyard and over the brick wall a handful of women loiter in front of the maternity hospital. They are round and wobbling and appear vaguely bewildered, whether by the snow that's begun to fall in heavy flakes or their circumstances, it remains unclear. They all wear nothing more than ratty bathrobes, white ankle socks and hospital appointed slippers fitted with cardboard soles. They stand separate in their bodily discomfort, like people waiting for a bus. One of them—the most rotund of all—smokes a cigarette.

You put the chicken in the sack, Magda is saying. Stella. *Dragă*. Are you listening to me?

Yes.

You tie the sack tight but not too tight—the bird should stay alive. You leave it outside your door. Then you call me. I'll send Tudor over.

Got it.

Magda makes lip-smacking sounds into the phone. Kisses-kisses, she says, and hangs up.

It's also a consolation prize, this chicken-noodle soup cooking. An apology for her behavior at the pre-holiday pig slaughter.

Magda had invited her. A family tradition, she'd said. There would be first, second, even third cousins at her uncle's farm north of the city. A real Romanian family tradition.

Stella didn't want to appear the delicate American; she didn't want to pass up on an important cultural experience. She didn't know what she was getting herself into.

It had all started off well enough. Warm early December sunshine cleaning up the dirtied winter skies, a jaunty ride to the country in the springy backseat of Magda's Dacia, flanked on either side by her two children Flavia and Tudor. There was mulled wine and bread with homemade apricot jam; the smell of crumbling leaves, burning wood; cold air watering, soothing Stella's tired eyes. There was cherry brandy and throat-burning *palincă* and lots of dirty-joke telling, most of which she'd missed but laughed along with anyway. She was having such a good time that when they paraded the pig out of the barn she felt only delight at the sight of it. It looked so eager, so happy, the way its ears were pricked forward, the surprisingly dainty steps it took as it trotted, its eyes squinting, snout wriggling, snorting a little pig-song.

A crowd formed. A large knife with a blackened blade was drawn. This was what fooled her—the blackened blade. Somehow she didn't believe it could have been sharp enough to slice quickly through tough, pulsing animal hide; she thought it was for show, part of tradition. Family tradition. It happened so quickly, the prancing sow, the raised, deceptive knife. The blood. People clapped. Were they clapping for the blood? She knew she should have closed her eyes but again: her pride. It was not so much the blood that moved her, but the way it spilled over the butcher's hands, as fast as water from a faucet. These two things, she thought, were incongruent—human hands, tumbling blood. She felt it rising inside her; there was no stopping it. She turned and ran behind the tractor shed.

Magda's anger surprised her. Her friend had been so patient with Stella over the course of the year, patient when she yelled at the superintendent for not renewing her visa, patient when she complained of the long lines at the station and the inefficiency of the trains, patient when she criticized the bureaucracy of the orphanage, the incompetence of the director, the resignation and passivity of her colleagues, all that *ce să i faci?*—what can you do? All that shoulder shrugging, the defeatist attitude; a self-fulfilling prophecy. Patient when she called Romania sexist and racist; as if Stella's own country were excluded from such labels.

But even Magda, patient Magda, had limits. Where do you think your precious bacon comes from, *dragă*? she said as she slapped Stella's hunched back and shoved a tin can filled with water under her nose. It's a fact of life. This is how they get meat in America, too, you know. In fact, it's probably less humane there than here. At least that pig back there had a good life before it went.

Sipping from the can, Stella inhaled the scent of iron. She retched some more. Magda rolled her eyes and leaned against the shed, turned to her children, who'd been watching wide-eyed, and told them to go find their father; they would need to head back home early.

If she could have talked, Stella would have apologized to her friend. She hadn't meant to seem superior. It was just that she preferred her meat in abstractions—drained of its blood, de-boned, de-hoofed, chopped and quartered, frozen, preferably ground—before she came in contact with it. She understood this: she had lived a sheltered life, something her friend would never understand since no one here had ever lived that way.

From the back of her kitchen cupboard, Stella digs out some plastic shopping bags. They are covered in images of naked women, their once flawless bodies now made grotesque with use. One woman's rich tan has faded through to plastic; another's face has branch-like wrinkles that bleed from her profile into the beach scene background. The third's bare breasts and brown nipples stretch down and out like carnival taffy.

Stella feels deep satisfaction at seeing how her repeated use of the bags on which these naked women appear is whittling away at their impossible genetics. She wonders how much longer these ladies and she can withstand another shopping excursion together. She's been holding out on purchasing new bags, waiting for more appealing images—kittens, perhaps, or flowers—but alternatives haven't yet appeared around town. For now she must suffer the indignity of it, getting by with tits, tits, and nothing but tits.

Stella reaches under her wool sweater to cup one of her own breasts. Sometimes she's unaware how this place is changing her until something shocks her out of her stupor. Only last month she went to Bucharest for a physical and discovered she'd gained ten pounds. Ten pounds in nine months.

I thought the Peace Corps was supposed to make me lose weight, she said.

The staff nurse took her pulse, smiled. That's Africa, Asia, the South Pacific. Dysentery. Malaria. Here it's high blood pressure, cholesterol.

Are you sure the scale is correct?

The nurse didn't answer.

It's just not possible, whined Stella. There's nothing here to *eat*.

Take for instance, now. She hasn't yet had breakfast and knows she'll be ravenous if she skips it. What she wants—what she thinks she'll need for this little chicken-shopping adventure—here is akin to manna from heaven. Wheaties or raisin bran, a half of banana, skim milk, some medium-roasted breakfast blend. But what she has is the dried heel of a loaf of bread, a lump of unsalted butter that changes its shape each time she removes it from the refrigerator, some mint tea.

During the summer, the *piața* where Stella and the rest of the city shop had been a carnival, busy and colorful and boisterous. The variety! The bounty! Dozens of tomatoes—beefsteak and heirloom, cherry and plum. Full-sized and pickling cucumbers; red, yellow, orange, green, and purple peppers; fat, glossy eggplant. Beans she snacked on as she strode back from the market to her apartment. The items weren't beautiful, but the tastes were unlike anything she'd ever experienced before. How could a scarred, mottled tomato, something that would never be displayed in her local Giant, taste as sweet as Swedish Fish? She'd never enjoyed them as a child but biting into a plum here, juice running down her fingers, sugar crystallizing in the crevices of her skin, she thought that maybe she'd never tried this fruit before. The abundance of flavor lit up her mouth; she wasn't eating but breathing it, experiencing it, from tongue to toes.

And then: autumn. Things began to thin by late September; by the end of October there were only a handful of farmers still selling alongside tables stacked with toilet paper, gray blocks of laundry soap, vinegar in greasy recycled bottles.

Now as Stella makes her way through the long tables of food items, all various shades of dull earth tones, the *piața* is nothing but winter-hued sadness. Like me, she thinks, indulging her self-pity. The holidays are a week away. She's never celebrated Christmas without her family. Thanksgiving, just another Thursday here, passed without ceremony. There are Christmas decorations, twinkling electric lights along the main boulevard; they are her only reminder of the impending holidays. She realizes she misses the incessant din of carols. The frenetic searching for gifts, last-minute mailing of holiday cards. The holiday cartoons, Hallmark movies, the savings commercials on TV. She'd never imagined she could miss these things, but it is their familiarity, their constancy for which she yearns. She doesn't have a TV here.

What a difference a single bright banana would make on this market. When Stella happens upon three pathetic little bunches that have traveled from Ecuador—not bright and lively but stunted, shriveling, freckled—she is reminded of the last time she bought them. That had been one splurge she'd regretted. She made them into bread to share with her neighbors. It's my mother's recipe, she explained as she handed out the moist slices, something special she's made ever since I was little.

Her neighbors munched politely.

An expensive loaf of bread, someone said.

Yes, murmured another. However do you afford it?

Wouldn't it be better to enjoy the fruit as is? someone else suggested.

It seems a waste, they all agreed, to use such fruit for bread.

She picks up a bag of cornmeal, a bag of flour. The bags leak onto her wool coat, her cold, bare hands. She buys spaghetti, a jar of tomato sauce. That is her special treat for the day.

When she approaches the kiosk where she usually buys eggs, the woman shakes her head, tells her the eggs have all been bought up for holiday baking. Same goes for the man who sells the white cheese she likes, the milkman. A little late for holiday shopping, no *domnișoară*?

Stella heads for the produce.

The apples' bruised, damaged flesh smears the insides of her bags. The cabbage—well, it's cabbage; if ever there is Armageddon, she thinks, the one thing that will survive is cabbage. The potatoes are small and already growing their eyes; they poke through the bag, stabbing the woman with the taffy breasts through her belly. The carrots are shriveled, pale runts. The onions are the only things that seem to be thriving, their papery skins flaking away in her hands when she takes hold, their layers upon layers so tight they are surely impenetrable. She raises a bare hand to her nose, smells the vegetable deep in her flesh. She's eaten so many onions she swears her skin secretes them.

As she moves down the stalls toward the bread, something catches her eye. It is a bright spot, so much so that for a moment Stella thinks it must be the sun—the sun has poked through the stony covering of clouds and illuminated a small corner of this gray *piața*. But upon closer inspection she realizes this is artificial brightness, a color only human hands could make, the packaging of something special, imported. It is a box of Cheerios or rather, a Hungarian rip-off of Cheerios. Still. Dried breakfast cereal.

Stella reaches out, picks up a box. She hasn't seen cereal since she left the States back in the spring. A single box costs more than she has left in her purse. If she were to return some of the items she's already bought—the pasta, the cornmeal . . . but there is no such thing as a returned item here, not even with a receipt. She looks up at the man standing behind the stall and smiles. He frowns, sucks snot deep into his throat, spits between his shoes. The frozen wind rustles her half-empty shopping bags, making the naked women tremble. She returns the box to its spot on the table.

Stella heads to the eastern side of the market where the chickens—that is, to say, the meat—are located. This particular section of the market retains some of the liveliness of the summer, in part because the chickens themselves are lively. Lively and alive.

They are lined up on tables. They cluck and stretch their necks and strike out at customers who get too close. Thankfully Stella won't be responsible for the butchering and plucking; that's up to Magda. But as Stella's gaze passes over the chickens she is reminded of a show she used to watch as a child that occasionally featured puppet chickens, their many personalities. Singing and dancing chickens! She begins to silently name each and every one—Edith, Betty, Mary Jo, Susie, Janet—imagines them bursting into song, performing the cancan then and there. She is certain if she goes through with it, she will be haunted by the ghost of one of them, those birds she has named. They will creep into her room at night, flap their way into her dreams, crow sadly, mourning over eggs never lain.

But she must do this, if only to prove to herself that she's worth something here. If this is a test, she's determined to pass it. She reaches down into her bags, begins to fish out the burlap sack Magda has given her but pauses when she sees three sets of glamorously made-up eyes casting doleful gazes at her. She shakes the contents of her bags to hide the eyes of those women from her. But this only causes the hens to tense up. One of them stands, steps boldly forward, jiggles her scarlet wattles at Stella. Hey there, lady, Stella coos doubtfully, reaching out to stroke the hen. It snaps at her. *Not so fast.*

Magda is going to kill me, thinks Stella and wheels around on her heels, scurrying away from the market.

Back home, Stella places the few items she's purchased on the otherwise empty shelves that cover the wall of her kitchen. Then she grabs the bottom of the second bag and upturns it. Produce rattles out, knocking disjointed rhythms against the table; a single potato rolls onto the floor. She doesn't bother to pick it up.

Outside in the courtyard, two of her neighbors stop their squabbling and murmur. *Zăpadă. Dumnezeu, zăpadă.* Stella looks out her window. Good God, more snow. Scattered, heavy flakes fall from the slate-colored sky, float in the air. She goes to the sink, scrubs her hands for several minutes, dries them, and puts her fingers to her lips, inhales. Onions, still.

She should start the water for tea. Take the butter out of the refrigerator so it will soften. Get out the knife for bread. But when Stella looks back at those dirt-coated items scattered across her kitchen table, inexplicably edible, she realizes she has lost her appetite. Anyway. Ten pounds overweight.

She watches the snow fall harder. The patients of the maternity hospital are still standing out front, as if they'd never moved. A nurse opens the door. Get inside for Christsake! she chastises. But the women just stare at her and then turn their faces back and upward, toward the sky. The snow lands on their cheeks, their eyelashes. They blink and blink, their lips quivering with smiles.

The telephone rings.

You sound funny, Magda says. Is something wrong?

I can't come over tonight, Stella says.

Are you feeling okay?

There wasn't any milk. Or eggs. Or *cheese*.

I'm sorry, says Magda.

And I didn't get the chicken.

No. I figured.

I'm sorry.

Nici-o problemă, dragă. We can make your mother's world famous chicken-noodle soup another time.

Stella sniffles, wipes her nose with the back of her hand, places a pot of water on the stove for tea. But the worst part?

Yes?

There was cereal, she says. Of course I couldn't buy it. It was too expensive.

Why don't you come over for dinner?

But chicken soup *was* dinner. What are we going to eat?

Well. I made *sarmale*.

Sarmale, repeats Stella. *Sarmale*? In her Polish grandmother's house it was called *gawumpki*. She used to help her grandmother spoon the ground meat and rice stuffing onto cabbage leaves, her grandmother demonstrating, pulling the leaf up, folding the ends over, rolling the leaves up.

Her mouth begins to water. Let me just get this straight: you *made* sarmale?

Magda pauses. I had a feeling about the chicken shopping.

They both laugh.

Sarmale. Are you sure it's okay? What can I bring? Stella removes the butter from the refrigerator, begins to slice the bread.

Magda snorts. Based on what you've told me? Nothing.

Monday morning and the orphanage is uncharacteristically active. When Stella bumps into Magda on her way in, she is given an explanation: a church group from Kentucky is here for a visit and has brought a shipment along with them.

So what will it be today? asks Stella. A box of left-footed shoes?

Magda laughs, loops her arm through Stella's. Let's go check it out.

The donations are being unloaded in the cafeteria. It is a good thing the children are at school right now; otherwise the scene would be impossible to manage. Stella has seen them ignore orders and reprimands and crack open boxes, rifling through clothing and toys, racing from the room before anyone has a chance to stop them. When she visits the living quarters, she is always surprised by the collection of contraband items the children have stashed away under pillows and beds—stuffed animals and Walkmans and jeans and board games.

Anything special you're looking for? Stella asks Magda. Stella's own rule is that she leaves the donations alone, but she's willing to help out a friend. A kind, good, patient friend.

I really shouldn't, says Magda.

C'mon.

I guess Tudor could use a new jumper, says Magda cracking her knuckles, her eyes dancing over the boxes. And if they're left and right-footed, Flavia needs a new pair of sneakers.

They settle into opening boxes, taking inventory.

Nothing here but books, reports Stella.

Girls clothing—but it's all summer apparel.

I think there might be some sweaters here.

Oh! Look at this doll! Better leave it for the kids—

How're these sneakers?

For a half hour they go on this way, ignoring their responsibilities, searching the boxes for gems Magda can take home to her children. The donations are not so bad, all things considered. The clothing and toys are new, the books conservative and Christian-leaning but not extreme in their messages.

This is a good shipment, says Stella, stepping back for a moment, resting her hands on her hips. Something here for everyone.

Even you. Magda is grinning, holding something in her hand. A bright red box.

What is it?

Magda shakes the box; it makes a sound like leaves rustling. What do you *think* it is?

Stella steps forward, reads the label. Frosted Mini Wheats.

Maybe we should go to the kitchen, says Magda. I, for one, want to see what all the fuss has been about.

Stella takes the box, gazes at it. We can't do that. It's for the kids.

There's plenty more where this came from. Besides, the kids won't even like it. Magda waves the box back and forth, runs her hands seductively along the bottom like a product model. Then she stops to take a closer look. Is it better than chicken-noodle soup? she teases.

The cafeteria kitchen is empty, the cooking staff on break before lunch preparations begin. Stella and Magda pull out bowls and spoons, a fresh bag of milk. Stella does the honors, cracking open the seal on the cardboard, tearing open the plastic bag. It lets out a sigh, as if it had been holding its breath for this moment, releasing the scent of sugar and grain.

Magda takes a sniff. I hope it tastes better than it smells. She grabs the box from Stella, pours cereal into their bowls. I hope it tastes better than it looks.

Hush!

Stella pours milk into each bowl.

Magda spoons up a single square, holds it high. *Poftă bună.*

Poftă bună.

For several minutes the only sound in the kitchen is the two women crunching, their spoons clinking against glass bowls, their throats gurgling when they swallow. Stella is waiting for something—a feeling, a flicker, a Polaroid gradually clarifying in her mind. Instead, she thinks of the *sarmale* she ate with Magda and her family on Saturday evening, the crowded, cozy space of their dining room, the homebrewed wine that warmed her cheeks, made her quick to laugh. Romanian seemed to stream off of her tongue that evening and later that night she had a dream that had been eluding her, a dream her language tutor had promised her would eventually come: a dream in Romanian.

She continues to wait. Perhaps it's that the cereal arrived unexpectedly, when she wasn't in need of it. This morning she awoke well-rested, content. There was a new layer of snow on the ground, crackling in the sunlight. She reheated leftovers from the dinner at Magda's, so much delicious food, enough to supply her for days. She doesn't know why she's agreed to this now; she's not even hungry.

The two women finish their meal, lay their spoons on the table, daintily wipe crumbs from their mouths with their fingers. The kitchen staff begins to filter in, eyeing the opened box and milk, the bowls, not speaking a word. Pots clatter, water is run. Magda glances in their direction, then back at Stella. She smoothes out the skirt of her dress, clears her throat.

So, she says. Was it everything you'd hoped it would be?

National Cherry Blossom Day

Gabriela runs her fingers over the embossed lettering of the party invitation, an insufficient Braille, and holds it to the light coming through the car window as if she might discover a watermark, some clue to a mystery she's been trying to unmask for a long while. The paper is substantial, a gold-colored cardstock bordered with an Asian-inspired print of tree branches coming into flower, but that look instead like question marks. "It is a holiday? National Cherry Blossom Day?"

"*Is* it," corrects her husband Joe; a bad habit acquired nine months ago, shortly after they moved from Romania to Washington. "And no, not officially. Christina was just being cute."

The traffic is bumper-to-bumper; they jerk their way in silence through Dupont Circle. The longer it takes, the harder it is for Gabriela to resist flinging the car door open, leaping out, and sprinting in the opposite direction. All morning she paced the apartment, rummaging through closets and squinting under furniture, searching for some excuse. But she knew what Joe would say.

"You never know who you'll meet at these things," he says now, immediately ducking as if he were expecting Gabriela to lob an axe in his direction.

Gabriela winces. Another bad habit. She would prefer nail-biting or nose-picking—anything—to this. "Maybe," she offers, trying on hope even though she knows it won't fit. She has attended enough of these parties to identify a lost cause when she sees one. And anyway, she isn't interested in who will be there because she already knows who won't: her mother, her sisters, her niece and colleagues from the university; Marta and Corina, her oldest childhood friends. "Do you realize there are holidays for everything here? Groundhog Day and Valentine's Day, Presidents' Day and St. Patrick's Day . . . "

"We have a lot to celebrate."

Or nothing worth celebrating enough. Gabriela's feeling about holidays is the same as friendships: if you have too many, the quality of all of them suffers. "The cherry blossoms haven't even *blossomed* yet."

Joe reaches over, pats her knee. "They will."

She gazes at his hand where it rests on her leg. With the exception of meticulously trimmed nails, it is the very same one that insisted she give him a chance four years ago. She knows she should place her own over his, that this is the right thing to do, but her arms feel heavy at her sides, impossible to lift.

She turns her face away, looks up through the closed window at the crocheted dome of fresh leaves bursting from the trees above them. The branches shiver. There are starlings and sparrows hopping from one limb to the next, shaking out their feathers, snapping their thorny beaks at invisible bugs. The skin on Gabriela's knee where Joe touches her begins to itch. The car lurches, bucks, stops. A pigeon veers dangerously close to their windshield before careening upward and away; car horns bleat at a cyclist weaving through the jam. And just when it seems he will never move it, Joe gives the tight flesh of her knee one final tug before placing his hand firmly back on the steering wheel.

"Cherry blossoms? Why, they're fashionably late, of course," jokes the hostess of the party, Christina Neufhausen Bryant the Third. Her manner suggests years of acting classes. As she speaks, her long hands flutter like they are caged and seeking escape exits; they land, fingers extended on her collarbone when she is pretending to listen. Gabriela does not like her. "Never count on Mother Nature to provide cohesion to a thematically-based festivity."

Other guests chuckle. Gabriela sips her drink and presses herself hard against Joe, her heartbeat slowing only when he puts his arm around her. She hates that this is what it takes. She does not know this person she becomes at such events, the person she has become more and more lately.

"They'll be here eventually," continues Christina. "In the meantime: bottoms up." She raises her glass, her eyes meeting Gabriela's, and winks. Gabriela drops her gaze into her drink, slurps.

"Gabriela's dying to the see them," says Joe. "Aren't you, sweetheart?"

It's true that she has wanted to see the blossoms since their very first date when Joe had described for her the Jefferson Memorial and Tidal Basin in April; the way the blossoms smelled so delicious you'd want to stuff your mouth full of them; how once they'd passed their peak, the wind swept them up and spread them like ticker-tape, the city besieged by a full-on floral assault. *I'd love to see that,* she'd said. *I'd love to show you,* he'd replied.

But now his eagerness and effort make her wilt. Stop trying, she wants to say. Instead, she mutters: "Yes. I am dying to see them."

The unseasonably cold spring is the official reason why the trees are unrelenting. But sometimes, during evenings of insomnia, Gabriela thinks the cherry blossoms were nothing more than a ruse Joe thought up to convince her to leave Romania.

"Blame it on global warming," one of the other guests says.

"That's right. Bizarre weather patterns are a sure sign of it."

"It's really unusual, isn't it?" Joe adds. "The weather, I mean."

"You always say that," blurts Gabriela, immediately regretting it.

Joe blinks at her. "Always say what?"

"Nothing." She shoves her hand in her purse, searching for something on which to cling.

"But I want to know." The arm that protects her begins loosening its hold. "What do I always say?"

Mere minutes into the evening and Gabriela realizes she has already broken some unspoken rule of party etiquette. The other guests smile close-mouthed at each other or comment on how delicious the freezer-burned mini-quiches are, but Gabriela knows underneath their politesse they are waiting for conflict the way seagulls wait for a tossed bagel, popcorn spills. Plucking a strawberry that looks to be hand-painted from a proffered tray, Gabriela tries to sound casual. "You always say: 'It's really unusual.'"

He'd started saying it last summer, when they arrived to Washington amid a drought. The lawns up and down the street in Mount Pleasant where they'd rented an apartment burned through to dried dirt, the leaves on the trees became as brown and shriveled as worms trapped in the sun; the air outside settled sap-like in their lungs. Normally the summers were hot, he explained to her, but this stretch—the drought?—was highly *unusual*.

By the look on his face, Gabriela can tell Joe is hurt. "But it *is* really unusual," he says.

"Bourbon chicken skewers, anyone?" shrieks Christina. "They're a nod to my Kentucky roots!"

Their first month in Washington they'd sought refuge in the air-conditioned bar of a local Salvadoran restaurant, numbing their uncertainties with cheap merlot and plate after plate of *papusas*. While at the university, Gabriela had had a colleague who spent a year in California on a Fulbright exchange and had come back thirty pounds heavier; now she was certain the same thing was happening to her. She pinched the skin on her waist, whined. Joe tried to buoy her spirits with chirpy pseudo-scientific explanations she could never fully comprehend—something about the gulf stream, weather patterns that ran on a seven year cycle—and suspected he was making it up. At night they had lain spread-eagle on a mattress their landlord had loaned them until the rest of their belongings shipped from Romania, their bodies too hot for embraces, spooning. Windows and doors were open wide to encourage a cross breeze that never came; sweat pooled in the small of their backs, in the shallow valley between Gabriela's breasts. She pulled her thick black hair up onto the pillow, pounded fists against the mattress. "Is it always this *hot*?"

"It's definitely strange." Joe patted her damp thigh. "But wait until next spring. You'll see. Rain, rain, and more rain."

He never said *Bucharest is just as hot* or *At least here there is air conditioning*. Sometimes Gabriela wished he would; at least if he retaliated she'd feel she had a reason to be mean.

"Liberal conspiracy theorists, the lot of you," laughs Christina Neufhausen Bryant the Third, taking charge. "Just wait till my boy wins the election. He'll debunk all your environmental mumbo-jumbo."

This induces a cacophony of cheers and groans, the inevitable political debate. Voices rise and people jockey for position in the crowd, the circle growing tighter. A wedge is created between Gabriela and Joe, releasing the loose hold they have on each other. The next thing Gabriela knows he is standing opposite her, engaged in intense conversation with a woman who resembles Hillary Clinton. Someone bumps Gabriela, splashing her cocktail. After inspecting her blouse for damage, she looks up, expecting to meet an apologetic face, only to discover she's been squeezed entirely outside of the circle. Sighing, she bites into the strawberry. It tastes of nothing but water.

"Do you know the drink you're holding is the precise color of cherry blossoms?" A stout, eagerly smiling woman stands next to Gabriela, she too having been excluded from the inner circle. "It's true." The woman nods in agreement with herself. "Christina did research."

Gabriela considers the half-drunk glass in her hand. "This is what the cherry blossoms look like?" The drink goes down easily enough but is the same artificial color as the farm-raised salmon Joe insists she buy for him each week, eschewing her famous fried meatballs and cheese omelets—all the foods they'd enjoyed together back home—for food with packages that advertise "all natural" as if it were a modern invention. "Aren't eggs natural?" she sometimes chides him when he refuses a plate of something she's cooked. "What's more natural than pork?"

"Sorry, sweetheart," he always replies, patting his belly good-naturedly. "Time to lose some L-B-S's."

"I'm Louisa." The woman is offering Gabriela her hand. "Christina really knows how to throw a party, doesn't she?"

Christina Neufhausen Bryant the Third had been the former ambassador to some East African nation and the ethnic bric-a-brac of her Woodley Park townhouse—woven baskets and freestanding carvings of giraffes and dark bowls made of illegal woods—clashes with the tastefully bland china plates stacked on linen tabletops and cocktail napkins printed with the presidential seal. The hostess herself wears large, brightly beaded bracelets on her slender, liver-spotted arms; a misdirected choice, thinks Gabriela, when the hand on the end of that arm holds an Irish crystal goblet filled with Californian pinot noir. All the hors d'oeuvres appear color-coordinated, segregated, earth-tone nuts and breads here, vibrant tropical fruits and pink-frosted cupcakes there, none of it homemade.

Music Gabriela has come to associate with expensive home furnishing stores—something instrumental, repetitive, with bongos and steel drums, Latin American-Caribbean fusion—trickles out of tiny speakers mounted to the walls. It is a festively insipid choice, one that urges guests to have fun but not too much fun. Dancing, for example, is not on the schedule for tonight. Party games, yes; Charades or Celebrity if enough alcohol is consumed. But absolutely, positively, under no circumstances will there be dancing.

Earlier in the week Gabriela had spoken with her mother and sisters. What were her plans for the weekend, they all were eager to know. *Another party?* they'd gasped. *Good lord! How lucky you are, Gabița!*

It was what her family had been saying all along, ever since Gabriela had been hired to provide translation services to the American Embassy in Bucharest. Like the rest of the world she had decided to take advantage of the post-revolutionary influx of the West, earning some extra money to supplement her meager professor's salary. She'd been translating a document reporting the breeds and numbers of fish counted in the Danube Delta during spawning season when Joe approached her one afternoon, his soft frame casting round, uncertain shadows over trout and pike percentages.

"Aren't you at the wrong embassy?" he'd joked when he learned that in addition to translating, she had a job as a French professor at the University of Bucharest.

She did not smile back. "I double majored."

"I see." He jiggled the keys in his pocket. "The last communists, the first capitalists."

Gabriela knew he was only repeating something he'd heard. Still, she set her jaw. "You've got that wrong. I wasn't a communist at all." It was a source of pride; she'd refused party membership, her name, she liked to imagine, still appearing on some torn, yellowing blacklist buried in the back of a forgotten government file.

Joe's forehead rippled. "But wasn't everyone?" He wasn't joking this time.

"No. Everyone was not." Gabriela turned her back on him.

The shadows wavered, but remained. "I'm sorry. I think we got off on the wrong foot." A hand was thrust under her nose. "I'm Joseph."

She considered the hand. It was plump, smooth, suggesting privilege, an easy life thus far. But then there were the nails like the edge of a serrated knife.

"And your name is?" The hand wasn't going anywhere.

He started bringing her coffee and tea, snacks from the embassy shop, things she'd never seen before—granola bars, Doritos, a jar of peanut butter her mother had taken a sniff of before shoving it deep into the recesses of the kitchen cupboard. Eventually, Joe asked her to dinner.

They went to an exclusive Greek restaurant and sat among expatriates, members of the Italian and Russian mafias, local celebrities from a newly privatized television company. They talked about his job, his travels; he told her about the cherry blossoms. She described for him her mother, sisters, and niece and taught him how to ask for another bottle of wine in Romanian.

She liked his modesty, the way he was quick to blush. She liked the way he spoke in exclamations (*How interesting! You don't say!*), his enthusiasm so infectious she found that by the end of the evening she was mimicking him. His optimism, particularly for the future of Romania, struck her as endearingly naïve, his opinions those only an American could have.

She realized she was having a good time and, amid him telling her a story, she snatched his hand up, rendering him mute. "What are you doing next weekend? I'm having a party."

Joe stood on her doorstep with a bouquet of flowers and a box of baklava purchased from the same Greek restaurant. When he saw the empty room, the pots on the stove only just boiling, he apologized saying he'd thought Gabriela had said the party started at six.

"I did. But that doesn't mean you *come* at six."

He shrugged, took off his coat, tossed it over the back of a chair, and began rolling up his sleeves. "What can I do?"

He stirred soups, sliced bread. He charmed her mother with boisterous, ungrammatical Romanian and compliments on the apartment and her daughter. When other guests arrived, he served up drinks. Later, furniture was pushed back, the lights turned off; dancing ensued. Joe gamely twisted and spun. "Does this happen at every party in Romania?" he shouted over the buzzing, distorted bass beat of the Macarena.

"What's a party without dancing?" Gabriela shouted back, laughing as he spun her again and again.

Her three sisters, niece, and mother were the only people in attendance at the wedding a year later. It was held in the living room of her mother's apartment—Gabriela's apartment—a place formerly known to her as home.

Joe has moved away from the Hillary Clinton doppelgänger and appears, from Gabriela's perspective, to be helping Christina Neufhausen Bryant the Third refill glasses. She had thought at that very first party back in Bucharest that his help was intended to impress her, but has since learned Joe is like a golden retriever, panting, smiling, always eager to please just about anyone. It is a truth about him others admire but that disappoints her, just like so many other things here.

The room continues to fill up; people break into conversational huddles. In one corner guests consider the impact of Texan culture on Washington fashion (*Would there be black ties and ten gallon hats? Cowboy boots on Capitol Hill?*); in another they compare the work ethic of their various Senate offices. Gabriela bounces like a pinball from one group to another. Above the party din, Joe's voice rises.

"It takes time to adjust," Gabriela overhears him rationalizing. "Especially if you're not well-traveled." And then: "No, she isn't working . . . She's fluent in French . . . I keep saying she should call Luc at Alliance Française . . . "

Gabriela's fingers flit over a shot glass filled with toothpicks. She plucks one up, chewing on the end of it before piercing it through a cube of florescent cheese and dropping it uneaten onto her plate.

" . . . I keep telling her maybe she could get an adjunct position at one of the universities or a community college . . . "

Gabriela snaps up another toothpick, stabs another cheese cube. That's the thing about Joe: he believes all problems can be solved with something as straightforward as a new job, hobby, car, house, religion. He'd suggested as much when, after nearly two years as husband and wife, he'd told her about being transferred back to the States. "There's a lot you can do there," he'd explained. "If you didn't want to work right away, you could go back to school. Take up painting. Or yoga." *Yoga?* Even though she had quit smoking years before, Gabriela locked herself outside on the narrow balcony of their single bedroom apartment, her body trembling with the indignity of it all, and puffed her way through an entire pack of Snagovs.

" . . . Her German isn't half-bad either . . . "

She blamed herself, mostly. Joe had warned her from the beginning that he wouldn't be able to stay at the embassy forever. It had been an agreement they made; at some point they'd try the States. Was it his fault that Gabriela had secretly prayed it never came to that? After she'd finished her Snagovs and come inside, lungs afire, Joe suggested that maybe he was being too hasty, maybe he could find some sort of work in Bucharest. It is the thing she still loves the most about him, the thing that makes her stay still even though every other part of her yearns for flight: his willingness to try.

Gabriela was, in the end, a good wife. *Of course you'll go,* her sisters and mother said. *Get out of this hellhole! Live life! There's nothing worth staying here for. Except you,* she'd said. *Us?* They'd waved their hands. *Bah.* How could she explain? She loved this hellhole.

"It'll all work out for the best!" Joe had insisted as their plane took off from Bucharest to the United States. If he was so willing to try, then surely it was the least she could do for him in return. She reminded herself of this as the plane broke through cloud coverage, sunlight glinting off the metallic wings. She pressed her forehead against the small oval window and looked out across an infinite blue sky. Below, she saw a wall of solid white cumulus clouds heaped on top of each other and veiled by gauzy cirrus. All of them absorbed the colors of the sun so that they bled through with pink.

"Like the cherry blossoms," Gabriela had offered to Joe, gesturing at those clouds. "Something like them," he said, flipping through the in-flight magazine.

She wonders now, gazing down at the perfectly symmetrical orange squares on her plate, each one pricked through its heart with miniature stakes, if she didn't set them both up for failure.

A full tray of shrimp cocktail sits untouched on the kitchen counter. In the freezer, behind several boxes of miniature spinach quiches, Gabriela finds a half-full bottle of vodka.

A dog lies on the bed in the master bedroom, lifting its head when she opens the door. Gabriela immediately identifies the breed of the animal as a Viszla, the Hungarian national dog. Its yellow, intelligent eyes receive her with an open curiosity and interest she feels she is experiencing for the first time in months. Her best friend Marta, who still had distant relatives living in Budapest, used to declare these dogs the most superior breed in the world in order to rope Gabriela into nationalistic debate. But as she thinks of this now it only makes Gabriela feel a hunger for something that isn't on the menu.

Placing the shrimp on the nightstand, she strokes the dog's smooth head with one hand while taking gulps from the vodka bottle with the other. Then she picks up the receiver on the telephone that sits next to the bed.

"Gabița! Are you okay? Is something wrong?" Her mother's voice is a whisper.

"Wrong?" Gabriela has forgotten: the time change. She glances at the clock on the nightstand. Nine thirty-seven. It was hardly morning yet in Romania. "No, Mama. Nothing's wrong. Just thought I'd give you a call."

"Ay, dragă." Her mother's deep sigh crackles so loudly in her ear she swears she can feel her breath on her skin. "You'll give me a heart attack one of these days."

"I'm sorry."

"Where are you anyway? Weren't you supposed to be at a party? Where's Joseph?"

Gabriela takes another sip from the bottle, leans back on the pile of pillows, kicks off her shoes. She imagines her mother as she would be in this moment: curlers, hair net, full-length nightgown she's been wearing since Gabriela was little. A heavy pain presses against her chest. "He's here," she says, casting a look around the empty bedroom.

"You tell him I said *ciao*, yes? Dear, dear man."

"I will, Mama."

"How was the party tonight? Did you enjoy it?"

"It was fine."

There is a pause on the other end of the line. Gabriela waits through the scratching and scraping of fabric against the telephone as her mother adjusts her position. She imagines her lips moving, counting off the six-hour time difference between them. "You're home early, aren't you though?"

"Happy hour."

Her mother chuckles. "Happy hour. Those Americans."

"Yes," Gabriela agrees, squeezing her eyes shut. "They're something."

"Are you okay? Your voice sounds funny."

"I'm eight thousand kilometers away. My voice *should* sound funny."

Next to Gabriela, the dog stretches and moans before plopping its head into her lap.

"What's that?"

Gabriela gazes down at the dog, rests her free hand on its head. "Just Joseph. He's tired."

"Is he working too much? You tell him I said not to work so much."

"I will, Mama."

"Good. Now listen, before I forget: Alina saw a department store on television—Saks Fifth Avenue? Have you heard of it? She said the clothing looked *foarte fine*."

Gabriela holds the cool vodka bottle to her temple. "It's expensive. *Foarte fine e foarte scump.*"

"But maybe good for bras, *dragă*. You know how bad they are here. Look would you? For me?"

Of course, Gabriela replies. And yes, panties, too. Whatever they need, she'll get it for them.

"Good," her mother says, satisfied.

"Mama?"

"Yes, *dragă*?"

She knows what she wants to say, but doesn't know how to start. And even if she is able to muster up the courage, her mother will say the same things Joe and her sisters have been telling her for months. She will say it is too soon, she needs to give herself more time to adjust. She'll say her marriage is still young, that these are the sacrifices you make, the risks you take, for love. She will ask Gabriela in a gentle, reprimanding tone if she and Joe have given any thought to expanding the family.

Gabriela feels tired from talking; she needs a cigarette. She pulls open the drawer of the nightstand, rifles through the pens and half a dozen varieties of birth control and emery boards until her fingers discover the crumpled package at the very back and pull it out. Menthols. Just her luck. But at least there are matches.

"Gabița? Are you still there?"

The dog's head pops up at the snapping sound the match makes. Gabriela blows out a slow trail of smoke, stroking the animal until it lays its head back down in her lap. "I'm here."

"Don't forget those chocolates, too. The ones you sent the last time? There's nothing like them here. Absolutely nothing."

After hanging up the phone, Gabriela smokes first one and then a second cigarette, alternating drags with careful sips of vodka. She realizes she is playing a game, waiting for Joe to come find her. Surely he's begun to wonder about her absence. The dog is dozing now, its nose making a high-pitched whistling sound each time it exhales. She likes the way its head feels in her lap, likes to watch it sleeping. Perhaps they might get a dog. Perhaps Christina Neufhausen Bryant the Third no longer wants this dog and they could take it home with them tonight.

This isn't the first time pet ownership has crossed Gabriela's mind. She'd first suggested it to Joe last summer, when stories of animal sightings not associated with urban-dwelling—deer, coyotes and, most frighteningly, a mountain lion—began to circulate in their neighborhood.

"A mountain lion?" Gabriela was unable to hide her alarm. She'd been peering over Joe's shoulder at the Sunday newspaper and saw the amateur photo included with the article, the picture taken at dusk, grainy but unmistakably that of a large shadow, something lurking on a side street blocks from their apartment.

"Coming down from the Shenandoah Valley," Joe had read aloud. "The drought is happening there, too. The animals are looking for food."

"There are mountain lions here?"

"They're supposed to be extinct on the East Coast."

"But people are *seeing* them."

"Sweetheart, I'm sure it's not a mountain lion."

But over the next several weeks the reports continued—one seen rummaging through the garbage of a nearby grocery store, another slinking off with what looked to be a rabbit dangling between its jaws. Overnight, bulletin boards in neighborhood coffee shops and telephone poles up and down the streets were covered with flyers announcing the disappearance of toy poodles, declawed housecats.

But it wasn't just the mountain lions that had given Gabriela the idea of getting a dog. One afternoon, when she stepped outside to throw away a bag of garbage, she'd found a line of rats larger than any she'd ever seen in Bucharest balancing on the edge of the dumpster. As she approached they turned skillfully on their haunches, sticking their blunted snouts into the air, making terrifying, high-pitched noises that sent tremors through Gabriela's hands. She'd dumped the bags where she stood and scurried back to the security of their apartment.

"The city's built on a swamp," Joe explained. "They're swamp rats."

"Why are there rats at all?" she asked. "Isn't this the capital of the free world?"

"Rats are everywhere, Gabi. At least they're not something worse."

She waited, half hoping for him to say it, overcome with the urge to argue. Bucharest had a terrible problem with stray dogs; Joe had been bitten not once, but three times. But instead of speaking he rubbed her back, trying to calm her.

Gabriela wiggled away from him. "We should get a dog," she said.

"A dog? For what?"

"Protection."

Joe began to laugh but stopped when he saw her expression. "Sorry, sweetheart. I'm allergic."

But now, as this dog rouses itself from its nap, yawning so Gabriela can see the ridges on the roof of its mouth, she thinks that surely in a land where there is cheese for the lactose-intolerant and sausage for vegetarians, there must also be hypoallergenic dogs.

She gulps down more vodka, wipes her mouth with the back of her hand, picks up a shrimp from the tray on the nightstand. The tags around the dog's neck jangle pleasantly as it gets to its feet. It lets out a quietly possessed whimper; wags its stump of a tail so the entire bed trembles.

"What? You like shrimp, do you?" Gabriela hands a piece of the food to the animal. It consumes it, tail shell and all, its gums smacking, and swallows with great effort. She holds up a second shrimp. "Are *these* the color of cherry blossoms?" she asks the dog, but this only seems to make it more excited as it snatches the food from her fingers.

Gabriela alternates between taking swigs from the vodka bottle and feeding the dog, occasionally tossing the food up in the air so the animal makes a show of leaping from the bed, catching the pink morsel in midair, the sound of its teeth snapping together like a knife blade falling onto the neck of a chicken.

She must not have been asleep for long because when she wakes, a lit cigarette left on the nightstand is still burning down, its ash hanging threateningly over the edge. The tray of shrimp is empty; the vodka bottle still contains liquid but less than Gabriela hopes. Her throat is raw, her eyelashes feel glued together. Next to her the dog is passed out once more, its mouth hanging open, a small line of drool running from its tongue onto the bedspread. She gives it a pat on the side. It is unresponsive and for a moment she is seized with the thought that shrimp, like chocolate, is poisonous to canines. But then the dog's hind legs kick out and she realizes it is deep in some doggy dreamland, chasing cars, digging holes.

The party is still in full swing; through the crack in the bedroom door she hears the voice of Christina directing someone who sounds like Joe to the bathroom down the hall. As his footsteps approach Gabriela realizes he is coming for her and puts out the cigarette on the tray, brushes back her hair, searches for her shoes. But then the footsteps continue past her; the bathroom door clicks shut. The clock on the nightstand reads ten thirty; she's been absent from the party nearly an hour and still no Joe. She wonders if he will ever come for her.

She slinks down onto the floor, finds her shoes, slips them onto her feet. Willing herself not to cry, she makes a plan: she will call a cab, insist to Joe that she is fine heading home alone, that he should stay and continue to enjoy himself, that tomorrow morning, after they've both had a good night's sleep, they will talk about what is to be done. But Gabriela cannot move. Instead of picking up the phone, she remains seated on the floor for five, ten minutes. Eventually the dog stirs and jumps down off the bed, seating itself beside her. It licks her hand, her cheek, gives her arm a nudge with its wet nose. When none of this works, it gives up and shakes itself out before squeezing itself through the narrow crack of the bedroom door.

Although she tries not to, her ears are still trained for outside noise, voices—Joe's voice asking people if they've seen her, Joe's voice calling out to her—and it is then that she notices something has shifted in the tenor of the party. It seems louder but it's not that it has grown in volume; the quality of noise is different. She places her hands on the ground, pushes herself up, listens. What is it that has changed? Vibrations thrum through the ground; she feels the rhythm in the palms of her hands and knows now what it is. The music. The Macarena.

Before that party in Bucharest, she'd never really liked the song or the silly dance that accompanied it. But ever since then she can't help smiling at the sound of it blaring from a passing car window or included in some television or movie soundtrack. She remembers now how she, her sisters, and her niece had cajoled her mother into joining them on the floor of the living room, how they all kicked off their shoes and did the dance in unison, slapping their shoulders and arms, wiggling their hips, laughing. She remembers how good it felt knowing that Joe was watching her, admiring her, already falling in love with her, and how the knowledge of all that lit her up more, gave her the energy and strength to continue.

Remembering that evening, she feels it now, the feeling that energized her, that made her jump. She knows it because she hasn't felt it for nearly a year and has desperately missed it. As she stands her body quakes with it; her head is dizzy with its power. She hurries out into the living room. She needs to get there before the song ends.

Gabriela does not pause to take stock of the living room where, besides the musical selection, little else has changed.

She does not care that no one else is dancing or that people gawk at her, their expressions as uniform as strip malls as she gently presses them to make room, carving out space for herself so that she can begin. She does not care that they murmur to each other as she flings her arms across her chest and waist, bouncing her knees to keep the beat, singing at the top of her lungs, jutting her pelvis forward before jumping a quarter of a turn, the dance repeating itself over and over again. She does not care that no one—not even Joe—joins her; that he does not watch her with joy and admiration as he had four years ago, but with shame that causes his face and neck to go splotchy. She will not let any of this ruin the moment for her; she closes her eyes, dancing blindly, singing, singing.

Excited by the commotion Gabriela is causing, the dog dashes into the room, barking and leaping up at her flapping hands, bounding around her. Finally, a dance partner.

Earlier in the evening someone had opened a window and Gabriela can feel the cool night air on her damp skin as she flies about the room. She inhales, the air burning her lungs, and that's when she tastes it on the back of her tongue, tickling her throat; something entirely new to her even though she knows immediately what it is. Sugary, elusive but more abundant in flavor than the pink cocktail she'd consumed so much of earlier in the evening. Fecund earth, flower nectar, tree bark.

She squeezes her eyes tighter, spins faster. The flavor awakens her vision; they begin to bloom on the backs of her eyelids. Stars, she thinks, she is seeing stars—but no, she is mistaken; not stars at all. She smiles, drops her head back, the music driving her on. She sees them as she saw the clouds from the airplane window nearly a year before and wonders if they hadn't been there all along. It is not how she had imagined seeing them, not the way Joe has described them to her, but she'll take it. Outside, they have not yet broken free from their green encasings, haven't officially revealed themselves to the rest of the world, but tonight, on a night that surely translates into failure, they privately unveil themselves to her, their petals wings, lifting her up, away.

Palace Girls

One of the girls has hung herself from the chandelier in the Athenee Palace Hotel's dining room. In the lobby, the rest of them huddle together, trying to decide what should be done.

Ovidiu, the boss, steps forward and tugs at his pants, silencing everyone. His flip-flops slap against the dusty marble as he approaches Irina, who is seated on one of the velvet divans that bookend what was once the reception desk of the now dilapidated hotel. He reaches into his back pocket, removing a switchblade, and holds it out to her. "Cut her down," he orders.

She stands up, looks him in the eye. "Why should I have to do it?"

"You're the expert."

Irina resists the urge to swipe the switchblade from his hands, flip it open and run it deep into his gut. She looks past Ovidiu at the other girls scattered around the lobby. They inspect their cuticles, hold pocket mirrors up high and apply an unnecessary layer of lipstick. The men meet her gaze, snicker.

"Don't make me do this."

Ovidiu puffs out his doughy chest, grabs Irina by the wrist; yanks her close to him. His breath smells sour and is hot on her cheek. He pries her fist open, slaps the switchblade against her palm: handle made of mother-of-pearl, screws that have begun to go orange. It's the same knife she used the last time. Irina runs her thumb down the smooth handle, sucks in air.

"Just one more thing." Ovidiu holds up a fat hand. He smiles and it is nearly jovial. "You're assigned corpse duty."

Irina blinks. She cannot feel her feet, her hands.

"I don't care how you do it. It can be the same as last time. Just get rid of it."

A familiar image comes to Irina then: the delicate, beautiful foot, the bones so carefully aligned like some piece of African artwork carved from the tusks of elephants, toenails painted an iridescent pink, mixing with rotten food, disintegrating paper, flies rising up in a single black cloud with the final shove of the body into the dumpster behind the Russian Orthodox Church. Irina's vision blurs, goes white, comes back into focus. She looks up and sees Ovidiu waiting, watching her closely. Through the open front door she can hear the banner fixed to the hotel's façade rattling in the wind. *Pe curând, Hilton Hotel!* it reads. She looks again at Ovidiu. His mouth twitches; he's holding back laughter.

Irina does not plan to hit him, it just happens. One minute her hand is at her side and the next thing she knows she has hit him because her palm is burning and Ovidiu is crouching before her, holding his face, screaming things she cannot hear and the other girls and men are rushing toward them, telling Ovidiu to wait, *just hold on now, don't do anything brash*.

One of the other girls, Simona, steps in front of Irina. Ovidiu will not harm her because her beauty is the most valuable item he has, the reason they are able to stay in the hotel during its early reconstruction, she being a favorite of the construction-site manager. "She'll do it, Ovidiu. She'll take care of it. Won't you, Irina?"

Irina doesn't answer, focusing instead on the marks up the inside of Simona's left arm, constellations of stars as seen on film negatives.

Ovidiu straightens up. "I know she'll *do* it."

Still holding his cheek, he grabs Irina with his free hand and drags her across the lobby, giving her a final shove in the direction of the dining room. Irina pauses to look back over her shoulder and squints at the light from the street, which casts the rest of them in a strange forest silhouette, the girls spindly saplings, the men thick aged oaks.

As she heads down the long corridor, Irina swears she can make out the sound of the others exhaling. If she thinks about this it will enrage her, and she knows that in order to do this, she must not think, so she stops there. She is good at this, turning her thoughts on and off as easily as she does the faucet, the television, the lights.

The doors of the dining room are closed, their golden, S-shaped handles cold to touch. Irina stares down at the back of her hand gripping the door handle. Her skin is darker in the dim light of the hall, most of the light fixtures having been pulled from the walls. She closes her eyes and counts. *One, two, three, four*. When she opens her eyes, the hallway is completely black, the feeling of her hand on the door is the only thing grounding her in place. She counts again. She thinks of a girl she used to know, a thirteen-year-old Russian who was en route to Germany. She'd get high on paint, stealing it from the nearby hardware store, inhaling it in plastic bags so that her mouth would be ringed with silver. Lidia used to take care of her when things got really bad, bathing her, putting her to bed, ensuring she had enough to eat. But then Lidia was always taking care of everyone.

Irina wishes she had some right now. She'd never taken to drugs the way some of the other girls had, but now she wishes she had something to deaden her insides, someone—Lidia—to take care of her. *But there*, she tells herself, *you've gone too far already*.

Her eyes readjust to the light; Irina presses down on the handle. The mechanism inside makes a clacking sound as if a vault were being opened, even though the door has no lock. She keeps her gaze fixed on the grimy floor as she pushes the door wide.

The nights were cloaked in darkness, silence but for the demands men made on them, their grunts and later, their gravelly breathing, the smell of stale cigarettes and sweat lingering in the linens of tired hotel rooms. They did not talk to each other about the fear. Instead, they looked forward to daylight, which was theirs to do with what they liked.

Irina and Lidia always spent their days together, as far away from Piața Revoluției and the hotel as possible. One warm afternoon, nearly summer, they took the subway north to Herăstrău Park. Irina bought a loaf of bread from a street vendor and they selected a spot under a weeping willow tree located next to a small lake. The carp sensed their arrival, felt their shadows moving across the water, so accustomed were they to being fed by humans, and lingered close to shore. Irina tore the bread in half, plucked bits from its white, fleshy middle, tossing them to the fish until the loaf was hollow inside. Lidia lounged back on her elbows, squinted into the hazy sunlight, gnawing at a piece of crust. Occasionally she dipped a foot into the water, trying to stroke the slimy backs of the fish with her toes. Sometimes she succeeded and screeched in glee and horror, jerking her foot away, scrunching up her face, shuddering. The fish nearly threw themselves onto land in an effort to get at the bread crumbs, their gray and orange bodies writhing against and over and under each other, their round mouths opening up before Irina, waiting to be filled.

She did not know why she fed them. She found them vaguely disgusting, the way they swam in murky, shallow water and fought with each other. Their eyes were large but unseeing; some of them had gouges on their sides where scales had been torn away, or fins that were shredded like decaying leaves. They ate the bread in violent, snapping bites, the water kicking up around them, spraying the girls. But their desperation was familiar to Irina, and so she fed them until there was nothing left of the bread, not even the tough crust.

Later, they headed to another part of the park, their fingers laced together as they paid admission at the kiosk next to the gated entrance of the Village Museum. There were patterns etched into the wood of the enormous gate—the Tree of Life, the Twisted Rope, the Sun's Ray. Irina read aloud a sign that explained the significance of each pattern, Lidia smiling, correcting her when she got stuck on a word. She'd been teaching Irina to read. The Wolf's Teeth were at the top, looming high over the girls' heads; Lidia stared at them for a long while. "We could use some of those above our bedroom door." Wolves' teeth were meant to ward off evil.

The girls took their time among the small country cottages, admiring the handwoven rugs and orange, painted pottery that was displayed on front stoops. They had to duck their heads to enter one small cottage, the roof made of thatched hay, the floor of clay. Two small windows barely lit the room from outside, making it dark and cool. A perfect hiding place.

"Have you ever seen such a place?"

Lidia shook her head, her fingertips brushing the smooth surface of a table, the handle on a cast iron pan. "But I wouldn't mind going one day. Have you?"

"I told you. Bucharest is the farthest I've ever been."

"Then you haven't been anywhere."

Irina didn't respond but moved instead to a small bed adorned with red woven rugs and sheep skins. She took a seat.

"You shouldn't, Irina. The sign says *hands off*."

"And my hands are off. See? It's my ass that's on."

Lidia laughed, paused before sitting down beside her. Their bodies pressed against each other. "What if we left together some day? Went to Maramureș, had a cottage like this one?"

Irina looped a lock of Lidia's hair around her index finger, covering it all the way past the nail so that her finger looked like a miniature mummy wrapped in red silk. "Could we have cows? A pig to slaughter at Christmastime?"

"Do *ţigani* do that? I thought Gypsies didn't celebrate Christmas."

"But *you* do." Irina knew Lidia was Hungarian, Catholic.

"I haven't in a while. But maybe this year. With you."

Irina felt Lidia's eyes on her but could not meet her friend's gaze. The cool space had become hot, the air thick with their conversation, and she felt something heavy pushing against her chest. "I need some fresh air."

She made a move to rise from the bed, but Lidia stopped her. "*Wait*."

When Irina turned to look at her friend their noses bumped.

They kissed. It was different than any kiss Irina had known before, nothing like the usual abrasive cheeks of men, some of whom bit her lips until she bled, squeezed her arms blue. This was soft, playful, lacking fear. They held the kiss longer than it seemed possible, their lips continuing to press lightly against each other's. Irina watched Lidia's eyelids droop, then close, and for the first time she allowed hers to close as well, giving herself over to the sensation, relaxing in the comfort and security of it. She wondered if it felt the same to Lidia as it did to her.

Lidia's lips expanded, stretched; she was smiling. The faint peach flavor of lip gloss lingered in Irina's mouth when they finally pulled away. Her eyes flew open; Lidia's cheeks were flushed and she was still smiling.

They were both just barely seventeen.

For the first time, Irina is thankful that the dining room has no windows; she'd prefer to do this in as dark a room as possible. But despite the lack of light, the white linens left on the tables glow and she catches a glint now and then from the crystal pieces of the chandelier. They are in constant motion, shimmying now and again because of the vibrations of some truck rumbling across the cobblestone streets outside or one of the other girls running down the corridor on the second floor. She keeps her eyes upward, toward the top of the fixture where the crystal pieces dance, avoiding the black shadow that hangs below.

She steps forward and the floor of the room moves, things scurrying to darker places, finding cracks and holes to hide inside. Irina stops, squeezes her eyes shut, pushing away thoughts. She presses a hand to her stomach; waiting, waiting. Satisfied that the moment has passed, she climbs up on the nearest chair and then the table immediately below the chandelier. Even standing on the table she isn't tall enough, and so she rights the chair the girl had knocked over in order to get the job done and steps onto it. Irina isn't strong enough to hold the weight of another human being, even an emaciated prostitute, and so she decides that the best thing to do is to cut the rope and let the body fall.

She begins gnawing away at the rope with the switchblade. The crystal pieces of the chandelier tremble as she works, tinkling against each other, casting fractured rainbows across Irina's hands. She is careful not to touch the body, careful not to think. Dust motes float down around her, clinging to her hair, and electronic bugs drop like rotten cherries, ping-pinging as they hit the marble floor. Irina turns away as the last strand of rope is severed. The body makes a dull thumping sound as it falls to the edge of the table and then onto the floor.

Irina steps down, stands over the body, takes a deep breath before looking. It is the Kazakh, one of the foreigners lured here by promises of work at a modeling agency. She hadn't known how to speak Romanian when she'd first arrived and Irina had helped her. She'd pointed at horse-drawn carts, soft-serve ice cream stands, and posters of the soccer star Gheorghe Hagi as they strolled through the streets of the city, saying the words carefully so the girl could hear every last syllable: *căruţă, îngheţată, soţul meu*. Sometimes the Kazakh would sit silently with her on the construction scaffolding set up around the hotel, the plastic sheeting covering the windows behind them billowing out like ship sails. It was something she and Lidia had done and once Lidia was gone, she appreciated the Kazakh's companionship. They'd listen to the music drifting from the Athenaeum across the street and wait for the crowds of philharmonic-goers to exit the auditorium after the concert had ended. They watched the women in their furs and silk gloves, teardrops dangling from delicate earlobes, strings of pearls fitted round slender necks.

The eyes of the Kazakh are still open and look just the same as when she'd been alive. Wide as tea saucers, they used to fill up with liquid when she spoke. Her color, too, is the same, gray and chalky, blue branches of veins at her temples. Irina bends down, checks the pockets of the girl's jacket and finds a few bills, a necklace she's never seen before. She places the bills in a small purse she slings across her chest and puts the necklace on, fingering the gold heart before tucking it inside her shirt to keep hidden. The arms of the body are splayed, one leg bent back toward the shoulder blades, the skirt rising to the waist, revealing twisted, red-laced panties a size too big for the slender hips and ass. Irina knows she should straighten it but she cannot bring herself to touch the girl, not even the eyelids, which should be closed.

Irina turns and moves toward the door. She crouches over, retches, fluid running now from her mouth, nose, eyes. After she is through, she wipes her face with her shirt and begins to stand up when something on the floor catches her eye. It is one of the electronic bugs that had fallen from the chandelier. Even though she and the other girls find them all about the hotel—under lamp bases and chairs, behind loose bathroom tiles and doors—it is the first time she has ever inspected one closely. Sometimes girls find them attached to wires sticking out from behind light switches and pull until the drywall is torn away, leaving open wounds that run across bedroom walls.Irina knows they are all dead and have been for some time now, but still cannot resist holding the metallic device between thumb and forefinger, blowing into it, imagining that someone might hear her breath, her movements, her voice. *"Alo? Sunteți acolo? Mă cheamă Irina."* But no one is listening.

Girls were like that, affectionate, in love in a way, with each other. That was why the men never gave Irina and Lidia a second thought, not even Ovidiu with his anxious eyes, always on the lookout for something not quite right. Girls brushed each other's hair, rubbed each other's backs, told secrets. Girls—especially teenaged girls, troubled girls—took care of each other.

Lidia moved into Irina's hotel room in the Athenee. They met early in the morning, before the sun but after the men, and spent hours talking in bed before they grew too exhausted to go on. Lidia was full of questions about Irina's childhood, the village where she grew up until Ovidiu had taken her away.

"Describe it for me again."

"Which part?"

"All of it."

And so Irina would tell Lidia about the sheep whose milk her mother made fresh cheese from, how her father would sometimes take her along in the cart to Bucharest to sell it at the markets on Saturday mornings, the rich, salty scent clinging to her hair even when she lay down for bed at night. She'd describe the empty bottles that hung from the branches of a dying apple tree and told Lidia about the dubious business deal her father once made that brought him nothing more than a rusted out Dacia with a bad clutch that sat unused in front of their cottage. The last time she'd seen it, through the window of Ovidiu's car, there had been wild sunflowers bursting up through the broken windshield, the dense stalks impervious to the jagged glass. She talked of her sisters who, on rare occasions, sent her letters to a postbox Irina kept at the central office. They were the only ones who knew the marriage to Ovidiu was not legitimate, the only ones who attempted but were unable, in the end, to stop it from happening.

"Why can't you go back?" Lidia asked.

"They wouldn't let me. My parents wouldn't let me through the front door."

"But surely, if you explained to them . . . "

Irina adjusted the blankets, touched Lidia's thigh. "And you? What about Cluj?"

Lidia pressed her hair back from her forehead, held a hand there as if testing for fever. "There's not much to tell. Home was . . . bad. I ran away. Lived on the street until Ovidiu caught up with me."

Irina waited but knew that was as far as her friend would go.

Later, Lidia asked: "Why do you let him treat you the way he does?"

It had been silent for so long, Irina thought Lidia had fallen asleep; the question startled her. "Let who treat me how?"

"You know. Ovidiu. He's meaner to you than anyone else. It's like he's got a grudge or something."

"He doesn't like it when girls try to run away."

"But that was so long ago. You'd think he'd get over it. No, I think it's more than that."

"Well, of course it's more than that."

"So what, then?"

Irina grabbed Lidia's hand, laced their fingers together, held them up. "There, see? *Chei de pian.*"

"Because you're Gypsy? That's too easy. I think he's threatened."

Irina laughed. "Threatened? Because of you?"

"No. *Because of you.*" Lidia rolled over, finding the gentle indent of Irina's temple, and pressed her lips to it.

It was all they ever did, kissing the height of intimacy for the two of them. It was all they ever needed. Irina preferred to wake up first, Lidia's hair swimming in hers, the sheets wrapped around them as if they were sprung from the same cocoon.

The sight of Ovidiu waiting for her in the hall surprises Irina. He lingers several yards down from the door of the dining room, hands shoved in pants pockets. In the dim light she can see him troubling his lower lip, working it in and out.

"Did you take care of it?"

Irina pulls the door closed, looks up at Ovidiu.

"Good. I'll give you some extra time tonight, if you need it, but I want it out by morning. Get one of the other girls to help you." He is trying to sound forceful but Irina notes the tremor in his leg, the muscle twitch above his left knee. One suicide is a fluke, two a curse. She knows he blames her for some reason, just like he did for the last one. But the difference this time is she hardly knew the Kazakh.

A warm gust blows through the open doors of the lobby, spreads clouds of dust down the hall, circling around Irina and Ovidiu's feet. Ovidiu turns from her, muttering, *curent, curent, they all want to kill me here.* If it were up to him, they wouldn't be allowed to open a single window, despite the heat that has dried the city out. He shouts down the hall: "Somebody close the goddamn door! Do you want to catch the plague?"

Later, as she heads up the staircase to her room, Irina catches sight of Ovidiu through the window of the landing. He reminds her of the birds that occasionally find their way into the Athenee but cannot find their way back out. They spend the final moments of their lives flying in violent patterns around the hotel, rapping their wings against windows, throwing themselves at walls. He paces around the invisible confines of Piața Revoluției, past the National Museum of Art, the Senate buildings. She watches as he stops in front of the pile of rubble fenced in with red twine where the Memorial of Rebirth is being built. A flock of pigeons moves in sweeping arcs above him, dodging left then right before settling on the ledge of the University Library. Cars trapped in the labyrinthine circle raise pitchy cries; drivers curse out their open windows at no one in particular. Crowds of tourists congest narrow sidewalks, eyes shaded with a hand to follow the pointing finger of their guide. Ovidiu rests his arms across his chest, scratches his chin. She is too far away to know for sure, but Irina thinks she sees his lips move. If she didn't know him better, she'd think he was paying his respects.

Lidia began to travel with the men whenever it was necessary to transport new girls; there had been some problems and she told Irina that Ovidiu thought she'd be the best chaperone, the one most likely to gain their confidence and trust. She was eager for Irina to understand how valuable, how indispensable she had become. Ovidiu had begun to call her his chief recruiter; she was making the business more profitable than they'd expected.

Always she sent postcards to Irina, some which came weeks, months after she'd returned and left again; some which never arrived at all.

Budapest is amazing! If only you could see it, Ița. One day we'll come back here together. Everyone in this city—the women—are so stylish. I'll bring something for you. Don't worry, draga mea. I'm always thinking of you.

Once, she returned with a silk scarf dyed in red, yellow and black, depicting a blurry field of poppies. Irina wore it in her hair, around her neck. It was her favorite gift.

Hours later, napping in her room, Irina is aware of another presence, someone crawling into bed beside her. Still asleep, she feels woozy with recognition and longing, another body lying next to her, pressed against the curve of her own, warming her chilled limbs. Lidia, she thinks, and the dream confirms it: she appears before Irina, crystal-eyed, freckled lips parting to speak, trying to tell her something. What is it? she asks but the body beside her pushes hard, causing the dream to fade. It is persistent, aggressive, shoving her.

"Pretty soon there'll be two corpses to contend with if you don't do your fucking job."

Ovidiu's voice jolts Irina awake. He grabs hold of the back of her head before she can scramble from the bed and is pushing her face against the wall. His dry lips scratch the bare skin of her neck.

"If it's so urgent why don't you do it yourself?" Her fingers find the switchblade he'd given her but has forgotten about, hidden under her pillow.

"Because it's a dog's job."

He yanks her from the bed by her hair, the switchblade slipping from her grasp. The force is so great it breaks the chain of the Kazakh's necklace and knocks the clock, the lamp, a glass of water, from the nightstand. She won't give him the satisfaction of a yelp but claws at his wrists, his arms, her nails piercing skin. His knuckles meet her cheekbone, once, twice, three times and then he throws her backward. Long black strands of her hair dangle from his fingers, sweeping the floor as he heads out the door. She touches her scalp, finds the torn flesh; her fingers come away red. When she is certain he is gone for good, she grapples across the faded rug, searching for the necklace, pushes back the curtains so that the midday light from outside might help her. Under the bed she finds the charm, the cut-open heart, but cannot locate the chain.

"Irina?" It's Simona. She comes up behind her, lays a hand on her back. "It's okay. We'll help you with her. Me and the girls."

When Irina turns around, Simona's eyes go wide. "God. What a mess." She reaches down, hooks her hand under Irina's arm, supporting her.

The street sweeper came by everyday in the warmer months. "Irina, here's your boyfriend," the other girls teased, flicking their chins in his direction, laughing. They knew him by the squeak of his rusted cart, heard him before he appeared in the flesh. Lidia was the only one who didn't laugh. Instead she scowled, waved the other girls quiet, wrapped a comforting arm around Irina's waist. "Don't worry," she'd say, her mouth so close her lips brushed Irina's earlobe. "He never has enough money for you."

Irina didn't like the street sweeper, the way he came and loitered. He'd stop in front of the hotel, scraping at invisible trash with his broom made of twigs, occasionally pausing to flip the broom over and pluck garbage from it while stealing glances at the girls, his heavy-lidded eyes always landing on Irina, his cracked lips parting, metal and gaps where teeth should've been.

"Puţin nebun, eu cred," she whispered to Lidia.

"More than a little crazy." Lidia brushed Irina's black hair off her shoulder, combed through a snarl with her long fingers. "But don't you worry. I'll take care of you."

Irina resisted the urge to kiss her right there on the street, with the white sun shining down on them. Instead, she smiled, squinted at her friend. "You need to stop with my hair; it only makes him look more." The two of them gazed back at the man. Irina spit into the gutter.

The street sweeper eventually moved past the girls, stopping at the men. Soon he was heard to be negotiating with Ovidiu, trying to barter for a better price. "They're women," Irina heard Ovidiu roar, "not rotten apples you feed to your pigs!" For a very brief moment, she was grateful to Ovidiu. Lidia, however, wasn't persuaded.

"What a hypocrite," she said, stroking Irina's hair again.

"Who?"

Lidia gestured toward Ovidiu.

Irina shrugged. "At least he saved me from *nebunel*."

"But he doesn't save you from the ones that can pay asking price now, does he?"

Irina didn't respond. Lidia had been this way lately; the postcards belying the truth. The glossy pictures—most recently of the Alhambra, the canals of Venice—were still accompanied by chirpy notes, promises of gifts and future trips. They were traveling more; more girls being transported. But when she came home, Lidia skipped meals and lapsed into long silences when Irina met her later in bed. Sometimes she slept so late they were unable to leave the hotel before the evening work began all over again. Only this morning she had snapped at Irina when she'd tried to wake her. "Go to the goddamn park by yourself, Irina. Can't you do anything without me?"

The last postcard Irina would receive came from Istanbul. It had a picture of the Hagia Sophia, all red-hued stone domes and minarets. On the back, not even a salutation or signature; just the facts.

Today we transported five girls. All of them nine and ten years old.

Irina hangs back in the hallway while the other girls collect in the dining room to survey the body of the Kazakh—Katarina, someone says—her name was Katarina, can we call her by her name for chrissakes? She listens as the others agree to lay her out and with some effort get her off the floor and onto the bar.

Use the dining linens—not those—cleaner ones. These. Yes. They're perfect.

Over her body like that. Use two if it's not enough.

Cover her face. Cover her gorgeous baby face.

Where's Ana?

Over there. She's not feeling well.

Pussy.

Laughter.

Shouldn't we say something?

You mean a prayer?

Yeah, the Our Father, something.

Silence.

What's Irina gonna do with her?

Yeah. Why not a dumpster? It's the easiest solution.

Are you guys a bunch of idiots? Don't you remember anything? The voice is Simona's. There are mutterings, murmurings, silence.

After they're done, the other girls step out into the hallway, and Simona takes Irina's hand, guiding them all to the English Bar. Ovidiu likes to remind them that it is a place once known for its gorgeous hookers, so high-class they mixed with international spies and later, the Securitate. "Perhaps with a little bit of effort on your part," he occasionally lectures, "we can restore that old reputation." But they know they're on borrowed time at the hotel. And even if they weren't, the girls don't like the English Bar. The windows were shattered during the protests in '89 and haven't been fixed since. Rain water puddles up across the floor, mixing with grime, milky and gray, making the tiles bubble and peel, the glue from underneath catching on heels and the hems of long skirts. It reeks of mildew; the ancient velvet on the seats prickles. And then there are the rats. *Why couldn't she have hung herself in here instead?* grumbles one of the girls as they all pick their way among the booths and barstools, eventually seating themselves gingerly, unhappily.

"Simona: what about that guy—Mircea?" Irina asks. "Didn't he say his family owned a funeral home?"

"Mircea? Oh, *Mircea*. I'm not sure what happened to him. I wish I knew. He tipped the best." She takes a long, contemplative drag on her cigarette. "He couldn't stand to share me. That's probably why."

Irina winks at the other girls who all roll their eyes.

"Can't we just cremate her?" another girl suggests. "I mean, we could just set her on fire right here and now." She holds up a lighter, snapping at it, but the flame won't catch. The other girls break into giggles.

"If you haven't noticed, Laura, this place is a tinderbox."

"Besides, do *you* want to cremate her?" Irina asks.

"And remember that other girl?" someone else says. "The one that was addicted to paint?" Everyone casts an awkward glance at Simona. "Remember when she accidentally set her hair on fire? What a horrible stench."

"Lidia went around spraying perfume in the air for *weeks*." The girl who says this immediately realizes her error. The other girls fall silent, waiting, sipping at empty espresso cups, their eyes roving everywhere except to Irina.

"I'll come up with something," Irina finally says. "I have to."

Later, as Irina passes by the dining room, she catches a glimpse of the body once more—she can't stop herself from looking—and realizes that the girl's feet have been left exposed. Something about this unsettles her; the girl should be covered, all of her should be covered. She steps into the dining room, approaches the body, steadies her hand before pulling the sheet down. She can't help but notice how the feet are small and pudgy, like those of a child.

Ovidiu had left one of the other men in charge while he and Lidia and a handful of others were in Istanbul. That was how Irina ended up at the Lido that night, with the street sweeper.

The other girls smiled at Irina sympathetically when the street sweeper bartered for her, one of Ovidiu's men pocketing the money, pressing a finger across his lips as they all watched, the look on his face warning them. *Keep quiet*. Irina waited for the street sweeper to approach her and took his arm, unsmiling, explaining to him that she wobbled in her heels on the broken cobblestone, making it clear the gesture was a purely utilitarian one. Irina never bothered to ask any of her customers their names but this man offered his up, chatting eagerly. "My name is Radu." It was, he explained, his first time. He blushed. "Not my first time, just the first time for, well, this."

"A whore, you mean."

"Yeah." His head bobbed enthusiastically. "My first whore."

She didn't like how he said it, holding the word, as if savoring it in his mouth. "Where do you want to go? You know we don't take customers in house. Gotta be somewhere else."

"I wouldn't want to sleep in that pit anyway." He pointed up at the golden-lit sign of the Lido.

Irina laughed. "You can't afford the Lido."

"Like hell I can't." He was squeezing her hand tight against his ribcage, her knuckles pressing painfully against bone. "You think I haven't thought about this?"

It was the middle of the week; the boulevard was quiet. Even as they passed by the open doors of the casino, she could see that it was half-empty inside, a few tired faces lit up in red as they sat in front of slot machines, shadows of figures slumped over the bar. A block away from the hotel they walked uptown, passing another street sweeper who was pushing a cart. Irina was certain she saw the man give Radu a wink. Radu gripped her arm more tightly.

She scanned the lobby as they passed through the circular doors of the hotel. Here were the pay phones, the conçierge; there the women's bathroom, the hotel café. Radu's hands shook as he dumped a handful of bills onto the reception counter. The receptionist picked through them, smoothing each individual bill out before finally passing over two keys, sliding one to Irina. But Radu intercepted it, handed it back to him before Irina could even touch it. "She won't be needing one." He gave her a shove toward the elevators.

She'd been in the process of undressing him, trying to hold out a little bit longer so that she could inspect his pockets, be sure nothing was out of order, locate the telephone, the lamp, something she could grab, just in case, when someone pounded on the door.

"Irina! Are you in there? Open the door!"

Recognizing Ovidiu's voice, Irina reached for her clothes on the ground but Radu leapt from the bed, ordering her to stay put.

"I paid for you fair and square." He pulled his pants back on, not bothering to zip up before going to the door. "I'm not going to get dicked over now."

But the minute the handle turned on the door, Ovidiu was forcing his way in, Radu unable to stop him from entering.

"*Where is she*?"

Irina began pulling her blouse back on over her head, picking up her shoes. Ovidiu must have been tipped off by one of the other girls and had come to get her. But then she realized the question was being directed at her. Ovidiu grabbed Irina, pulling her off the bed.

"Where is she?" he repeated, shaking her hard.

She saw Radu watching them, his arms hovering at his sides, his trousers hanging open. "What the fuck is going on?"

"Don't worry. You'll get your money back."

"Where is who?" Irina managed to ask. Her arms were past pain, going numb now. She was aware of her blouse hanging around her neck, the straps from her bra sliding down off her shoulders, her skirt in a puddle under her feet.

"You know who. Lidia. Where the fuck is Lidia?"

Irina worked the words spoken to her like a piece of gristle. "Lidia's with you. I thought—with you."

Diesel fumes snuck through the open hotel window. The rug scratched the bottoms of her bare feet. Ovidiu's eyebrows slid upward; he leaned back as if to get a better look at Irina.

"You really don't know, do you?" He jerked his nose toward her, forcing her to look away from him, and then gave her a toss, throwing her back onto the bed. Blood flooded her arms and face, pressing behind her eyes. Ovidiu's mouth curled.

"She screwed you just like she screwed me."

"She wouldn't do that." But it was a whisper.

During the weeks that Lidia was gone, Irina found it hard to sleep alone in the wide bed they shared. No matter how much she stretched her limbs out there was no filling up the heavy space Lidia's absence left behind. She tried stacking pillows, piling up blankets. When she did sleep she woke with soreness in her ribs where the springs from the mattress had poked at her, or a crick in her neck from a pillow Lidia—and not Irina—had been accustomed to using. She read her collection of postcards over and over again, trying to hypnotize herself to sleep with words. And that was before Ovidiu had confronted her with Lidia's disappearance. After that she did not sleep at all.

Ovidiu brought Lidia back weeks later, tipped off by the very man who had agreed to help her escape. Irina could not bear to look at or talk to her when she appeared in the doorway of their hotel room. She held her hands up when Lidia moved toward her.

"Get the hell away from me. Don't you come near this bed."

"I can explain, Ița. Didn't you get my last postcard?"

Irina studied Lidia's face. Ovidiu had done a fine job on her. Her lips were fat and dark, the freckles now camouflaged, the skin stretched so taut the natural creases had disappeared. They were smooth and slug-like; Irina could not imagine them tasting of ripe fruit as they once had, could not imagine desiring a kiss from those deformed lips. Lidia kept them shut to hide the gaps where three teeth had been knocked from her mouth. Her jaw bulged from her white skin, the color of a bruised heart. She winced as she moved closer, held a hand to her ribcage, sucked in her breath. Still she managed to lace Irina's fingers through her own. Her touch cracked Irina open.

"You said you'd take care of me." Irina choked on the words. There had been no protecting her from Radu. Ovidiu had left just as quickly as he'd arrived that night, and on subsequent nights had handed Irina over to the street sweeper despite the lowered price. Guilt by association, Irina had supposed, and the times with Radu were punishment. "You said you'd protect me."

"I was protecting you."

"Why didn't you tell me?"

"I didn't want anything to happen to you. In case it went wrong."

Radu liked to press his hand around Irina's throat; she could feel her young pulse resisting his thumb and forefinger and saw, in those moments, how easy it would be for him to steal it from her.

Irina twisted Lidia's arms, a sudden jerking motion that made her friend cry out and release her fingers. She crumpled back from her, slumping on the floor. From the drawer of the nightstand Irina pulled out the gifts, all the pretty, meaningless trinkets. A tiny, carved, wooden box grazed Lidia's shoulder; an etched, gold lipstick case hit her temple. Irina grabbed the pile of postcards with their postmarks stamped *Paris, Berlin, St. Petersburg*, tore at the ribbon that held them together, flung them across the room. They fluttered like oversized tickertape, falling around Lidia. Irina imagined them landing on the surface of the pond at Herăstrău, saw the greedy mouths of those fish they'd once fed together gobbling up all of the words Lidia had ever written to her. Irina ripped her favorite gift—the poppy-strewn scarf—from her hair and tossed it. It floated, swirled, landed carefully across Lidia's bare foot.

Lidia wiped a cheek with the back of her hand, reached out; fingered the silk. Irina could see the effort it took, how Lidia supported her elbow with one hand, hunched one shoulder up so that she could maneuver her arm. Lidia stroked the silk scarf the way she had Irina's hair, cheek, the fuzzy top of her belly, the soft skin inside her thigh.

"Why don't you get the hell out already."

Lidia rose and walked slowly out, a long string of poppies dangling from her white hand.

The next morning Irina woke to the sound of someone calling her. It started from down the hall, then grew nearer, louder. The huskiness of the cries could only be Simona's. She recognized them before she was fully awake, Simona appearing in the final scene of the dream she was having, stepping from offstage, yelling in a way that people can only yell in dreams, so absurd and incongruous. The screams began to lose their incoherence, becoming more precise. Words were growing out of the screams as Simona drew nearer and was suddenly throwing open Irina's door, rushing toward her bed. Opening her eyes, Irina finally understood what she had been saying.

Lidia. My God. Lidia.

Irina has stuffed the scarf deep inside her pillow, sewing the seam back up again each time she needs to hide more money. The other girls and even the men are so obvious with their hiding places—under mattresses and beds, inside socks, tucked under layers of clothes. She has been collecting money ever since she met Lidia, taking small amounts that would go unnoticed from the other girls' purses, the men's wallets, an occasional kiosk, a dozing customer. It was her own plan for the two of them, one she'd never had a chance to surprise Lidia with.

As she removes the money from the cut up scarf and counts it out on her bed, she takes a moment to follow with her finger the jagged line the switchblade had left in the silk. She'd thought Lidia was bleeding when she came upon her in the dining room, the poppies so bright against her friend's birdneck, a neck she never had a chance to fully grow into, or was it just the circumstances, the way she hung from the chandelier, that had made it look longer? She'd cut her down without hope, knowing it was done. Now she presses the remaining bits of silk to her cheeks, covering her whole face in it, holding it there, breathing in to find some remembrance in the tiny fibers. But there is nothing left, so she goes back to counting bills. She'd found money among Lidia's things; she does not dare to consider what it had been for. Combined with what Irina has saved, there is more money than she'd realized, more than she'll need.

She goes to the bar at the casino, tells the bartender she needs to place a call for Ovidiu, is handed the phone without question, poured a glass of white wine. With the receiver cradled against her shoulder, the telephone directory splayed open across her lap, she dials the first number on the list and writes in the margins the rates quoted her, scheduling a pick-up time. *No obituary, no hospital, just buried*, she says and the voice on the end of the line seems to understand.

That afternoon, the other girls mistake the hearse that pulls up in front of the hotel for a limousine until the men enter the hotel lobby and pass by all of them into the dining room. Moments later they return with the bundle of white sheets, one at the head and one at the feet, carrying the body as easily as if it were a plank of balsa wood, stopping only briefly so that Irina can tuck a wad of cash into the breast pocket of one of the men.

Ovidiu is standing by the door, watching. "Where'd you get the money for this?"

"You told me to take care of it." Irina starts to leave but Ovidiu blocks her.

"Where'd you get the money?"

"Do you want me to call them back?" She makes a motion as if to follow after the men but Ovidiu holds up his arm. She looks hard into his eyes, waits. He opens his mouth, pauses, glances away and in that moment she understands for the first time what Lidia had meant so long ago when she said he was threatened. Something flutters against Irina's ribcage then, a feeling she cannot decipher, and it is as if the bones have parted, the world has opened up. Ovidiu steps back, watching her as she passes out into the *piața*. She imagines for the first time what it would be like to leave for good.

On the taxi ride to the cemetery she thinks to buy flowers and has the driver stop at a stand on a corner. She selects a bouquet of Gerber daisies, gold and orange and red, plucks one from the bunch to make it an even number, knowing odd numbers are for happy occasions only, handing the lone flower to the driver along with the cost of the fare. She wears the scarf on her head, tied under her pile of black hair, the pointy ends of it rising up toward the sunlit sky, catching the breeze, trying in vain to fly away as she walks. It is just the sort of day they would've enjoyed together, she and Lidia.

When she arrives at the plot, they are patting the last of the moist dirt down. The gravediggers tip back their caps, give her a nod, spit on the grass at their feet. She hands them the last of the money from her savings, notes the dark crescents of their fingernails, sticks her own hands in the ground after they have left so that hers might look the same. She takes from her purse the heart-shaped charm, digs a small hole, places it inside.

She is the only one at the funeral as, she thinks, it should be. She has requested a headstone and presses her now-dirtied hands to its confetti surface, runs her fingers down it, leaving brown streaks. She goes back to the gravel path that runs through the cemetery and collects stones, lining them up on the top of the headstone as she sees others have done around her. The sunlight catches the stones, and they glint like the crystals of the dining-room chandelier. She imagines that room as it once had been, the fine china they took pleasure in eating and drinking from, the expensive linens they pressed to their young mouths; they were teenaged girls playing at tea. They would turn on music that piped through a speaker system, filling up the room, and practice dance moves in front of the wall of gilt-framed mirrors. And when they were finally out of breath they stood close, arms over each other's shoulders, and studied the carefully drawn details of the other's reflection.

A strong wind shakes the trees; they splash shadows across the ground and over the cemetery plot. There is no engraving on the headstone. Irina explicitly requested there not be, knowing that in the future she will want to come back here to pay her respects, to beg forgiveness, from more than this poor girl, this Kazakh child, this Katarina.

Wood Houses

Thomas hears his parents talking about their neighbors' newly adopted son when they think he isn't listening.

He's sweet, his mother is saying, but there's something . . .

Maybe he just needs time, says his father. It's an enormous adjustment. For all of them.

They're brave to have adopted him at such an age.

You can't undo some things. Not at fourteen.

When Thomas has heard enough, he walks into the living room. Their tense, stiffened expressions dissolve into sweetened parental smiles.

His mother holds open her arms. Hiya, monkey, she says. Although he tries to dodge her, she still manages to plant a kiss on the crown of his head. For some time now he has wanted to tell her to stop doing this, but hasn't yet figured out a way that won't hurt her feelings. And then there's the fact that sometimes—only sometimes—he still needs her affection—yearns for it—in a way that shames him.

How about a little catch later? Thomas's father suggests. Get some work in on that pitching arm. Thomas agrees but senses that his father's invitation is linked to the conversation his parents were having only moments earlier about his neighbor, Stefan.

For his part, Thomas likes Stefan. He likes the way Stefan says *eat* instead of *it*, the way he gently rolls his *R*s. He likes that Stefan has a passport and that he has flown on a plane. He likes that Stefan doesn't care that he is two years older than Thomas; he'll play with him anyway. He likes how agile Stefan is when climbing trees, the way he latches onto a branch with his oversized hands, not even having to think about it, swinging effortlessly, trusting in the strength of nature to hold him up.

Stefan was placed in the eighth instead of the ninth grade. Sometimes he gets pulled out of class for special help. *Eat is so boring,* Stefan sighs, brandishing a tennis racket like an axe, beheading his adopted mother's just-bloomed tulips. *But my English is not so good, so I must to go.*

Sometimes, Thomas feels that Stefan is younger than he is. Stefan relies on Thomas to explain certain things because he still doesn't understand everything the other kids in the neighborhood say. *What does eat mean dope? What does eat mean pussy?* In other kids these details would make them easy targets for taunting and teasing. But something about Stefan, the way his jaw sets, the way he looks at the other boys, his eyes flashing metallic, holds them back. Sometimes he pulls out a bottle he's swiped from his adopted parents' cabinet—vodka, vermouth, one time crème de menthe—explaining that all fourteen year-olds in Romania drink alcohol. He offers some to Thomas. Always Thomas declines.

On the weekends and after school Thomas and Stefan spend time roaming on their bikes, drawing lazy, irregular loops around the neighborhood. Stefan's parents have bought him a high-tech mountain bike with shocks built into the frame and so many gears Thomas doesn't know how anyone could possibly use them all. Once, when Thomas complimented Stefan on it, his friend offered the bike up. Take eat. I don't care. But when Thomas pulled into the driveway, his mother ordered him to turn around and return the bike immediately.

Oftentimes when they are together, Stefan marvels over the things he sees, things that Thomas had never paid attention to before he knew his friend.

Houses are so weird here in the States, Stefan says. Big wood houses. And people wonder why their houses burn.

Thomas notices how when they are together Stefan is always commenting on things like this—the size of things, how large everything is here—people, cars. Houses. He talks about it so much that sometimes Thomas imagines that everything in Romania is like that place his parents used to take him to when he was little. Tiny Towne. At the age of five he towered over miniature replicas of the Colosseum, the Parthenon, Big Ben. Tiny Towne had little figurines of tiny people, tiny cars and trees, a tiny train that ran through the town, and even tinier mailboxes and dogs and children. Once, Thomas tried to step on the tiny children, but his mother snatched his wrist, scolded him before he was able.

Today their meandering has led them off road. They are resting on a rotting, damp log in the narrow strip of woods that border the back of their neighborhood. Thomas doesn't like it back here; it's swampy and smells of septic and mud. Even though it is early spring the mosquitoes are already out. But he endures it because Stefan likes to smoke back here.

Through the naked, rattling trees Thomas can see straight through to the newer, more expensive development opposite their own. He watches as lights blink on in bedrooms and kitchens in the dimming afternoon.

What're the houses made of in Romania? Thomas asks.

Stefan rolls a cigarette between his thumb and forefinger. His fingers are long, almost too long. Black spikes of hair have begun to sprout along the backs of them, the same hair that sprouts from his jaw line. He offers the cigarette to Thomas.

Thomas shakes his head. No thanks.

Pussy. Stefan grins, his lips stretching back, revealing a bright expanse of gums. He uses the word all the time now, ever since Thomas told him what it means.

Stefan pulls a silver lighter from his jacket pocket, lights the cigarette. He sucks his cheeks in, checks to see that the cigarette is lit, sucks some more. His eyes bulge, two brown, opaque marbles.

Thomas runs his fingers along a small patch of moss that grows across the surface of the log. It is as soft as a carpet, as soft as his father's hair when he gets it cut close to his scalp, like a Marine. He thinks the hair that grows on Stefan's face and hands is not as soft; he can tell just by looking at it that it's something entirely different.

He watches as Stefan presses the tip of the cigarette to a clump of leaves between his feet, trying to catch it on fire. But the leaves are rotting and moist. They trickle blue smoke that disappears as soon as he removes the ember. Minutes pass with Stefan smoking, Thomas waiting, so long that he thinks Stefan will never answer his question.

Finally, Stefan says: I never lived in a house in Romania.

Where did you live?

But Stefan just stares at him unblinking and Thomas wonders if his friend has understood him at all.

Wind picks up, shuffles some leaves and branches around as if it is searching for something lost beneath them. Thomas shivers through his sweatshirt. His pants are wet and cold from sitting on the log. They stick to the back of his legs when he stands. I think I better get going, he says, reaching for his bike. Are you coming?

Not yet, says Stefan. I want to finish this first. He holds up the cigarette.

Okay, says Thomas, wondering if he should wait for his friend or leave on his own. I'll see you tomorrow?

Stefan shrugs, yanking his collar up around his neck. Sure.

That night, when Thomas's mother comes in to say goodnight, her face lingers over his, her nose pokes about in his hair. When she pulls away, her eyes are like two emergency flares illuminating her shadowy face.

I smell cigarette smoke. Were you smoking?

No. The accusation stings him in a way that others that have come before it—sneaking cookies, playing video games when he should have been doing his homework—have not. He tugs his blanket up to his face, sticks the edge of it into his mouth.

You better not be lying to me. Has Stefan been smoking?

I wasn't even *with* Stefan today. The lie surprises him; he's not sure why he's said it.

That night, Thomas dreams that Stefan and he travel to Romania. The people there are all tiny; Stefan and he soar over them, their shadows darkening the cities and villages like clouds, blocking out the sun. Stefan holds the spire of a church in one fist and beats his chest with the other, imitating King Kong. The Romanians below seem not to notice them; they continue to walk around, ride in their cars, sleep and watch TV and eat in the rooms of their lives.

Their bones snap like brittle branches, their tiny bodies bursting like raindrops, when Stefan squashes them between his giant toes.

One day in late May, Stefan and Thomas find a robin's nest in a squat, fat blue spruce behind the garage of Thomas's house. Thomas knew that it would be there; birds seem to like this tree with its wide flat branches. Nearly every year for as long as he can remember, he and his parents have kept watch over the newest family, reporting back to each other on the progress of the nest's construction; the number, color, and size of the eggs.

Thomas remembers one time when his father paused over the pancakes he was making, put a finger to his lips. The three of them sat in complete silence, the spatula his father held extended like a conductor's baton. Thomas's muscles burned with the effort to sit absolutely still; he held his breath. It took a while but eventually the sound rose like small bubbles from the bottom of an ocean—up past the radiator clacking, up past the coffee pot burbling, up past the creaking of the house and trees, cars and lawnmowers whirring. The fine thread of sound, dry, airy. The sound of newly uncovered life.

The birds, his mother exclaimed, her hand flying to her mouth. Thomas wondered at the tears springing to her eyes. The mystery of the world, she murmured, looking away when she saw him watching her.

This year, there are only two eggs.

They are perfect, says Stefan, his eyelids flying up and then returning to their lazy hooded place, just above his pupils. Thomas realizes he hasn't stood so close to Stefan before. For so long he has believed that Stefan is larger than he; being around his friend sometimes reminds Thomas of his smallness and weakness in the way that being with his own father does. But it surprises him now to see that he is the same height as his friend and may, in a short time, surpass him in size. Then he realizes: it isn't so much that Thomas has grown but that Stefan has developed a slouch, the sheer weight of his broad, heavy shoulders and chest curving his back, making him hunched, the gravity of his body moving forward, pulling him down.

For a moment Stefan takes his eyes away from the nest, blinks his curled, dark lashes at Thomas. *What is eat?*

Flushing, Thomas looks away. Nothing.

You're too damn close, says Stefan, giving Thomas a shove. Fag-*got*. The word comes out deflated, like the dampened carcass of some already burst balloon. Thomas doesn't bother fighting back.

The bird's nest is made of grass clippings, dried leaves, a McDonald's straw wrapper, brittle twigs. Its construction is flawless, round and as tightly woven as a basket. The hollow in which the eggs rest is fit to their size and shape and appears so comforting that Thomas wishes he were small enough to fit inside there so he might curl up and take an afternoon nap. He used to have places like this in his life. The spot beneath his father's desk right beside his feet; the curved space his mother provided when she scooted over, opened her arm. But he's outgrown these places; they're uncomfortable for him to try and squeeze all his limbs and torso into, and he can't seem to find new ones that are large enough for his ever-expanding body.

In the past, the eggs have been a very pale blue, nearly white. Or they have been speckled with dots like the freckles bridging his mother's nose. This year, these eggs remind Thomas of the world map that hangs in his classroom at school. They are the color of the oceans—Indian, Atlantic, Pacific.

You flew over the Atlantic Ocean, right?

What? Oh. Yes. Stefan presses down the branches so they can get a better look at the nest. He reaches inside.

You're not supposed to do that. The mother will know. Over his shoulder Thomas sees a pair of robins embroiled in a violent, raucous dance on a nearby maple.

So what?

They'll reject the babies.

Birds? Stefan laughs and shakes his head. Stupid American schools.

This has been Stefan's new observation: how stupid all American kids are, how easy school is here.

If school is so stupid then why do you still need special help? argues Thomas.

Eat isn't for my studies anymore, says Stefan, but for other things.

What other things?

I talk to a doctor.

Are you sick?

No. *Pussy*.

Then why do you have to go?

I don't know.

So what do you do?

Sometimes we play games. I draw pictures. He gives me these. Stefan digs in his pockets, holds out some baseball cards.

Cool. Thomas reaches for them, hesitates.

Do you want them? Take them. Stefan nearly tosses the cards away, so eager is he to be rid of them.

In Romania you study study study, Stefan says. Here you play play play. Five-year-olds in Romania know more.

Well why don't you go back to Romania then? Thomas is getting tired of his friend's complaints.

You think *they* will let me? Stefan tosses a hand in the vague direction of his house which is located on the opposite side of the neighborhood from Thomas's. I can't go back.

Stefan reaches back inside the tree. When he pulls his arm out one of his hands is cupping an egg. The blue of it glows, pulsates with so much life that the longer he stares at it the more it seems to Thomas that the egg is moving, rocking ever so slightly, vibrating so that he begins to think it might crack open right now in his friend's hand.

Stefan moves the egg close to his face, holding it just under his nose. Dark hair covers his upper lip and has grown up into the shadows of his cheekbones. Once, when Thomas asked him why Stefan didn't shave it, his friend blinked at him. *I shave it every morning.*

Stefan brings the egg still closer to his nose and inhales. His lips part.

What're you doing?

Do you smell that?

Thomas sniffs but besides the sodium scent of his friend, he doesn't smell anything. He shrugs. What does it feel like?

Stefan gives the egg a gentle toss. Nothing. Here: want to see?

He tips his hand, rolls the egg onto Thomas's palm. It is weightless; if Thomas weren't looking at it he wouldn't have known it was there. But he knows that this belies its importance.

Can you believe a bird comes out of there? he says, moving to place the egg back into the nest.

Wait. Stefan holds out his hand. I want to see eat again. Thomas hands it back to his friend. Stefan stretches out his fingers. Then he makes a fist.

It takes Thomas a moment to realize what has just happened. When Stefan unfurls his fingers, where the egg had been there is now nothing but oozing clear gel and the tiniest fragments of oceans sailing within it.

Thomas shudders, punches his friend in the shoulder. What did you *do* that for?

Stefan stumbles back, regains his footing, wipes his dirtied palm against the thigh of his jeans. It leaves a dark, viscous smear. I don't know.

Stefan looks as stunned as Thomas feels; that's how he knows his friend is telling him the truth.

No babies this year, his mother says several weeks later. I knew this spring was missing something.

Thomas's parents don't like how much time he's been spending with Stefan. They never say so, but it's obvious when his mother suggests he call a friend from school, asking him if he wants to have a sleepover. When he asks if Stefan can come too, his mother says: You see Stefan all the time. And then his father signs him up for the summer baseball camp he's spent most of the spring begging him for.

Maybe you'll make some new friends at camp, his father says.

It's good, his mother says, to spend time with lots of different people.

Sure, says Thomas, but as far as he can tell, his parents only ever seem to spend time with each other.

Once summer and camp begin however, there is too much going on for him to think much about it. Just days after school ends Stefan and his parents go away for two weeks on vacation. By the time they return, Thomas has started camp. He leaves early in the day, his father driving him there on his way to work, and comes back late in the afternoon, sweaty and tired. Some afternoons he musters up the energy and hops on his bike, heads to the other side of the neighborhood. But more often than not, there is no answer at Stefan's door.

I'm sure they had no idea what they were getting themselves into, he overhears his father say to his mother one evening after dinner.

Those poor people, his mother says. They must feel helpless.

One afternoon, Stefan shows up on Thomas's doorstep.

Hey. Stefan is smoking and despite the heat and humidity wears blue jeans and the same satiny, black jacket he wore all throughout winter and spring. He scratches what is now a fully grown beard that Thomas thinks makes him look ten years older. Can I come in? He makes a move to step inside, but Thomas holds up his arm.

Not with the cigarette.

Stefan bares his sharp, yellowed teeth and snubs out the barely smoked cigarette on the front stoop, not bothering to conceal it. He shoves his hands in his pockets. Your parents are in?

My mom's at the grocery store, says Thomas. What have you been up to this summer? I stopped by a couple of times, but no one answered the door.

Stefan walks past Thomas and down the hall into the living room. His body cants as he moves, propelled forward by the weight of his shoulders. He doesn't step so much as lope, springing off the floor beneath him. As he follows him, Thomas realizes that his friend has never actually been inside his house before. He knows this because of how strange it is to see Stefan in his space, to observe his friend's body lurking about the bookshelves and his father's music collection. There's something about the way Stefan pulls CDs from the stand and flips them over that makes Thomas feel compelled to move closer to him and cautiously pry the items from Stefan's hands.

Do you want to watch TV?

Stefan glances at the couch and armchairs, grunts. It is a deep, growling sound, though unthreatening. He makes no move to sit.

Thomas finds his gaze resting on Stefan's feet; he hadn't told him to take his sneakers off. There are no traces of Stefan's path on the rug or the floor, but just over the tongue of the shoe Thomas spies a fringe of black hair.

Your dad likes some old music, says Stefan. But I like this. He holds up the Rolling Stones. And this. The Doors. He places the CDs back precisely where he had found them, shoves his hands back into his pockets.

Do you want to play some video games? Maybe go for a bike ride somewhere?

Maybe later, says Stefan, his eyes meandering over pictures and furniture, magazines, the television. How many rooms are in your house? he asks.

Dunno. There are three bedrooms.

There are four in Millie and Tad's house, says Stefan. Eat makes no sense—three people, four bedrooms.

Thomas realizes Stefan is talking about his adoptive parents. He laughs.

What's so funny?

You call your parents by their first names?

They're not my parents.

Stefan brushes past Thomas in the direction of the front door, knocking into him as he does so. Thomas is surprised by the solid force, the impact of sinew and protruding muscle. He hasn't ever heard Stefan talk about working out to build muscle. Besides riding bikes, all he seems to do is climb trees, sometimes kicking off his shoes, letting them tumble through branches below him before hitting the rooted ground, gripping the trunk of some elm or oak with the bottoms of his feet, his toes digging into the bark. Once, when Thomas tried to emulate his friend, he walked away with cuts on the soles of his feet.

Are you leaving already? Do you want to do something?

But Stefan isn't headed for the door.

Thomas follows his friend up the stairs, still eyeing Stefan's shoes. Each time he takes a step the legs of Stefan's jeans ride up and Thomas gets a closer look at his friend's ankles. Hair grows straight as grass, so thick he can barely see through to skin.

Where's your room? asks Stefan.

Just before the bathroom on the left.

But Stefan walks past Thomas's room without even glancing through the open doorway and slips instead into the bathroom.

I'll just get some shoes on, Thomas calls after his friend, picking his sneakers off of the floor of his bedroom. Let's go outside. As he ties up his laces he tries to slow himself down, to take his time, calm the anxiety that has surfaced inside him. It's not as if he hasn't hung out with friends up here before.

Stefan has left the bathroom door open and when Thomas steps closer he realizes his friend has been going through the medicine cabinet, opening bottles, draining them of their contents. A bright syrupy liquid has been splashed across the sink; Stefan squeezes a bottle of cold medicine in his hairy fist.

What're you doing? barks Thomas. *Don't do that.* He grabs the bottle from Stefan who doesn't resist him. That's private.

Stefan doesn't say anything. He appears to be holding his breath, the skin of his cheeks stretched taut as pregnancy. He coughs through his nose, a translucent line of snot catching in his mustache. When he cannot hold back his laughter any longer, Stefan spits a mouthful of pills into the sink, scattering them across porcelain and tile, shooting them at the image of Thomas reflected in the mirror.

Are you fucking insane? Thomas tears the hand towel from its rack, swipes it over the sink. As he cleans he can feel through the terrycloth the pills breaking apart, dissolving.

Thomas is so intent on cleaning up the mess Stefan has made that it takes him several minutes to register what he guesses is his friend's laughter; he has to look at his friend to be sure, it is too agonizing a sound to be joyous. But Stefan's head is tossed back, his lips pulled tight, teeth laid bare. Back arched, his chest convulses and then gradually settles. When Stefan is done, he runs the back of his hand sloppily across his eyes, his mouth. Thomas's heart and stomach knock against each other, some confused primordial dance of fight versus flight.

So? What's next? The words are tossed out recklessly; Stefan's voice jumps octaves. He shoves his hands in his pockets and for a moment Thomas thinks that he's stolen things from the medicine cabinet and is about to confess to pilfering his mother's antidepressants, his father's sleeping pills. Instead, when he removes his hands he pulls out the same lighter he always carries with him. He snaps the mechanism with his thumb a few times, sending up sparks but no flame. For a moment the two boys stand there, watching the sparks leap and disappear. Then Stefan turns and heads back out into the hallway.

You need to help me clean up the mess you made. Thomas's voice wobbles.

Fuck off. But the words trip off the tongue, fall flat. The absence of emotion terrifies Thomas.

Stefan puts his hand on the knob of Thomas's parents' bedroom. What's in here?

We can't go in there.

Why not?

It's my parents' room.

They don't let you in their bedroom? says Stefan, but he's already opening the door, stepping inside.

Thomas follows his friend and is immediately struck by the realization of how infrequently he comes in here anymore. There was a time when he was a child and preferred their room to his own; he'd gone through a phase when he asked nearly every day if he could move into their bedroom with them. It seemed unfair somehow, that they should have each other for comfort at night, while he had no one. He would spend at least one night a week, sometimes more, having suffered nightmare or illness or the side effects of an active childhood imagination—monsters under beds, goblins outside windows, gorillas behind closet doors—sleeping with his parents, waking up wedged between their immobile and somnolent limbs, their rich human scents. But over the past year or so, he's been managing nightmares on his own and when sick prefers the space that his own bed provides him, stretching out his sore arms and legs, comforted by the knowledge that his sweating, fevered body need not come in contact with another. From time to time he still seeks out his parents, craves their comfort, but less so and, if asked, couldn't explain what has happened to make this change come about.

Thomas watches as Stefan picks his way casually across the room, lifting his feet over clothing and some magazines strewn across the floor. Unlike the rest of the house, his parents' room is cluttered with living—unfinished crossword puzzles, a pile of clean shirts that have waited for over two weeks to be ironed, unpaid credit card and utilities bills, their envelopes torn, stacked on dresser tops. Only this morning Thomas's mother had asked him repeatedly to make his bed, finally standing over him to ensure he got it done. But here the raft-like mattress has been left hurriedly: the sheets crumpled and tossed about, one pillow on the floor, another inexplicably resting at the foot of the bed, as if his parents had had a fight when they'd woken or lost something inside the sheets and were scrambling about to find it. But nothing this morning had alluded to the frenetic environment he stares at now. At breakfast, his parents had smiled languidly, sipped their coffee. Thomas's father took his time getting ready for work; his mother packed him a lunch. He watched them, his spoon dangling above his cereal bowl as they kissed each other goodbye, their eyes closing, as if they were too ashamed to witness what they themselves were doing in the clear light of morning.

Stefan silently inspects the tousled bed and then, placing his hand on the footboard, vaults himself over it, landing feet-first onto the mattress.

Thomas can't help but envy the swiftness of his action. How'd you do that?

Stefan laughs. It's easy, he says. He begins to jump.

Get off there! Thomas rushes forward, swipes at his friend's pant-leg, trying to yank him down. But Stefan only laughs louder, jumps higher, now and then kicking a leg out, touching his fingers to the ceiling, counting the times.

Stefan. C'mon! You'll get me in trouble.

Stefan takes one final jump to the edge, lands in a seated position, and slips from the bed. He moves to a nightstand and picks up a heavy, blue-faced watch. It is Thomas's father's. Stefan struggles to slip the watch over his large hand, snapping the metal clasp into place around his wrist. Is it possible that in the weeks since last they met, his friend has lost weight? Or has Thomas grown? On second look it is as if certain parts of Stefan—his height, his head, his legs—have ceased growing, while other parts of him appear elongated, as if made of elastic. His arms, for example. Thomas inspects them now, watching Stefan tip the watch this way and that, tapping at the glass face. The watch is even larger on Stefan than it is on Thomas, slipping up Stefan's forearm when he raises his hand. But it's not this that catches Thomas's attention so much as how long it takes the watch to travel from wrist to elbow and back again.

Stefan curls his fingers under, trying to hide them in his palms. They remind Thomas of a picture in his science textbook, the stages in human evolution. They are the hands of prehistoric man.

Nice watch, says Stefan.

It's my dad's, says Thomas. You better take it off before my mom gets home. She might get the wrong idea. He moves as if to take the watch, but Stefan looks at him in a way that makes him stop short.

Stefan flips through the pages of books, picks up bottles of perfume and cologne, gives them a sniff. Thomas is ashamed that he isn't trying to stop him. If he were a good son, he would protect his parents from the threat that Stefan seems to pose. But something holds him back. It is as if Stefan is looking for something, solving some mystery or puzzle he hasn't yet told Thomas about.

Stefan gazes for a long time at a black-and-white photo of Thomas's parents at their wedding. He fingers change collected in a small glass dish, opens and snaps shut the container that holds what Thomas has recently learned are his mother's birth control pills; picks up a single pearl earring, raising it to the light from the window. Occasionally he pulls his lighter from his pocket, rolls the mechanism with his thumb, always sending up sparks—*snap-snap*—but never holding a flame.

Let's go outside, Thomas offers once more even though he knows now that his friend hasn't come here for him.

Stefan rifles through socks and underwear, pants and shirts. He holds up a T-shirt and drops it in a crumpled heap on the floor. When he picks up a camisole, his lips curling, Thomas steps across the room, snatches the clothing from his friend.

Quit it! Thomas pushes the drawer closed but Stefan holds out his arm like a shield, presses it against Thomas's chest, gives him a shove that sends Thomas stumbling backward. Thomas's heels hit the corner of the dresser; he bangs his elbow against the doorknob and falls into the open door, slamming it shut with the force of his body.

Thomas? What're you doing? his mother calls from downstairs. They never heard her return.

Stefan strokes and paws the camisole; his nails look to Thomas as if they could tear right through the fabric as tender as skin. Your mom smells good, says Stefan, and Thomas feels as if some invisible hand has closed around his neck, holding back air and words. Stefan raises the clothing up high in one hand while snapping open the lighter with the other. He dangles the straps over the flame. Bet this burns easy, says Stefan. He pants out the words, licks his lips, brings the flame closer.

Thomas? Are you home? His mother's voice is closer this time.

Just when Thomas is thinking how he might explain it all to his mother, Stefan drops the camisole, slams the dresser drawer shut, shoves the lighter back into his pocket. Thomas yanks open the door, and together they sprint into the hallway, meeting his mother on the stairs.

Hi Stefan, she says, smiling. You boys headed outside?

I'm just leaving, says Stefan. Eat was nice to see you.

Tell your mom I said hi, sweetheart.

One morning a week or two later, Thomas overhears his father ask his mother: Any idea where my watch could've gotten to?

In the fall Thomas starts eighth grade. The leaves go orange to yellow to brown, and the trees shake them off in great piles that collect in bushes and cover drains, backing up rain, causing it to pool and swirl out into the road. Thomas helps his father rake, holds the ladder when he clears out the gutters, but the leaves seem endless, always falling, always suffocating the earth, and a week later they must start all over again.

They go apple picking; they take a long weekend to visit his grandparents out of state. He surprises everyone come Halloween, when he decides that rather than wear a costume and roam the neighborhood, he wants to stay home and hand out candy instead.

I hate to see him growing up, he hears his mother say through their closed bedroom door one night when they think he's asleep.

Had to happen sooner or later, says his father. They both sound so tired and sad that Thomas thinks maybe next year he'll dress up as a pirate, trick-or-treat one last time.

Stefan's house feels as far away to Thomas as another country, another universe. He doesn't see his friend anymore. He has heard that Stefan's parents have transferred him to a different school, driving him into the city every morning, picking him up on their way home from work, late in the afternoon. Thomas's mother says the commute is an hour one way. *Such dedication.* She closes her eyes and shakes her head in a helpless sort of way.

Thomas doesn't see Stefan anymore but he hears rumors—that Stefan is responsible for the disappearance of Mrs. McCormack's cat, that he hit a kid in the next development so hard he cracked the other boy's jaw, that he started the fire at the abandoned barn on the edge of the Filmores' property, that he climbed a telephone pole and the fire department needed to get him down. Thomas's parents say you shouldn't believe everything you hear, even though the expressions on their faces tell him otherwise.

One evening, Thomas goes for a bike ride, retracing the loop he and Stefan had ridden countless times together. The night is heavy with darkness; there is no wind to lighten things, bring a respite to the silence that weighs everything down. The starless sky sags from close above. Only the purr of Thomas's bike offers a counterpoint, but it isn't enough to settle his nerves which clatter like silverware inside his empty chest.

He stops when he reaches Stefan's house. A *For Sale* sign stands at the edge of the lawn. The windows mirror night. Thomas drops his bike in the vacant driveway, begins a slow circle by foot around the modern colonial. Someone has been around to rake—bags of yard waste line up next to the mailbox—but the grass is long. Its moisture-tipped blades dampen the cuff of Thomas's pants, brush at his bare ankles so that from time to time he must stop to scratch the exposed skin. As he passes the front picture window, from the periphery of his vision he catches a flash of movement but cannot tell if it comes from inside or out.

He had seen the backyard of Stefan's house before his friend had been adopted by Millie and Tad Barnum; they had once been close acquaintances of Thomas's own parents, and all of them had been here on occasion for summertime barbecues. His own father had helped Tad build the wooden swing set that Thomas is surprised to discover still occupies a large corner of the yard. Stefan had never been young enough for it; it represented an earlier idea of family the Barnums eventually abandoned. But outside of the single visit Stefan made to his own house, he and his friend had only ever spent time together in neutral territory, territory that now Thomas strangely fears, as if all those afternoons spent watching Stefan smoke in the septic woods had had a potential for disaster Thomas hadn't at the time sensed or comprehended.

Thomas moves across the yard to the swing set, grips the solid frame. He imagines his friend must have climbed this at some point; it is tempting enough for Thomas and must have been irresistible to Stefan. He moves his hands up the beam, places his shoe against its side, tests his strength.

He has hoisted himself up, his legs wrapping around the beam, less than a foot from the top, when he hears it. A laugh? A growl? Someone speaking? He cannot be sure. Hearing it is like the times he has been woken by cats fighting into the night, their low guttural moaning strikingly human.

Who's there? Thomas calls out. He slides down from the pole, moves across the yard in the direction of the sound. Mrs. Barnum? He feels ridiculous saying it because he knows that neither she nor her husband is responsible for it. Somehow he knows it could only be Stefan but feels for a moment that he must pretend not to know. If this is one final game with his friend, then he will abide by the rules. But once more, the night is silent, cracked only when a branch falls from some tree behind him, knocking against other stronger branches, falling to the earth.

As Thomas nears the house once more he senses something moving—a reflection in the glass, a body moving behind it; he still cannot be sure. He squints but cannot see anything inside. When he turns to glance behind him there is just the dark scaffolding of the swing set, the edge of fields beyond that, and still further out, some vague twinkling of other lives. Something about this—the occasional flash of life—makes him think of Romania. It is as if those flashes are the place itself, as if he could hop on and ride his bike there right now, see for himself the place where Stefan comes from, as if it is the secret his friend kept from him, his home only a subdivision away.

Glass shatters against the night; Thomas reels around. The back windows of the Barnums' house tremble but none break. He realizes the sound must have come from the front of the house and follows it, but there is no sign of anyone, only the dark forms of people moving behind jaundiced curtains in the houses opposite the Barnums'.

The moon is out now, a finger-nail clipping littering the black rug of sky. Its dull light reveals shards of glass cluttering the Barnums' front yard just below the picture window. Thomas steps over to it, inspecting the damage. Whatever shattered the window did it from the inside. Whatever it was made a hole in the glass not quite large enough for Thomas to climb through.

Day of Lasts

His eyes were the color of the chocolate-covered cherries displayed in the shop windows Lidia passed on her way to school every morning. He removed his gloves, their leather as smooth as liquid, and pressed them flat in sideways prayer, on top of the envelope containing the train ticket and passport. He reached across the café table, flicking ash from the end of his cigarette, the sleeve of his camel-hair coat riding up to reveal a gold watch strangling his fleshy wrist.

"So. What do you think?"

At fifteen, Lidia was already familiar with the way boys looked at her, so different from even a year ago. But this? This was something entirely new.

Leaving on a jet plane. Don't know when I'll be back again. Her father used to sing that to her when Lidia was little and couldn't fall asleep. A friend who'd fled before the revolution had pulled some strings at the post office and sent him a collection of records he hid in the bedroom closet. Her father's English was terrible, but Lidia hadn't cared; she just liked the song, liked the sound of his unsteady voice—one she had begun to forget—wrestling with the tune. Now that she knew what the words meant, she imagined her father had played a part in this whole situation. Maybe he too would be in France, waiting for her and not, as her mother insisted, in Bucharest with his new family.

"What's that smile for, huh? I convinced you?"

"Listen, sir—"

"—What did I tell you? It's Gheorghe."

"Sorry. Gheorghe." Her cheeks burned. He was as old as her father. "Do you know a man named Marius Kovacs?"

"Hungarian? Not familiar with him, no. Should I be?"

He's my father, she wanted to say, but didn't.

Gheorghe smiled, the corners of his mouth turning up like the curlicues of bruise-colored smoke trailing from his cigarette. "You're gorgeous, you know that?"

Lidia's skin prickled. She imagined reaching up and plucking those delicious eyes from his face, popping them into her mouth, the flawless texture on her tongue, the flavor—something rich, forbidden—melting there.

"Sorry." He chuckled, holding up a hand. "That came out wrong. I just think you've got a career ahead of you. If you want it."

"There were other girls at the disco the other night, just as pretty as me."

Gheorghe put out his cigarette, leaned back in his chair. "They didn't have the look. Trust me. I've been in the business for years."

She glanced down at the plate in front of her where the croissant she'd ordered sat untouched. She understood now that she'd mistaken her hunger for something physical to be assuaged with chamomile tea and fresh bread, when the real solution was sitting across from her, adjusting his scarf, tucking it under the lapel of his coat.

She pushed back his sleeve with her free hand, rubbing the cuff between her thumb and forefinger. "Be careful," she warned. She spoke in a voice she used with Ivan or one of the other boys from school. "Coffee stains are impossible to get out."

"Thanks. I'll keep that in mind." He slipped his gloves back on and pushed the envelope closer to her. Lidia picked it up, began to open it, but he stopped her with a wiggle of his index finger. "Not now."

"Sorry." She pressed the envelope to her chest, felt her heart thrumming against the paper.

"Think about it." His tone was buttery, soothing. "I don't want you to do anything you don't feel comfortable doing."

"No," said Lidia. "I want to do this."

He crossed his arms over his chest as if he'd just finished eating a satisfying meal. "I'm glad to hear that, Lidia. I'm very, very glad."

Sunlight trickled through the cracks of her bedroom curtains, landing somewhere near Lidia's closed eyes. She knew without having to open them that the bed across from hers would be empty, the sheets thrown back, already cold, her nine-year old sister Marianna still too young to appreciate sleeping in on the weekend. She slid her hand under her pillow, felt for the envelope. She didn't bother pulling it out now; she'd looked at it every day over the past two weeks, pressed the paper to her nose to breathe in its crisp scent, licking a small corner of the adhesive as if to make sure it wasn't some figment of her imagination. She'd read the itinerary, which took her first to Bucharest, where Gheorghe said he would be waiting for her. There was one small detail with her visa he still needed to sort out, he'd explained; then, from there, they'd fly on to Paris together.

In the kitchen, plates were being stacked, water run; a radio voice rattled out the day's news. She'd never flown on a plane before and had only taken the train a handful of times to visit cousins a few hours south, in Timișoara. Tomorrow, all that would change. She ran her hand across the magazine pages she'd taped to the wall above her bed, her fingers coming away with the faint scent of perfume samples: Destiny, Obsession, Fantasy, Euphoria. She pressed her palm to her neck as she'd done so many times before, hoping a shadow of the scents would stick. Sometimes when Marianna saw her do this, she clambered over her, rubbing her own small hand to the paper, thrusting her palm under Lidia's nose, asking: Did I get some?

Lidia stretched and took a deep breath, her nostrils tingling from the cold. Today would be the last day she would wake to the impossible garbage stench from the apartment-block dumpster, the last day she would be subjected to her stepfather's roars and belches as he watched Saturday-afternoon soccer, the last day she'd loathe her mother for marrying him.

On cue, her mother called to her. "Lidia? Are you ready?"

She tugged a wool sweater over her head and socks on her feet, and headed to the bathroom. She began to brush her teeth, then pulled the toothbrush from her mouth and pressed her face close to the mirror, inspecting her pores. A cluster of pimples had bloomed overnight, just below her lip, and were sure to attract the attention of her sister. When will that happen to me? Marianna's tone was always more inquisitive than anxious. Why does it happen? How do you make it go away?

Usually, Lidia didn't mind Marianna's questions. Even if she was only providing answers about the mundane details of her life, her sister's inquiries gave her a sense of authority she otherwise never experienced in the day to day. It was as if, by asking, Marianna imbued Lidia's existence with meaning. Since meeting Gheorghe, however, Marianna's questions had become bricks, each one stacked onto Lidia's shoulders so that the simple act of moving through the day had become difficult for her to bear.

"Lidia! Can you hear me? We need to get to the market before it closes!"

Lidia squeezed her eyes shut. The last day she'd hear her mother yell in a voice that could curdle fresh goat's milk. "Go without me!"

Someone rapped on the bathroom door. "Don't you want to see Ivan?" a muffled voice asked. Lidia knew that Marianna was standing on the other side, her curls springing from a knitted cap, her oversized boots already pulled on, her face twisted into such silent agony that if Lidia were to see her sister she'd want to kiss and smother her all at once.

Lidia smirked at her reflection in the mirror. "No," she said to the door, "I don't want to see Ivan."

For a moment, her sister's confusion hung silently between them.

"Go tell Mom I'll be ready in five minutes." She listened to the receding *shush-shush* of her sister's footfalls as she went to deliver the message.

Lidia shoved the toothbrush back into her mouth, the bristles making furious noises against her molars. The last day she would read bedtime stories to Marianna, feel the tickle of her sister's blond curls underneath her chin.

Firsts were just around the corner. Once she was settled, the first thing she would do would be to send for her sister.

Lidia unlatched the bathroom door and waited until she could hear her family's voices coming from the kitchen. Then she slipped outside and into the next room, certain no one had seen her.

Her mother and stepfather's bedroom was cast in dirty shadows, the heavy curtains not yet drawn. It didn't matter; Lidia had memorized its layout and moved swiftly across the cluttered space, careful not to trip over loose shoes, a pair of trousers, a strewn belt—anything that might sound an alarm bell. Her stepfather's dresser was on the far wall. Sometimes in the night she'd be woken by her mother yowling and scolding, a hip or elbow caught unexpectedly in the dark against the jutting corners of its top drawer, which he always left open.

Sliding her hand through the narrow crack, Lidia's searching fingers grappled under the piles of cloth—graying underwear and mismatched socks and wrinkled handkerchiefs—until she felt what she was looking for. From the thickness of it, she could tell that the pile of bills had only just been replenished. This was her revenge, most recently for the parallel lines of welts on the back of both of her thighs, welts her stepfather claimed not to have recalled giving her.

She'd begun taking his money years before, whenever he harmed one of them. Later, when he scratched his head over its disappearance, her mother unwittingly—indeed believing the truth of her words—provided reasons. "The drink, Daniel," she'd say. "It makes you forget how you've spent it." Normally, he accepted this explanation. Still, every once in a while he turned on Lidia's mother, accusing her of stealing.

Today would be the last time. This time, to insure there would be no wrongful accusations, Lidia did something she'd never done before. Where the money had been, she left in its place a slip of paper. She thought of the expression on her stepfather's face when he finally found the note. She'd signed and written simply "I.O.U." Later, she'd reimburse him; she was composing the letter of explanation in her head already. *I'm as good as my word*, she'd say, enclosing a clipping from her latest shoot—*French Vogue, Elle, Mademoiselle*—the money wrapped inside the magazine pages like a pearl.

Turning around, Lidia nearly crashed into Marianna. "Jesus Christ! What are you doing in here?" Her sister didn't speak but remained standing, the expression on her face illegible. Lidia pinched Marianna's chin between forefinger and thumb. "Not a word of this, you understand?" She gave her sister's head a jerk before releasing her hold and hurrying past her, too shocked and ashamed by her own behavior to wait for a reply.

"You want some of my sausage, Lidi? It's fresh."

Lidia gazed up at the string of salami that hung from Ivan's steaming hand. What was it about the winter that held the saline smell of blood? She swore she could see droplets of it hanging like rubies in the crystallized air around her.

"I saved it just for you." He was trying to look nonchalant but his tone was panting. The boys standing behind him laughed, slapping each other's backs. Lidia's lip curled. The last day she'd flirt with the butcher's son (so immature, a child really), or any boy for that matter. The last day she'd endure the fresh smell of death for the promise of something fleeting, fickle, something that always left her feeling dissatisfied.

Ivan had been with her at the disco the same night she met Gheorghe. He never knew she'd spoken to anyone else, the pick-up happening right under his nose. But of course that was the wrong expression; it wasn't anything sexual but a business transaction, the beginning of a career.

"How old are you?" Gheorghe had asked, setting a drink in front of her.

"Twenty."

"Like hell."

The business card he tossed on the table said *ABC Modeling Agency*. "I'm only in town for a day or two. Looking to recruit." He was studying her, his eyes moving from her face to her neck, chest, waist, legs. He wrote a time and location of a proposed meeting on the back of the card. "I think we could make something of you yet," he said. He was gone before Ivan had returned from the bar.

Later, Ivan gestured at the unfinished drink. "Where'd that come from?"

Lidia pushed it away from her. "Someone must have set it down and forgotten it." She could feel the business card, which she'd slipped into her back pocket, pressing against her skin through her jeans.

Now, standing before Ivan, the frigid air was clarifying so that everything around her—the marbled slabs of meat, the stack of raw bones, the bleached cap against his dark head, the scarlet fingerprints on his butcher's apron—was crisp, fresh, the intricate designs and details, the sharp edges and distinct shades and shadows magnified. She considered Ivan's eager, open face, the jowls still soft and smooth, childhood not having entirely left him. What would he say if she told him the truth? Would his adulthood begin there, in that moment?

She stepped closer to the kiosk. "I'm not interested in your sausage," she said. "I've found better."

The boys roared, widening their eyes and mouths. Ivan blanched. "What's that supposed to mean?"

"It means—"

"Ivanko! Get back here and help me with this rack!"

Ivan jumped, the string of salami tumbling onto the countertop. "Call you later? Maybe the disco? Paradiso again?"

Lidia shrugged. "Maybe," she said, then once he'd disappeared to the back of the kiosk: "Maybe not."

From behind Lidia, a voice said: "What do you want with the Russian anyway?"

She turned. Anita was hatless, gloveless, and already bringing her face toward Lidia. As she leaned in to kiss her friend's cheeks, she was struck by the ease of this gesture, the familiarity that had been there since grade school. Surely, if there was anyone she could trust with her news, it was Anita?

"Don't you know they drink worse than Romanians?"

"You can have him," Lidia said. "The Russian and I are through."

Anita shivered at the meat displayed in glass cases and looped her arm through Lidia's. "C'mon," she said, directing her away from the butcher's stand. "All those sheep heads give me the creeps."

The girls wove through the huddles of people, shoulders hunched and stiff against the cold, until they'd reached the *langoș* stand and took their place in line. Lidia wondered: would there be Hungarians and Romanians in France? Would there be *langoș* for her to eat on Saturday mornings in the wintertime, after a long, luxurious sleep-in? Never mind. In France, there'd be something else, something better: café au lait and croissants with a view of the Eiffel Tower.

"So are you serious about the Russian? You're kaput?"

Lidia didn't answer, placing her gloved hands over her friend's bare ones.

"Well, do you mind if I give him a whirl?"

"Sure."

Anita pulled her hands away. "I don't get it. It doesn't get much better than Ivan."

"So people tell me."

"It's true. He's hot. And after college, he'll inherit his dad's business. You'll be all set up."

Lidia couldn't get past the laundry she'd be expected to do, how it would stink of raw flesh, crushed bones, wet animal hair. She imagined water in a white bathtub going pink the way it had the time her father had gashed his hand—a clean cut that wouldn't stop bleeding—on the saw blade he'd been using to trim the lilac bush at the old farmhouse. She missed that farmhouse still, even though it had been more than six years since her mother had remarried and they'd moved into town.

Once, not long after he had left, Lidia had asked her mother for her father's contact information. "Don't you think he'd have called you by now if he'd cared?" her mother had said and then, frowning, had flipped through the back pages of a beaten-up address book and written down a number. Lidia called several times before anyone answered. When someone finally did, a voice she didn't recognize—a woman's voice—told her Marius wasn't home, whom should she say had called? Lidia hung up. She never tried the number again.

"Blood stains are impossible to remove," she said now.

"You'll be rich enough to send them to the cleaners."

She handed Anita a piece of the fried dough, still dripping with hot oil. "I'm rich already. See?" She revealed the wad of bills stolen from her stepfather before stuffing them back into her coat pocket. "It's on me today." She asked the man behind the counter for two cups of mulled wine. He took a long look at her but eventually ladled them out.

"What's with you today?"

"Nothing. It's just . . . What if I have other plans that don't include Ivan?"

Behind the stand they found some empty buckets to sit on while they ate. Lidia devoured her *langoș*, barely tasting it, taking bite after bite without swallowing, as if she feared someone might snatch it from her hands before she'd had a chance to finish. She hadn't been aware of her hunger and felt mildly embarrassed when, wiping her mouth, she saw Anita had hardly begun to eat.

Anita grinned. "It's like my mom says. Hollow legs. How else to explain you're not as big as an ox?"

"So which leg do you think it is?"

Anita gently rapped her raw knuckles on each of her friend's thighs. "The left. Most definitely the left."

Lidia crumpled up her napkin, tossing it for the frigid wind to pick up and blow away. She wondered how to tell Anita without the whole story sounding unbelievable. *I met a man, the head of a modeling agency, he's promised to take me to France.* She didn't know why she was worried. After all, it had been Anita who'd first given her the magazines from which she'd cut out the pictures that now decorated her bedroom walls. Most of their time together was spent imagining a life beyond this place, a life like the ones they watched endless hours of on television. If she confessed her news to her, Anita was sure to pepper her with questions. When are you leaving? she'd ask. When can I come visit? Will there be a job for me someday?

"What if you were given the chance to live your dreams?"

Anita stopped chewing. "You mean movies, modeling, that stuff?"

Lidia nodded. "What if someone told you you could do it? Would you?"

"It's fun to think about." Anita considered the food in her hand. "I'd miss my mom and dad. Could they go?"

"No, they couldn't *go*. It'd just be you alone."

"It's hard to think of leaving home."

"But it's your dreams, Anita! You'd travel the world, date movie stars!"

Anita shrugged. "It's not gonna happen anyway so what's the point in talking about it?"

Lidia swished the remaining liquid around in the bottom of her cup and watched the spices settle like tea leaves before swallowing down the last of the wine. A bitter, vinegary taste lingered on her tongue.

The last day of eating *langoș* with Anita.

"Lidia? What's wrong?"

"Nothing." Lidia wiped her nose with the back of her hand and got to her feet. "My mom and sister are probably looking for me now. I better go."

Leaving their mother behind at the market, Lidia and Marianna were on their way to buy sweets when Lidia spied him: the back of the camel-hair coat, the broad shoulders, the heavy wrists. It didn't make sense, his being here, but there was no mistaking him. He was buying a newspaper off the street, the salesman and he sharing a joke, looking at a picture Lidia couldn't see. Gheorghe was lecturing, instructing, his fingers running lines and curves over the paper as if it were a masterpiece and they were debating shade and shadows, brush technique, color pallet, use of light. When he folded the paper backward she saw what they'd been discussing:

the page 10 pinup in the regional newspaper. Lidia stopped on the sidewalk, not knowing what else to do.

"Why are we stopping?" Marianna asked. "Who's that?"

When Gheorghe turned around, the look of surprise was no more than a camera flash on his face before he was tucking the newspaper under his arm and kissing Lidia on her cheeks as if they were old friends who met like this all the time. "What a pleasant surprise."

She felt Marianna's hand wriggle in her own, felt the pressure of her sister's small body against her as she moved closer.

"Who's this?" Gheorghe was grinning stupidly at Marianna.

What are you doing here? Lidia wanted to ask. "This is my sister. Marianna."

"A beauty, just like you."

Lidia could feel both Marianna and Gheorghe's eyes on her but couldn't bring herself to return their gazes. Instead, she focused on the newspapers, silently reading the day's headlines. A fatal, ten-vehicle pile-up on a nearby stretch of highway. The arrests of several county officials after it was uncovered they were taking bribes from the Russian mafia. The impact loss of revenue had had on municipal hospitals.

These, Lidia thought, are bad news. Not *this*, right now. This, she told herself, is nothing, an encounter easily explained. She met Gheorghe's eyes. "You stayed—in town, I mean?"

"I was visiting some relatives in the area," he said squinting past her. "Killing two birds."

Marianna began to jiggle at Lidia's side. She was trying to twirl, using her sister's arm as a point of center when she tripped, twisting it around, yanking Lidia so that her arm popped in its socket. "Goddamnit, Marianna! Stop it!"

Marianna blinked at Lidia, wriggling her fingers free from her sister's hold.

"I'm sorry—"

"Don't worry," Gheorghe replied, thinking the apology intended for him. He was tucking his wallet into the inside pocket of his coat and kept his hand there, over his heart, as if making a pledge. "So. I'll see you soon?"

Lidia watched as he dashed across the street, whistling to hail a cab.

The wooden shingle creaked back and forth above Lidia and Marianna's heads, the name of the shop so worn it was impossible to make out any letter except the E, which had been painted more elaborately than the rest, with a tail that swooped down and curled back over on itself. Although she had accepted Lidia's conciliatory hand, Marianna hadn't spoken since Lidia had yelled at her, even as Lidia considered out loud what treats they might buy.

She herself didn't have to decide; she knew already what she wanted to get. She felt for the money inside her pocket, her fingers wrapping around the bills. "How about some of those?" she asked her sister, pointing at the neat row of chocolate-covered cherries.

Marianna exhaled as if she'd been holding her breath for several minutes. "You *can't* get those."

"Why not?"

"They're too much money. Mom will be mad."

But Lidia couldn't leave without an entire velvet box. "We're entitled to something special now and then." She gave her order to the woman behind the counter.

"Who was that man?"

Lidia pretended not to have heard the question, focusing her attention on the chocolates being selected and placed one by one in the box.

"*Lidia*." Marianna tugged at her sleeve. "Who. Was. That. Man?"

"What man?"

"You *know*."

"Gheorghe? Just someone I met at the disco."

Marianna wrinkled up her nose. "He wears too much cologne."

Lidia paid for the cherries and opened the lid in front of her sister. "Here. Take one."

"Why did he say he'll see you soon?"

"Why do you ask so many questions?" She pressed the box on Marianna. "I said take one."

She watched as her sister plucked up a cherry and bit into it, holding the uneaten half up, inspecting its insides while she chewed. Red liquid oozed as slow as tree sap onto her pale thumb. "Well? How is it?"

Marianna swallowed. "Here." She placed the uneaten half back into the box, wiping her hands off on her coat. "I don't want the rest."

"Is something wrong with it?"

"I don't like it."

Lidia laughed irritably. "But it's chocolate. You love chocolate."

"It tastes funny."

"Really?" Lidia popped the uneaten half into her mouth. Cocoa, cherry, a hint of liqueur: it tasted just as she'd imagined it would. "There's nothing wrong with it. Don't be stupid."

Marianna's chin quivered. She played with the buttons on her coat. "Can we go home now?"

Marianna's hair hadn't yet darkened to the rich auburn color of Lidia's but remained strawberry blond, the same as their father's. As she washed it, Lidia hoped it would never change but grow only fairer, something she knew was unlikely but struck her tonight as important.

Marianna sat in the tub between Lidia's legs, both sisters naked, bathing together on Saturday nights something they'd begun doing shortly after their father had left. Whatever had transpired earlier in the day seemed to Lidia to have dissipated and now things were back to normal between them. Using a coffee cup, Lidia poured lukewarm water over Marianna's head and squeezed the last of the shampoo out of the bottle, the sickly apricot scent forcing her to turn her face away as she worked the soap into lather. Marianna's boney arms were clasped around her knees, her back facing her sister. She never fussed—not when suds from the soap ran down over her eyes and lips or when the water was ice cold or when Lidia combed the tangle of damp curls, jerking her sister's head backward, the only way to get through the dense hair.

When Lidia finished, she ran her fingertips down Marianna's knobby spine, watching tiny pricks of goose bumps rise up under her touch. She kissed each white shoulder, licking her lips. She enveloped Marianna with her arms and squeezed until her sister squirmed. Gray soap scum thickened on the surface of the water and milky waves sloshed over the edge of the tub when they moved, making clattering noises against the floor tiles. Dinner smells crept under the door, clinging to the steamy post-bath air.

"Cabbage, again."

Marianna screwed up her face. "I hate cabbage." Lidia watched her rise to her feet, water falling away from her sister's body like thousands of tiny, silvery fish. It was as if she'd just been born.

"Pretty soon we'll both be eating steak and hamburgers every evening for dinner."

Marianna pursed her blue, trembling lips. "Really?"

Lidia didn't answer, instead reaching for a towel, draping it over her sister's shoulders, rubbing the tail end against her hair.

"Bend over so I can wrap this around your head."

Marianna leaned over and stared at her bare feet, wiggling her two big toes. "Did you see his shoes?"

"Whose shoes?"

"That man we saw today. They had metal on the tips."

Lidia covered the towel over the back of Marianna's hanging head and scooped up cloth and hair, twisting it together before tucking the end under. The way Marianna kept mentioning Gheorghe unsettled her. "There." She gave the terrycloth turban a pat before wrapping up her own hair. "Come on. Dinner will be ready soon."

"You're not going out with Ivan tonight?"

The question surprised her. Lidia knew her sister didn't much care for Ivan; he was, in Marianna's eyes, the one responsible for the unfortunate deaths of all those innocent animals heartlessly slaughtered at the butcher's stand. He was also the one who took Lidia to discos when she wasn't allowed to go. But Lidia had sworn her sister to secrecy. "Not tonight."

"Why not?"

"For months you've been begging me not to go and tonight you ask why not?"

"Are you mad at him?"

"No, I'm not mad at him—"

"—What's wrong with him then?"

"Would you *shut up* with the questions already?" Lidia's words reverberated against the walls of the tiny room. Marianna shrunk back.

"I'm sorry." Lidia pulled her sister toward her, pressing her against her chest in the way she'd seen her mother do so many times before. "I'm sorry I said that." Her fingers patted the toweled head. She tried the truth. "Honestly, I just want to spend the night with you."

"What did I do?" Marianna sobbed into her belly.

"You didn't do anything."

"Then why are you mad at me?"

"I'm not mad."

Marianna pulled away from Lidia, tears still streaking her cheeks. She turned and held her two arms up. "Can you put my nightgown on now?"

Sighing, Lidia unfastened the towel wrapped around her sister's head and folded it over the rack on the door. Hair unfurled down Marianna's back in tight, damp springs. She tugged the clothing over her sister's head, helping her when she couldn't get her arms through the narrow sleeves. Then she slipped on her own bathrobe, cinching the belt about her waist. When she reached to hug her sister, Marianna wriggled free.

After dinner, Lidia returned to their room to find Marianna buried under blankets, their bedtime story ritual cut short for the first time she could ever remember.

She waited until her mother and stepfather turned out the lights that leaked from under their bedroom door and then waited two hours more. The warped, bubbling tiles just outside the kitchen that creaked whenever she stepped on them were all it would take to wake someone. It had happened once before, when Lidia had wanted to go to a party her stepfather believed her too young for. She remembered the terror she felt, her hand still gripping the knob of the front door as the figures of him and her mother close behind appeared at the opposite end of the hall. Where the hell do you think you're going, Missus? The following Monday at school Anita's endless chatter about the party had angered Lidia so much she'd snapped at her, telling her to shut her fat mouth, nobody cared about some stupid, high-school party.

Oh! the parties she'd soon attend! She smiled to herself, hugged the manila envelope to her chest as she lay in bed, waiting. There would be so many parties, like the ones she'd seen on television and in the magazines. "Anita's mother lets her spend money on these?" her mother always tut-tutted as she flipped slowly through the slick pages, unable to resist a glimpse herself. "Who wears such clothes?" Lidia could tell by her tone that her mother had been just as awestruck as she was.

The streetlamp outside her window illuminated the room enough so she could make out a few of the pictures on the wall above her head. Women in satin party dresses, holding cocktail glasses, pouting at men who stared at them adoringly. Women who smirked out from the glossy pages at Lidia, as if to ask her: don't you want what I've got? Lidia would have ripped those pictures down from the wall in that moment, shoving them into her mouth, swallowing them whole they looked so delicious, if she'd known it wouldn't have woken up Marianna.

She peeled back her covers, placing her feet flat on the floor. "Marianna? Are you awake?"

No response.

Marianna slept with her back toward Lidia; she needed to get up and stand over her sister in order to see her face. This close, she could make out the rhythmic whistle of her sister's breath, the rising and receding of blankets, which Marianna clasped in fists under her chin. When they were still living with their father, the sisters used to share a bed. Marianna slept so soundlessly that sometimes Lidia would panic, shaking her sister until she sputtered and moaned, complaining: "What is it? What do you want?" She did not know where this fear of her sister dying in her sleep came from. When the impulse gripped her, there was nothing Lidia could do about it; she had to wake Marianna.

"Marianna?" The soles of her feet were already cold as Lidia tiptoed across to her sister's bed. Brushing her sister's still-damp hair with her fingers, she worked hard to resist the impulse now, giving her a half-hearted shake. She knew waking Marianna was too risky. There'd be the usual litany of questions that might be hard to answer and more terrifying, Marianna begging her—persuading her—not to go.

She made a mental note of Marianna, studying the gently upturned nose, the lips pursed but turning down at the corners, the brow furrowing and releasing, as if she were dreaming of an argument or something she found disagreeable. All these details would be captured in Lidia's mind, the last image she would have of her sister for a long while.

From under her own bed she removed a small, packed duffle bag that contained a change of clothes and the remainder of her stepfather's money, and slid the envelope containing the passport and train ticket inside. Her fingers grappled until she found the rest of the chocolates; she placed the box on the desk she and Marianna shared, and on top of it a note she hoped explained everything. Then she picked her shoes up off the floor and slunk out of the bedroom and down the hall.

Even the apartment door, warped, resistant, normally requiring a firm tug or two to get it open, tonight relented, smooth and soundless on its hinges. It's a sign, Lidia thought as she stepped through the opening, even as her throat tightened, closing up, making it difficult for her to breathe.

Song of Sleep

The earth is coated in a fine, crystallized sugar that crackles under Dragoș's feet. In the vague morning light, he picks his way to the outhouse, and after, to the wood stacked under the kitchen window. His fingers numb up so quickly it's difficult to carry in the logs, but he manages somehow, and once inside stokes the fire in the stove. Through the open grate the logs spit red onto his sleeve; he quickly tamps the coal out, cursing the burn mark left in his jacket. He likes to do this for his young wife, to heat up the cottage before she wakes, so that rising from bed will be easier for her to endure.

He peeks through the kitchen door to the single room of the cottage, getting one last look at Lucy before he goes out. She is buried so deeply under the wool blankets and sheep pelt that he can only make out a single strand of orange hair curling out and over the down pillow. This is all he needs to stir him. He wants to run his fingertips through that piece of hair, wrapping it gently over knuckle and skin, and would if he knew it wouldn't wake her. He misses those first few months of their marriage before she'd grown accustomed to her new home and bed and would wake when he did, her eyes struggling to focus in the dark, her lashes catching the illumination of a candle he'd lit. She'd groan, too tired to express her irritation, and roll away from him, her hair streaming across her face like a veil. He'd brush it back, press his palm to her cheek (he was amazed at how hot she'd get, her slender, muscled body a furnace), and kiss her. Only then, she'd offer him a gift: a faint smile with closed eyes, as if she were dreaming of him.

Te iubesc.

Her dry lips barely moved when she whispered it, the words not directed at him but into the open air, the space between them temporarily filling up.

I love you.

What Dragoș doesn't know is that Lucy has been awake since he got up, and is aware that he is watching her now. Although her arm is squeezed awkwardly under her chest and throbs, she is careful not to move. She wants to savor this moment just before life takes over. Her ears strain for that distinct note from Dragoș, the way he sniffs the air, stands taller, muscles silently gathering themselves up before he turns away from her, stepping through the kitchen and out the front door.

Lucy holds her breath. Still Dragoș does not move. He seems to be taking longer today, leaning into this moment. She opens her eyes but all she sees are the peaks and valleys of blankets. Outside the cows low, a sound like deflated squeezeboxes. She can hear the rooster, who never warbles on cue, flicking stones against the side of the cottage, searching for grubs in the soft spot of earth just outside the window. The world outside is vibrating, ready, but Dragoș remains where he is.

Okay, she thinks, you win. Lucy flexes her ankles, the popping noises they make shattering the silence of the room. She sighs in resignation, and in love. "*Te iubesc, dragă mea.*" Rolling over to face Dragoș, she reaches out a hand, fingers stretched, blindly grappling for him.

"You're awake."

"Come here." The heat from her hold penetrates past frozen skin, muscle, tendon, bone. "No gloves again, huh? One day your fingers will fall off."

"Not if I have you to warm them back up."

She shudders at his sentimentality, though he does not see it. She knows he will forever be this way: naïve, boyish, even when he is fifty, sixty, seventy. It is there when he refuses a hat despite the snow, insists he can lift something three times his weight, drinks milk on an upset stomach and spends the rest of the evening clutching a bucket. I've been taking care of myself since I was six, he tells her, and she doesn't doubt it. But it doesn't mean he's been taking good care.

"Go back to sleep, Luciana. Rest up."

But this: taking care of her. He is very good at this.

Lucy yawns, arches her back. "I am rested up. I slept like a baby last night."

Dragoș knows this is a lie; the past few nights he's been waking to the sound of her sighs. She rolls in bed as if covered in fire ants and yet when he asks her in the morning how she slept, the answer is always the same. *Like a baby*. He doesn't say he's never understood the expression: in reality babies are fitful, inconsistent sleepers. He doesn't tell her that he hears everything. Hears especially in the notes she plays when she practices, her fiddle straining to sound exulted when the hand that leads it is weighed down to earth. Surely this is a happy time, the arrival of her parents.

"Just stay in bed an hour or two longer. You have plenty of time before we need to go to Baia Mare."

"Okay." She rolls away from him. "Just watch out for Goat."

Dragoș chuckles. "I'll do what I can."

He walks back across the room and waits in the doorway, listening until her breath slows and takes on a measured, waltzing rhythm—six-eight time, she told him once, snapping her fingers to demonstrate. One-two-three, four-five-six. This is the song of her sleeping.

Outside, a thin line of orange drags itself across the dark contours of surrounding hills; the cows stand in the front pasture, breathing out puffs of white air, snorting in nervous recognition when they see Dragoș, their leaf-like ears missile scopes, trained on him as he lugs pails of water from the well to their trough. He wasn't born into farming but he may as well have been. After Lucy, it is his favorite thing in the world, growing things. He likes the self-sufficiency of it, producing crops they sell and eat, feeding animals that bring them milk and eggs. Maybe it is because for so long he relied on others of dubious trustworthiness to get by, raised as he was in an orphanage. Now, if there isn't any food to eat, he has only himself to blame.

Dragoș hears Goat's bleating before he sees him round the far side of the barn, entering the yard from outside the fence. There must be a break in it or—more likely—the animal has figured a way to wiggle himself into freedom. Dragoș wouldn't put it past this one. He's seen him flatten his chest against the ground, arch his back like a cat, just to get his teeth around some clover. This morning, Goat paws at the frozen earth and teases the milking cows, sneaking bites of grain from their trough before they give him a bump with their hindquarters. In boredom he sometimes chews at the wooden shutters on the cottage or climbs up onto Dragoș's truck, remaining on the hood even when Dragoș turns it on, lays on the horn, revs the engine. Goat meat's as good as lamb, he sometimes tells Lucy. But she raised the animal from birth, and Dragoș knows her affection runs deep.

Lucy gets out of bed and takes up her post at the kitchen window, a blanket thrown over her shoulders, her feet bare on the cold cement floor. She watches as Dragoș shakes a pail full of feed at the goat, clucking to him, trying to draw him closer. Goat, as she calls him—for she has never met an animal that better embodied his species than this one does—has clearly been in places he shouldn't have been, spots that make him easy prey for wolves. She knows her husband wouldn't mind if this happened: Goat is one of many compromises Dragoș makes for her.

When he is within reach, Dragoș lurches at the animal, catching him by an ear, and begins tugging off the gnarl of burrs matted to his chest. Goat bleats and ducks, attempting to butt his head into Dragoș's ribcage even when he loops his strong arms around the animal's neck, holding him in a headlock, pinching down on his muzzle to get him to stand still. Lucy sees the animal immediately blow all the air out from his lungs, relaxing his neck muscles, but she knows it's a trick and one her husband is falling for. Dragoș smiles, but his sense of victory is short-lived: the animal leaps, wrenches free, strikes out with a sharp hoof, spilling the bucket of feed Dragoș has set down on the half-frozen ground. Laughing, Lucy opens the door and steps outside just in time to see Goat take a swipe at her husband, catching hold of his sweater, trotting off with tufts of gray wool clenched between triumphant teeth.

"Guess we know who won that battle," Lucy calls out.

Dragoș jerks around, surprised to see her there. "You'll catch cold with your feet like that."

"My feet are fine. They're the feet of a farmer."

"I told you to rest." He goes to her then, cups his hands over her ears, bringing his face close to hers. They are nearly the same height.

"There might be a few more things to take care of. I wanted to be prepared."

"Everything's ready. Cosmin's mother is making the sausages and Danica's taking care of the party. All you have to do is pick them up."

"You say that as if it's so simple."

"Are you worried about the trains? We'll leave earlier."

"You have an answer for everything." Lucy immediately regrets saying it; she can see that it has hurt him.

Dragoș looks away, casting his eyes across the pasture where the cows now graze, beyond the barely visible dirt road that marks the edge of their property, across to more fields, dark forest, pointed hills. Clouds stretch and shift above them, covering and then revealing the sun. Its rays hit him full in the face and he squints, raises his hand for shade. "How could they not love it here?" He drops his hand, closes his eyes, and tips his head back, succumbing to the sun.

"Of course they'll love it," Lucy says, her brow wrinkling at the light.

Dragoș had been living in Maramureș for three years, had bought a house and some land, had finally finished his apprenticeship with a neighboring farmer, when he'd begun to hear about Lucy.

Americanca was how people referred to her then. Overnight she popped up in stories at the local bar, the bakery, the weekend market. Foreigners were still a novelty in this part of the country; a foreigner that stayed was something entirely new. A fiddler, a great talent, come to study our music all the way from America. Can you imagine? Of course they mentioned her youth, her beauty. Dragoș imagined a flirty blond with a violin pressed to an ample, suggestive breast, smiling wickedly, charming them with her pretty accent, for it was also known that she'd nearly mastered the Romanian language, spoke like *un român*. Her performance at a funeral for a famous matriarch in the region had become the stuff of folk legend. The music was said to have made men keen and women thump their heavy chests; children sat in a paralyzed, silent trance.

Friends invited Dragoș to a holiday party and then a wedding to hear her play—by then Lucy had been adopted by a local musician and had joined his band. Dragoș declined the invitations. His own arrival to Maramureș had not received such an enthusiastic welcome. He'd heard how they'd referred to him when he'd first arrived from Bucharest. *Țigan*. Gypsy. *Orfanul*. Orphan. When he talked to the villagers the men slipped their trilbies lower over their brows, the women pulled their scarves tighter about their chins. It took a year before they met his eye, called him by name; another before he was invited to a table and a shot of *țuica* at the local bar, to dinner at a neighbors' house on Orthodox Easter. He did not like the ease with which the community seemed to accept *americanca,* and decided to steer clear of her.

But that was all before she appeared on his doorstep, clasping and releasing her hands, fumbling with the space where a fiddle should have otherwise been held, blushing all the way down her neck and beyond the V of her parted blouse. He was surprised that she wasn't blond at all, but a redhead. He'd seen ampler breasts more than once in his lifetime.

"I think it's what back home they'd call a 'set up,'" she said, glancing over her shoulder at a retreating car—the local musician's car—that tooted before a hand shot out the window, waving goodbye. Her accent was clumsy and slow. The skirt and traditional embroidered blouse she wore were too big for her—clearly borrowed—and hid her small frame under folds of heavy, graying cotton. She shifted her weight; her hair blew about her face and got tangled up in the strong wind sweeping across the pastures. "Listen," she said batting at her wild hair. "It's silly, I know. But can we at least make the most of it? My ride isn't coming back for another two hours. The alternative is I sit on your front stoop for all the world to see."

Dragoș stepped back from the doorway. He didn't tell her that it was unlikely anyone would see her rejected and camped out on his front step: her ride had been the first car in weeks besides his own truck to pass the dirt road mottled with potholes and patches of deep mud.

They saw each other several times a week after that; their courtship grew to one, two, three months. He asked after her music but she was coy, saying always there was time for that. Then one afternoon, Lucy brought her fiddle to his cottage. She played for him nearly everything he'd requested; it had turned out she'd been studying Romanian folk music long before her arrival to Romania. A college professor had piqued her interest, she explained, suggesting it for her graduate work. How strange, Dragoș commented, but Lucy only shrugged, lifting her bow to play one more song.

It was something he didn't know but that sounded strangely, comfortingly familiar to him. Perhaps, he thought, it was a rendition of a popular American song, one of the many he'd heard on the radio, although the tune did not sound as light and carefree as others. Lucy kept her eyes fixed on Dragoș throughout the song; it seemed she was measuring his response. There was something underneath the notes, a tidal sensation that pulled him. He moved closer toward her and watched the strings dance. Later he realized he'd never asked her the name of the tune.

Lucy smiled at his applause, blushing like she had that first day, all the way down her chest. With his hand he wanted to follow the stream of color that spread across her but resisted the urge to reach under her blouse. Instead, he asked: "Why are you embarrassed? You perform all the time." Her family had formed a successful band back in the States; Lucy had grown up on stage.

"It's just me," he said.

"I blush *because* it's you."

She rose from her seat and leaned her fiddle against the wall by the kitchen stove. She was wearing the same oversized blouse she'd worn the first time she'd shown up on his doorstep, and when she pulled it up over her head he saw the fine machinery, the mysterious craftsmanship of her.

Her shoulder blades moved smoothly under skin; her back arched and curved with the ease of a willow branch. The bottle of wine Dragoș had set out for the occasion sat neglected, perspiring on the kitchen table. The flames of the lit candles lined along the mantle stretched left, then right. So close to the fire, Lucy's skin took on the hue of freshly churned butter; her hair was a mass of copper wiring. She pulled it off of her back and across her chest before sitting back down beside him.

There was symmetry between her body and the instrument she played, the curved outline of her figure running parallel to the fiddle that gazed with its drooping, S-shaped eyes at the scene unfolding before it. It was this that made Dragoș hesitate, the fiddle with its strange stoicism, its reticence in the hour of something that was to him extraordinary.

Her smile was a crooked, unbalanced line that seemed ready to topple over and fall right off her lips. "What're you *waiting* for?"

Dragoș turned in his seat so he was facing her and placed his hand in the valley of her waist. His hand rose and receded with the slow rhythm of her breathing. He felt in that moment that he was as good as a taut string plucked sharply, vibrating from the inside out, singing a note only the two of them could hear.

Lucy stands outside the international-arrivals gate. Next to her, a mother with two young children waits as if for a photo, the woman's hands resting on the children's shoulders. Airport employees lounge in plastic chairs scattered around the terminal, sipping espressos out of plastic cups, puffing on cigarettes that leave trails of yellow smoke. The last time Lucy saw her parents was nearly two years ago.

She tugs at her oversized sweater, pulling straw from the back of one sleeve. She unfastens her hair, which is much longer than when her parents last saw her, and combs it with her fingers, ties it, starts all over again. A runner in high school, she now looks the part of a Golden Gloves champion. She is ten pounds heavier, much of it muscle gained from the manual labor the farm demands. She rubs her palms together in slow, rhythmic circles, a sound like sandpaper. She thinks of Dragoș waiting for them back home and begins to hum the only song she's ever written. Yesterday morning the tune had come to her as she drifted away from dreams already forgotten. It stayed with her in the car to the train station and then on the train, the thrumming of the wheels on the tracks adding percussion, filling in for the bodhran that she'd always imagined her brother would play.

The song lacks a name; it's been a long time since she's played it. The performances she does now with the band consist primarily of traditional Romanian folk songs, songs people know how to dance to at weddings and parties. Dragoș has preferred to hear her play songs he can sing along to; he does not know he was this particular tune's inspiration.

Her parents couldn't contain their surprise when she'd announced she wanted to do her thesis work in Romania. They'd expected Appalachia, New Orleans; no further east than Scotland. They imagined she'd study the songs they raised her on, the songs that had made them successful bluegrass musicians. But she'd heard a recording in the music library at school and knew she'd found something special. It was at times slow and methodic, but what drew her in most were those songs that ran frantically, pitchy and sharp, desperate, dashing up and down in unexpected ways. She wanted to yelp when she'd heard it but instead pressed the headphones hard against her ears. The notes felt to her as if they were throwing themselves from cliffs; she imagined a hundred little half, quarter, and eighth notes followed by a fat treble clef all falling in a bundle from the stave. She tried to follow the tune with an imaginary fiddle, her fingertips tapping on the wooden desk until the man in the cubicle next to her glared.

She noted the instruments—of course there was a fiddle, and then some sort of horn or clarinet, a hammer dulcimer, an accordion. The constant wobbling and screeching in the background came from a single guitar string pulled between thumb and forefinger, the player adjusting the tension to get those eerie, voice-like noises. This, she later learned, was called a *zongora*.

If her parents were surprised by her academic choices, she refused to consider how they felt when, a year and a half later, she told them she was ending her studies and marrying a local farmer.

Lucy raises a hand to her mouth and chews on the cuticle of her thumb until it begins to bleed. She sticks it inside her mouth, trying to stanch the blood. The loudspeakers crackle and screech unintelligible announcements. The sliding doors fly open; her parents appear. This is how they find Lucy: slouching slightly, sucking on her thumb.

Her mother gives a hug that hurts her spine. Lucy wonders if she notices that her body is larger, giving more than it did before. Her father watches, his mustache twitching, and sets down his guitar so that he can peck her on the cheek, another painful embrace. “You look terrific, Lu,” he says.

They are older, but not as dramatically as Lucy had envisioned. Her mother has cut off her long hair and colored the salt and pepper a brassy shade. She’s also taken to makeup, each of her cheeks displaying small blossoms of color, her blue eyes carefully lined in gray. The overall effect is more Nashville than Appalachia. Her father feels shorter somehow, less demanding a presence than she remembers him to have been all those years they traveled on the road, directing the band, securing motel reservations, haggling free drinks out of bars, playing peacemaker between squabbling members. She studies them for clues, but they give nothing away; they seem joyous, relieved. Only once does she catch her father eyeing her hands—toughened by water and dirt—when he thinks she isn’t looking. She nearly tells him that despite appearances they are still as lithe and agile as ever, perfect fiddler's hands, there's no need to worry. But it's too soon to make excuses for herself, too soon to apologize for the life she's chosen. They will be staying with her and Dragoș for two whole weeks.

Lucy is unable to secure a sleeper car back to Maramureș, even when she attempts to bribe the conductor.

"Your father always sleeps best sitting in his rocker anyway," says her mother.

"We're used to roughing it," her father adds, "Or don't you remember the Roses of Picardy?"

Her mother whoops with laughter, slaps her knee. "Roses of Picardy! Now I forgot about that."

The memory of the dumpy motor lodge they made their home for three nights while touring through Virginia calms Lucy. She recalls the two televisions stacked one on top of the other, both broken; the toilet leak that covered the bathroom floor with water, the beds with mattresses that felt as if they'd had their centers scooped out. She'd only been eleven at the time and liked the way the mattress felt like a giant palm that held her. One evening, local teenagers rented out rooms next door to theirs and threw a party, keeping everyone awake. Eventually her parents and the rest of the band had taken their instruments out into the parking lot to provide the revelers with musical entertainment.

"Yeah, I guess you guys have your share of war stories," concedes Lucy.

Still, she can't shake the feeling she's already failed them as she watches them stare out the window, eventually dozing off in upright positions, their heads slumped in unnatural angles, the two of them hugging their coats to their chins. They are not at all like the people Lucy recalls on stage. These people are vulnerable, small, and she wonders if she is to blame.

For the remainder of the train ride, Lucy sits up and watches through the window as blackness passes by. She imagines what lies beyond it, giving herself over to childhood fantasies, only to discover what was there all along and is revealed when the dawn emerges: fields of hops, the browned and drooping heads of wilted sunflowers, squat cottages, earth. Dragoș.

Dragoș feels the vibrations first, heavy tires on dirt, the vehicle rattling over potholes and rocks, sending tremors out across the pastures to where he squats. He pulls one oversized spud from the cold ground, brushes away the dirt, checks its mottled skin before tossing it into the basket at his side. When he sticks his hands back into the dirt he feels the desperate retreat of earthworms and the vibration again, the ground as loose and flimsy as bed sheets being shaken out. From above, the overcast sky absorbs sound; it takes Dragoș minutes before he finally detects the call of an engine, a useless Dacia cab from the high-pitched buzz of it, that he is certain is now heading in his direction.

He stands up, looks off toward the north. The draft horse, who has been dozing while she waits for Dragoș to finish, springs her head up, suddenly alert, and nickers: she hears the car, too. They watch together as it finally reveals itself on the horizon, a speedy beetle careening in their direction, a wake of dust and rocks shooting up behind them like the tail of a comet.

"Here they come, Flora," Dragoș says, giving the horse a slap on her rear flank, as if this might make up for the wobbling he feels in his gut. The horse swishes her tail in response, snapping at Dragoș as if at a greenhead. He picks up the basket of potatoes, drops it into the wagon, and yanks at the reins, hurrying the horse back to the barn, his mind droning with the sound of the Dacia's engine.

When Dragoș walks into the cottage, he finds the three of them crouched together over the luggage, laughing and talking. Lucy's parents have brought gifts from the States, things they say both Dragoș and Lucy will enjoy. After introductions and stiff-armed hugs, Dragoș watches silently as Lucy rummages through the bags.

"Look!" She is sitting on the floor and holds up a large jar and a smaller, narrow bottle filled with crimson liquid. "This is *unt de arahide*," she awkwardly translates, "peanut butter. And this, well, we don't have a Romanian word for it. It's barbecue sauce."

Dragoș tries the English. "Barbecue sauce."

All three of them smile at him. "That's right," says Lucy.

Dragoș sees how Lucy could only have been sprung from these two people. When she turns in profile she has the same slightly crooked nose as her father, and when someone tells a joke, the same booming laugh. Even though he cannot understand the words, he hears her mother's voice in her, the intonation that draws itself out, turning up at the end, as if she were in a perpetual state of inquiry. These similarities fascinate Dragoș and are also foreign to him; he has never been aware of looking or sounding the same as anyone else in the world.

"*Unt de arahide*, you say? It must be very expensive." He takes the jar from Lucy, opens it; sniffs. "People eat that?"

"You'll like it, you'll see. I can't wait to eat it. You're in for such a treat, *dragă*." She hugs the items to her chest, laughing. "Isn't it so great?" she says to him now. "Isn't it so great they've finally come to visit us?"

Dragoș nods. He cannot recall the last time she seemed so pleased with a gift he'd given her.

The second evening of their visit they gather in the kitchen with friends for a dinner party. Lucy had worried about this event, parties in Maramureș always leaning toward the rowdy side of festive. But when she had raised this concern with Dragoș, he laughed. "Aren't your parents musicians?" he asked.

Now she sees he had a point. Lucy's father has been mixing homebrewed beer with shots of *țuica* made by a neighbor, ignoring her warning that if he empties the shot glass the others will simply refill it. He is gripping Dragoș by the neck playfully and seems more like the man she recalls from the stage than the one she met at the airport days earlier.

"Lulu? Don't Dragoș have a bit of a Cherokee look to him?"

Lucy sees her husband wince behind his public smile.

"Daddy! Go easy on him." She reaches across the table to pull her father's arm away.

Her father smiles apologetically. "You tell your husband I'm sorry," he says, and then: "How do you say it again, sweetheart? Remind me. *Îmi pare rău*, Dragoș . *Îmi pare rău*."

Dragoș nods back, mutters *nici o problemă*. This is the most they've directly spoken to each other in the past forty-eight hours. Already Dragoș and his in-laws have tired of playing charades and when left alone together lapse into long silences until Lucy reappears.

"Cherokee?" asks their friend Danica, picking out the single word she's understood. "Like Dr. Quinn?"

Lucy laughs. "Like Dr. Quinn." She explains to her parents that *Dr. Quinn, Medicine Woman* is a popular show now in Romania. Danica has a satellite dish and they go every Wednesday evening to watch the episodes.

"Dr. Quinn!" laughs Lucy's mother. "That show hasn't been on TV in ages."

"It's a good show," Dragoș says, then shows his mother-in-law the thumbs-up sign. "Good. Tell her, Lucy."

"She knows. We used to watch it when I was a kid." But Dragoș just blinks at her; she's spoken to him in English. "Sorry, *dragă*. I'm not used to playing translator."

He waves away her error and grabs a bottle of wine, moving around the table, refilling glasses.

"It's amazing how well you speak the language, sweetheart," Lucy's mother says. "How it just comes out of you like that. The way you talked to that man at the train station. I was impressed!"

"Thanks, Mama." But her mother hadn't looked impressed so much as disturbed when Lucy attempted to haggle with the conductor, as if the spirit of another person, one she'd feared, had possessed her daughter.

Lucy watches now as her mother fingers the hair at the base of her neck, her eyes lighting on this and that face, the fragments of conversation she cannot understand. She sips at her cherry liqueur, nibbles at homemade sausage. When Danica asks her if she likes Romania, she nods exaggeratedly, widens her eyes, says: "It's delicious. Thank you!" She gestures to Lucy. "How do you say *thank you* again?"

The room has become stuffy with the fire and large crowd, but looking around the table of animated faces, Lucy feels only she has noticed. She opens the window, breathes in the sharp night air. A shadow of something moves across the yard. She hears the dull clop-clop of footsteps, sees small clouds of vapor flash, and there is Goat, his marble eyes reflecting the light of the house. "Oh, you." She sighs, looks behind her. She tries to shout to Dragoș so that she might tell him the animal has escaped from the barn again, but cannot be heard above the din of conversation and laugher.

"Dragoș!" she calls again. "Goat!"

But it is useless. When she reaches out through the open window to grab hold of his halter, Goat stands just an inch shy of her. His lips curl back, revealing yellowed teeth; he nods his head, taunting her. She clucks to him, sweetly beckons, leans farther outside. "Come here, you silly boy." The animal smacks his lips, bored now, and wheels around, trotting off into darkness, his pointed tail the last thing she sees. Now there is nothing outside, just stars and silence.

"Goat?"

But still, silence. Lucy takes one last deep breath, holding the cold air in her lungs before closing the window.

Something Lucy's father has communicated makes everyone at the table guffaw; everyone, that is, except for Dragoș, who appears to have missed it. "What is it? What did he say?" he keeps asking while the others wipe tears from their eyes and belch through chuckles.

Anxiety rises inside her; she yearns to go to her husband, but cannot see her way past the benches and bodies cramped into the tight space to where he stands at the far end of the table, clutching a now-empty wine bottle in his hand.

Lucy's band mates are all in attendance, having been eager to meet her parents. The accordion player has taken out his instrument and begins to play. Another guest offers Lucy's mother his hand. She is a good sport, jumping up, warning him of her two left feet ("Tell him, Lucy! I might be a musician but I can't dance to save my skin!"). They bump about the small space, eventually careening out the door into the other room, knocking into chairs and people on their way out.

The voices grow louder; there are too many bodies. Lucy cannot find a place to sit; she hasn't had a chance to eat or drink anything. Her stomach rumbles in its emptiness, and it seems every second someone is tugging at her sleeve, pointing at her parents, her parents pointing back. *Tell them, Lucy! Tell them!* And then there is Dragoș. She looks once more across the room to catch his eye but he is gone. Where is he?

She jumps when someone squeezes her elbow. "Only me," Dragoș says, eyebrows raised. "I was trying to get your attention."

"*Dragă*."

She clutches his hand and he laughs, jokingly rubbing her palm against his pant leg as if to wipe away sweat before lacing his fingers through her own. "Are you alright? Do you want me to open the door? It *is* getting hot in here."

Lucy shakes her head even though she can feel a slow rivulet of sweat running down her spine.

Lucy's mother reappears with her dance partner. They pretend to still be dancing but then her mother winks at her father and with the final spin reveals the arm that has been hidden behind her partner's back: she is carrying Lucy's fiddle. Their friends roar with appreciation and enthusiasm, slap their hands hard on the table, making plates and flatware jump, sloshing glasses of beer.

"Bravo!" Dragoș says. "Show your parents what you've learned."

Her mother holds the fiddle over her forearm as if she were a waiter presenting her with a bottle of Dom Pérignon.

"Maybe later, Mom," Lucy says and turning to Dragoș, "I'm tired. How about later, when things are"—she casts a glance around the room, shouts above the conversations and laughter—"calmer."

"Now's a perfect time." He takes the fiddle from her mother's hands and they bow to each other. Dragoș appeals to their friends, waving his hands to get their attention. "I was telling *soția mea* that now is the perfect time for a song, no?" Once more, pounding fists, unanimous agreement.

"Are you playing?" her father asks. "I'll get my guitar."

Lucy gives Dragoș a look but he grins after her father. "See: he wants to hear."

"Okay," she says to Dragoș, "but not without an accompanist," and gestures to Danica, who is always eager to sing.

They perform one and then another *cîntec de pahar*, drinking songs, the men banging their beer steins, slapping their hands on the table in messy rhythm. Then comes a popular *doina*, a mix between blues and lullaby that quickly tames those same boisterous, drunken men, who now burble tears when they hear Danica's voice, one of them begging her to put him to bed later. While they play and sing, Lucy is aware of her parents, looking for clues in their flushed cheeks, the way they clasp each other's hands. They applaud with everyone else but seem restrained, polite almost; her father hasn't yet reached for his guitar. Dragoș stands by the mantel, smiling at her but squeezing yet another bottle of wine by its sickly neck so that she can imagine him shattering it, splintering glass flying across the room.

Cosmin—the leader of the band in which Lucy plays—eventually jumps up from the bench and picks up his *zongora*, resting the body of the guitar-shaped instrument on his knee, plucking at the three strings as if he might pull them right off. Now a trio, they launch into a series of Transylvanian tunes that make the others whoop; three women stand up and clasp their hands on each other's shoulders, forming a tight circle, and bob up and down, giggling and bumping off the walls and chairs and musicians. Dragoș sings along between generous swigs from the wine bottle; the Bob Dylan of Maramureș is what she jokingly calls him although he has only a vague notion of who the singer is.

Her father watches Cosmin closely, the sight of this new instrument transfixing him; he grabs up his guitar and now they are four as he follows Cosmin. Lucy closes her eyes, her body settling into the music. She's regained her confidence; she feels the notes inside fluttering against her ribcage, a thousand songbirds trying to escape. She raises the voice of her fiddle above everyone else—she's decided to open up, let them loose—and cues the others to follow her. They oblige; she feels them leaning in toward her, their voices deferring to the fiddle's. Out of Danica's vocal harmonies, the *zongora*, and her father's guitar rises the singular pitch of her mother's song: she sings opposite Lucy, trading riffs with the fiddle, providing melody that does not need lyrics to sustain its feeling. Her mother's voice is inebriating; it swirls through the cottage, a benevolent tornado of sound, drawing everyone up in its funnel. Lucy has an image then: the three of them on stage, the song and their instruments so perfectly aligned, her father's rhythmic guitar, her mother's voice so engrossing, linked by their blood to Lucy and her fiddle so that Lucy—only fifteen at the time and in a trance—tumbles from the stage, the last sound she hears the gasp of an audience of two thousand, rising up like a cloud of dust.

The windows and floor boards hum; flames lick at the roof of the black iron stove. Out in the barn the animals, woken and now wracked with insomnia, shudder and paw through the straw, digging holes in the dirt floor. Goat gallops in circles around the cottage, bleating wildly, before his legs lift him off, down the dirt road, away. The last of the night clouds flee, and thousands of stars shake loose from their posts, some of them jumping, falling, burning through invisible gases, flaring one final time—the brightest they have ever shone for Lucy—before disappearing forever, no one there to witness them.

Lucy opens her eyes and sees her mother there, hands floating at her sides in the way Lucy remembers them doing whenever she has been taken over by song. Her father bows his head low toward his instrument, the guitar giving him instructions he must be careful to hear, guiding him along in song. She hadn't realized how much she has missed this but now she knows: this longing is a gray disruption in her that she's mistaken for a headache, an oncoming cold, a menstrual cramp.

Later that night, Dragoș lays awake in the makeshift bed they have set up on the kitchen floor. Beside him, Lucy sleeps deeply, dreamlessly, her breath telling him so: One-two-three, four-five-six. Her back is to him, the covers rising and falling, and he places his hand on her hip, feeling its bone through the layers of blankets. He understands now what it means when people say you can be taken over by a spirit.

"Lucy?"

One-two-three, four-five-six. Perhaps it wasn't a spirit at all but something he suspects he doesn't know all that much about.

"*Luciana*?"

His father he cannot remember; he is just a dark stain on the back of his mind. But although it's been over twenty years since he last saw his mother, Dragoș still thinks of her every day, remembers her as she was on the afternoon she left him at the orphanage: his red duffle containing a single change of clothing clenched in one hand, a toy soldier she'd bought for him at the *piața* in the other, her hair braided and collected on her head like a crown. She asked the director if she couldn't make up his bed, ignoring the sniggers of the employees there, and while Dragoș watched, she lingered over it, tucking and untucking the sheets; the corners, she'd said, weren't quite right. She was crying but then so was he; at the time he hadn't understood her tears for what they truly were: she knew she'd never see him again.

Lucy swallows, sighs, her right leg twitches and then is still. *One-two-three, four-five-six.*

His mother had promised to return. That was the plan, she'd explained to him, she'd go to Germany, find his father, and then together they'd come back for Dragoș, start life over. Her voice trembled as she spoke. She gripped his small shoulders so tightly in her hands he'd gritted his teeth with pain, knowing to try and wriggle free would only upset her more. He felt that underlying the information she gave him she was reprimanding him for some mysterious misdeed, something he was anxious to put right.

"*Lucy*," Dragoș whispers louder, fervently.

"What?" The rhythm is broken; the body lying next to him jerks, rigid, alert. "What is it?"

The blackness is suffocating, a blanket thrown over him and pressed to his mouth. He has realized something just then and cannot respond to her.

"Dragoș? What is it? Are you okay?" The hand that lands on his bare thigh is frigid.

He cannot say for certain he has ever known the person behind this voice.

The next morning, still reeling from the night before, Lucy rolls over, lays her head on Dragoș's chest, runs her fingers down the length of his arm.

"All things considered, it went well, don't you think?"

"Sure."

His arm is loose around her shoulders; she burrows into his body, trying to get closer. "I haven't played like that in a while. It felt good."

Dragoș removes his arm from around her, sits up. "I better get the morning started." As he gazes over his shoulder out the window, she sees the dark circles under his eyes, the way his face slumps with exhaustion. She touches his bare shoulder.

"You look tired. Let me take care of the barn this morning."

He shakes his head. "Your parents are visiting, Lucy. This is your time with them." He stands up, stretches, tugs his pants on, smoothes back his hair.

"Okay." She rolls back, hugs a pillow, smiles. She did sleep well last night, the first time in weeks, and is reluctant to sacrifice her position in the bed just yet. Dragoș kisses her forehead, strokes her cheek. When he opens the door cold air rushes in, as if it has been waiting for this opportunity all morning.

"I forgot to tell you," she calls out, suddenly remembering. "Goat got out again last night. Dragoș? Did you hear me?" But he is already gone, the door clicking shut.

During the day, they are visited by curious friends and neighbors; by night there are dinner invitations impossible to refuse. Always Lucy is asked to play, and so too are her parents. People marvel, joke, tell them Why not stay! Play with Lucy! You have nearly a full band right here! Lucy realizes how much she's missed playing with her parents, her father wielding his guitar, challenging her with a spontaneous lick, a friendly sparring with her fiddle; her mother's voice one of her earliest memories, its richness and complexity enveloping her, making her feel protected, safe, understood. Sometimes she gets so wrapped up in the music that she loses herself, forgets where she is: it could be Tennessee, it could be Edinburgh. And then she will see Dragoș's face and smile or bob, a gesture to let him know she is still with him despite the musical fever that fills the room. She can never tell if he has seen her efforts or not; his habit is to sit far from her when she performs so, he says, he can have the best view.

At night after traveling around the countryside they relax, sitting in the main room of the cottage. Her parents lounge on the bed. She and Dragoș sit side by side on the floor, legs sticking out straight in front of them.

"Do you remember," Lucy says on one such evening, "that drummer you guys hired the summer before I left for Julliard? The one Jonathan had recommended?"

"Oh, god," her mother laughs. "Don't remind me. That poor child."

"Why'd Jonathan recommend him to us anyway?" her father asks, holding up his glass of beer to Dragoș—something between men—before taking the first sip.

Dragoș sips his as well, asks Lucy: "What're you talking about?"

Lucy's mother reaches for her husband's glass. "He was his sister's boyfriend, remember? I think they got married. But Lordy, that child hardly knew how to hold a stick, much less keep time."

Lucy puts her hand on Dragoș's thigh. "*Stai puțin, dragă*. One minute." Then to her mother: "I heard they were divorced a year later. Just a few months before you guys dumped Jonathan and hired Eddie as manager. Was it the drummer that did him in?"

"It was more than that," her father says and they all cast knowing looks at each other.

"What? What is it?" Dragoș asks, but Lucy only replies, "Nothing, *dragă*. Just old war stories. Nothing worth translating."

Later, she can't remember when he had actually left the conversation, although she remembers him rising from the floor, stretching, scratching his chest, smiling pleasantly at all three of them, saying *noapte bună, somn ușor*, her parents repeating back, *somn ușor*, Dragoș.

While her parents manage bedtime routines in the outhouse, Lucy checks her watch. Two forty-five. It must have been hours ago that he'd gone to bed; his day will start in just two more. How had she managed to stay up so late? All that beer, she thinks; she normally doesn't drink so much. But she wants to take advantage of every moment spent with her parents. They've barely completed a week of their visit, and already she is thinking about the end of it. She wonders when she will see them again; they haven't spoken of this with each other.

Dragoș had suggested moving to the States once. If it's something you really want, he'd offered. She clasped his hands in hers then, laughing and shaking her head. "But what on earth would you do there?" He pulled away. "They don't have farms in the United States?" Her words had come out all wrong; Dragoș never brought the subject up again.

Lucy pushes the kitchen door slowly, trying to keep it from creaking, and feels for the iron latch, fumbling to lock it into place. Without the fire or a candle to light it, the room is thick with darkness, and she must move about the space using only the mental image she carries in her head, and instinct. She looks to the window but it offers no assistance. There is no light to reflect off of the glass panes; they absorb the blackness like everything else. She undresses, barely able to see her own limbs as she pulls off her sweater and shirt, removes her bra and panties, slips wool socks off of her feet. In the morning she will see that she was closer to the door than she'd thought; her clothes will lie in a heap only a foot from the threshold. She tests her sight, waving a hand in front first at arm's length, then closer until she can make out the shape of her long fingers.

Lucy feels as if she is swimming in a vast lake of India ink. She knows she isn't far and reaches out, feeling for the covers. Finding them, she slips underneath the blankets, searches for her husband's body. Her hand brushes the sheets, the wool blanket, the sheep pelt. Touching Dragoș causes an electric shock, a spark that clicks, flashes, and for a split second lights up a spot on his arm, just above his wrist. He jumps, groans, rolls away from her, muttering something but not waking. She covers her mouth, holding back laughter and surprise, and moves closer to him. But when she moves to touch him again—intentionally this time—it happens once more and then a third time, blue light, sparklers that will not stay. Dragoș moans in his sleep and moves even farther away from her, pulling the covers over himself so that no part of his body is left bare. She settles with spooning him through the layers of blankets, her arm resting on the outside, her hand and fingers going cold.

The next morning, Dragoș stands outside on the threshold of the house, listening to the three of them through the closed front door. They are laughing at the kitchen table, talking in English. He has never heard Lucy speak in English so much before. At the beginning of their courtship she would share words with him, holding up *un păhar, o furculiță, o lingură* when there was a lull in conversation. A glass, she would say, a fork, a spoon. Once, she provided translation services to an Australian couple who had backpacked through the area, negotiating a room rate for them with a neighbor. He had never made an effort to learn English, and she had said she'd never cared. But now he wishes he knew more. Her voice as it forms unfamiliar sounds and incomprehensible words makes him feel as if she is standing on the other side of the pasture, unable or unwilling to walk forward, meet him halfway.

Her parents are nice to him, in the limited way they are able. He sometimes wonders about the way they look at him, the way they look at Lucy, and he senses they are speaking about things Lucy doesn't want him to know about. Sometimes when the three of them speak in English she answers questions in short, clipped words, glancing in his direction. It reminds him of the way Danica tries to have an adult conversation when her children are in the room. The few times he's attempted English with Lucy's parents they squeeze their faces up, as if it causes them great pain to understand him. He finds himself wondering what their motives were in coming to Maramureș and suspects it has little to do with meeting him.

Dragoș squeezes the broom handle, gazes out across the pasture, stiffening for a moment when he thinks he sees something moving. It seems to be munching at grass, moving daintily—could it be? But then it splits in two. Nothing more than birds feasting on something out there. They fly up, batting their wings at each other when a third comes to fight over whatever they've discovered. Goat has been gone for days now. Dragoș believes it might be for good this time, but hasn't yet told Lucy; he doesn't want the visit with her parents to be tainted by unhappy news. Still, he thinks, he should go and take a look.

The door swings suddenly open.

"What're you doing out here?" asks Lucy.

"What does it look like?"

She looks surprised; he normally doesn't speak to her like this. "I was just *ask*ing."

She heads toward the back shed. He watches her from behind, notices that in the week since her parents have been here she's lost a couple of pounds, maybe more. It's no surprise; she's hardly been eating, turning down even Danica's eggplant dip and polenta.

When Lucy returns, she is holding a sweater and some other clothing, jeans maybe, trousers that she no longer needs, her old American wardrobe having been replaced long ago by the utilitarian country attire of the region, Lucy having explained once that she wanted to fit in, not stick out.

"My mother's cold," Lucy says, hugging the clothing to her chest.

"She's free to use my sweater. I've offered it to her before."

Lucy scrapes at the ground with the toe of her shoe. "The wool itches her." She looks back up again in time to catch Dragoș's expression and explains: "She has very sensitive skin."

"I see."

"Dragoș," she begins but seems to catch herself. Her eyes widen, unnaturally bright; it is hard for him to look at her. "Are you going to Săpânța with us?"

"Of course I'm going. Do you not want me to go?"

"No, no. *Dragă*." Lucy sighs and grabs his wrists in her hands. "Of course I want you to come. They're my parents." What she doesn't say—what he wants her to say—is that they are his parents now, too. A Romanian wife, he thinks, would have said so.

"Is something wrong?"

He takes up the broom, starts sweeping. "No. Is something wrong with you?"

Her eyes narrow. Her hands are on her hips. He can feel her watching him, carefully considering her words. "We'll meet you out here," she says and steps back inside.

While Lucy and her parents get ready, Dragoș pretends to keep busy with morning chores and goes off to the barn to hide. The truth is he is ahead on work around the farm, having taken refuge in the care of the animals, the fields, equipment repairs. Anything to keep from being caught alone with them. At times, anger gets the better of him. Why should he be made to feel a stranger in his house, unable to sit by the fire, have a cup of coffee, a glass of beer without worrying about his guests and what they might think of him? Why should he be unable to spend a single moment alone with his wife?

The draft horse follows his movements, waiting for a handout. When nothing comes, she clenches her teeth on the wood of her stall door and arching her neck, sucks in air. Dragoș has applied coats of a repugnant-tasting liquid on the wood to stop the horse, but despite his efforts, she has still worn down the top of the stall with her chewing and cribbing. The sound of her is too much. Dragoș swings around, bangs a bucket against the stall door. "Quit it!"

The horse spooks, her hooves banging against the walls of the stall. Her head jerks high in the air; her eyes are ringed in white. When he takes an apologetic step toward her, the animal shakes her head at him, jumps farther back. Her withers twitch.

"Come now, Flora," he says. But the horse remains where she is, casting a haughty, disappointed look at him.

Only when Dragoș offers a carrot from his pocket does she relax and move toward him. He rubs the flat, wide spot between her eyes, fixing her forelock, which has gotten twisted up in her halter. "I'm sorry, Flora. That's a good girl." The motion of stroking her soothes the two of them; the horse's eyelids droop, her jaw goes slack. Dragoș breathes in the earthy smell of the barn, feels the firmness of the ground beneath him.

He fixes the cap on his head and steps out from the barn into a patch of sunlight. Closing his eyes, he feels it on his face, seeping through his jacket into his chest. The warmth of it calms and reassures him. There's still a week left; things can be turned around. He is smiling when he opens his eyes and sees Lucy and her parents coming toward him. Lucy holds the keys for him to drive, jangling them flirtatiously, her movements jaunty and playful.

He grabs her around the waist, kisses her on the cheek. He is so swept up in the good feeling of this moment that it isn't until they are in the car and on the road that Dragoș finally notices: she is wearing the sweater and jeans she'd taken earlier from the shed.

Though she wants to appear interested and eager, Lucy wishes her parents would stop talking about their latest tour. She doesn't like hearing about the fiddler named Arthur, a person she's never met but who plays in the band with her parents. When they mention his name, she finds herself wondering if he's handsome and tall, but mostly if he's as good a musician as she is.

She remembers as a teenager having crushes on some of the men in the back-up band. There was a drummer, a long-haired guy from California who had hazel eyes and a degree in philosophy from Berkeley. He would entertain Lucy when they traveled between gigs by telling her various Greek myths. The story about Penelope was her favorite; she had a distinct image in her head of the shroud Penelope wove and unraveled each night, waiting for Odysseus to return home, trying to fight off her suitors. Dragoș hadn't finished high school, had never traveled beyond the borders of his small country.

Last night, her parents had asked Lucy if she and Dragoș would ever consider moving back home. "I don't think so," she'd said. "This is our home." But she's always felt that musically speaking, doubt was an A flat, and that was the note she heard when she'd spoken. She knows it is the right answer, the true answer. Still, that A flat had unnerved her. She'd soothed herself with the thought that a night's rest always brought clarity. But even now things still feel out of order, choices like pennies jangling around in her brain.

And then there is Dragoș. Normally so sensitive to the safety of others, on the road to Săpânța he drives erratically, swinging around turns, slamming on the brakes. At one point she catches him glancing in the rearview mirror at her parents after a particularly harsh stop, sees the hint of a sneer playing on his lips. She knows she's in part responsible for his behavior, but she can't think of anything she's done wrong, not really. She reaches out to him and places a hand on his knee, squeezing it, but he does not appear to notice.

The road spread out before them is a narrow black ribbon that cuts the country in half, ending at some distant point Lucy imagines she'll never see. The sun strikes great godlike rays down on the pastures and meadows they roll past, drawing attention to the small angled roof of some cottage, the flat of a lean-to, a cluster of white cubes, a distant village. Up ahead a man leads an ox along the narrow side of the road. Lucy glances at Dragoș, but his eyes stay directly forward. As they pass by she swears she can hear the swish of the animal's tail striking the side of the vehicle.

They pass through a village where a group of men sit on the ground, their backs resting against whitewashed houses, some of them with one knee bent, propping up an arm with a hand that holds quickly burning cigarettes or small cups, shot glasses. A cluster of women carrying burlap sacks over their shoulders stop and turn at the sound of the approaching car. They stare, flick their wrists like shrunken, useless wings, some yelling out "*Băi! Măi!* Give us a ride!" Dragoș beeps, yells out: "Find your own ride!" never breaking speed.

Lucy clutches the handle of the passenger side door. *"Dragoș."*

He glances at her. *"What?"*

"Look there," her father says, trying to lighten the mood, "A *zongora*." He points to a man walking ahead of them, the instrument—without a case to protect it—fastened with bailing twine to his back.

"It'll be ruined," Dragoș says.

Lucy looks at him. "What do you mean?"

"Rain's coming." He gestures to the sky. There are purple clouds on the horizon.

"So *stop*."

Dragoș shrugs, thumbs over his shoulder at the man who is now behind them. He never once slows down. "Too late."

Once in Săpânța they head to the *Cimitirul Vesel*—the Happy Cemetery—to view the headstones painted in scarlet, saffron, violet and royal blue which depict in cartoonish fashion the lives of the deceased. Lucy translates for her parents the silly epithets carved into the headstones, chuckling over them together, while Dragoș lurks several paces behind them. Only when she reads:

Here lies my mother-in-law
Had she lived another year
I would have lied here

does Dragoș snort.

Back in the car, Lucy asks Dragoș if he is okay, if anything is bothering him. "No," he says, looking forward, concentrating on his driving, "Nothing is bothering me." Lucy defers to him when her father asks questions about local history, farming, the weather, but always she is met with shrugs and a mumbled reply. *Nu știu*. I don't know. Furious, she thinks that if he asked her now if she loved him, she'd give him the same hurtful reply. *Nu știu*.

But of course she can see how unfair this would be. Of course she still loves him. And of course, she isn't going anywhere.

They go to the village of Ieud to see the wooden church there, one of the oldest in the region. Dragoș pulls the car onto an unmarked dirt road, the four of them riding in silence until they come upon the church, which is surrounded by a large cluster of pine trees the shape of trumpets. When the priest who still holds services there comes out to show them around, Dragoș is suddenly chatty and animated, asking questions about its history, inspecting the manner in which logs have been laid on top of each other at the corners, noting the mud and stone used to fill in gaps and keep out inclement weather, admiring the icons and frescos of Saint Christopher, Judgment Day. They follow the priest outside, walking a slow circle around the building as he points out to them specific features of the building's construction. Dragoș gestures to Lucy, prompting her to translate for him.

"Tell them," he says, "tell them there is no such church like it in your country."

Lucy blinks at him. "What?"

"Tell them there is no such church like it back home. Not in America."

She laughs.

Dragoș stares at her. "I *said* tell them."

She realizes her parents have stopped talking and are listening to Dragoș. They don't need to understand the language to understand his tone; they are musicians after all.

"I'm not telling them anything," she says, staring back.

The muscles in his jaw pulse, he clenches his fists. "Suit yourself." Dragoș walks back inside the church. Minutes later, when her parents are ready to leave, Lucy must go inside and get him.

She finds him sitting in the front pew, kneeling, his forehead pressed against the knuckles of his hands. When she places her hand on the slope of his back, she feels him bristle.

"Are they ready? I still have work to do before dinner." He stands and without waiting for Lucy's reply, exits the pew from the opposite side. Thunder rattles the dim lights of the church; rain grows in a widening crescendo, soon beating, timpani-like, on the roof.

When they return home the rain still hasn't let up. The clouds darken everything around them, making it feel much later in the day than it is. Dragoș retreats once more to the barn, pitching hay just outside the door into the pasture where several of the cows wait once more. Chickens peck at the dirt around his feet, searching for stray bits of feed. He grabs a handful from the bin in the storage room and lets the feed fall through the spaces between his fingers. The grains form small piles on the ground, the chickens choosing one, hoarding it, pecking at each other for space and sustenance.

The windows from the cottage pour orange light in long sheets out across the yard. The sound of the rain covers up Lucy's footsteps so that Dragoș is surprised to see her when she appears in front of him.

She is still wearing the jeans and light sweater from before; she stretches the sleeves down over her hands, covering them up from the cold. She doesn't say anything at first but instead watches him working. There is a smell, something rising above the earthy, sweet scent of hay, the pungency of the cows. It is crisp, sugary, entirely new.

Dragoș stops working. "Are you wearing perfume?"

"It's my mom's. Do you like it?"

He shrugs and returns back to work, the pitchfork making gentle scratching noises against the hard ground.

"I thought we might talk."

Dragoș keeps pitching hay, moving it from one side of the barn to the other, unable to do anything else, afraid of what she might say if he does.

"Dragoș."

He is certain it's bad news but needs to prolong the moment so that he can remember things the way they are now. It isn't until much later, months later perhaps, that he realizes his efforts had been unnecessary; things had subtly shifted long before that single moment inside the barn.

"Dragoș, please look at me."

He scrapes at the ground until nothing is left, the pitchfork leaving crisscrossed lines in the dirt of the barn floor so that it looks as if it is covered in netting, like a giant trap that will pull from above, scooping him up, dangling him in the air so he cannot break free.

He stabs the prongs of the pitchfork into the floor, leaning heavily on it. Still unable to look at her, he asks: "Are you going to leave?"

"Leave? No. Of course not. Why would you ask such a thing?"

It's not her answer that makes him look at her but a timbre in her voice. It reminds him of something; a song she played for him once.

A wind shakes the flame in the lantern he had hung earlier just inside the door, and the light flickers across Lucy's face, altering her features from one second to the next.

"But you want to leave. With them."

"No." Lucy steps toward him but stops short. "No. I don't know. I don't know what I want." She shivers, pulls the thin sweater tighter around her.

Dragoș removes his jacket, hanging it over her shoulders. "I do."

She furrows her brow. "You do what?"

"Know what I want."

She sighs as if she knows what the answer is going to be. "Oh, yeah? And what do you want?"

The words are easy, the easiest for him to say. "I want you." He can tell his answer has surprised her, and for once in over a week he feels he's said the right thing.

Lucy places her hands against his cheeks and holds them there. They are cold and dry and on one side he can feel the small calluses across the tips of her fingers, the hand that works the neck of her fiddle. He feels, too, a tiny sliver of a spot, a bit colder than the rest of her hand: her wedding band. He remembers then which song it was he'd been reminded of moments earlier.

"Remember that song you played for me? The first time?"

This makes her smile.

"What was it?"

"I never told you?"

"I never asked."

Lucy starts to pull her hands away from Dragoș's cheeks before he catches them in his own, his touch searching out that sliver of cold on her left hand. "It doesn't have a title. I wrote it just a few days before . . . I was inspired."

"I want you," he repeats, waiting for her to respond, but the words seem to have less of an effect on Lucy the second time around.

She presses her thumbs to his lips, runs them over his mouth. "I've got to get back inside," she says finally. "Dinner will be ready soon."

"I'll just be another minute."

He watches her as she walks back to the house, her arms swinging loosely at her sides.

After Lucy has left, Dragoș realizes that the rain has stopped. The sky is taking on a lighter, jaundiced look, like a fading bruise.

He walks out and around the barn, whistling to the cows and horse, calling them in for the night. As he watches the animals lumber toward him he sees once more a pair of turkey vultures on the far side of the pasture and decides to finally take a look.

His boots make messy sucking sounds as he walks through the saturated dirt; mud clings in thick layers to his pants. A dim buzzing has begun to grow in the back of his head, making it difficult for him to walk, messing with his equilibrium. Twice he stumbles, once nearly falling completely, his arms sinking elbow-deep into mud.

The birds fail to take note of his approach until he is nearly upon them. Only then does one of them look up, flapping and squawking at him. Its wingspan shocks him, the sharp feathers spreading gracefully like fingers on a harp. But Dragoș marches forward, clapping at them, shouting, "Get out!" and the birds rage, jump up into the air, their claws pointing down at him before they take off into the sky.

As he approaches the spot where the turkey vultures had been busying themselves, Dragoș prays that his instincts have been wrong. The buzzing is loud now, pressing against his skull. He holds his hands against his cap and squints through the dimming light at the ground in front of him.

Goat is still fully intact, his neck, head, and legs stretched out as if he had chosen this spot to take a nap, but the flesh around the barrel of his body has been torn through and all that remains are his ribs, the haunches too nearly gone, his heart-shaped hipbones having been plucked clean of fat and muscle, glowing white against the black earth. The birds appeared to have been working on what remained of his legs and head; where there had been eyes there are dark holes. His lips are pulled back, revealing teeth that nearly form a grin. There is something peaceful about it.

Tutors

"You're late," Dana says, stepping back from her apartment door to let me pass. As I cross the threshold, she tilts her face toward mine inviting, despite her displeasure, the obligatory cheek-kisses.

I check my watch. "By five minutes."

"*I'm sorry, Dana,* will do just fine."

I roll my eyes, but she doesn't see it. Two hours, three even, I have waited for Dana. Once, when it reached nearly four hours, I concluded it was best I start coming to her. I was, I explained, tired of waiting. "What's the rush?" she asked. "It's not like you've got other things to do." She wasn't wrong on this point, but Dana isn't much different. She has no kids, and it is her family—her brothers and mother—who take care of her, not the other way around. She would be the first person to reject her own impossible standards if ever they were thrust upon her.

I follow her into the kitchen. Dana gestures at a chair and waits for me to sit before seating herself. She will not offer me her beverage of choice, Nescafé and Coke, today. It is her way of punishing me, though truth be told I'm relieved; I only drink the concoction because I have been raised to be unfailingly polite. Living here, I find myself doing many things I otherwise would not out of sheer politesse. I eat blood sausage and gelatin molds, accept movie invitations from twelve-year-olds, wear to school a handmade sweater, a gift from a student's mother, which has uneven sleeves and the head of a smiling horse on it. During training, we volunteers were told that while in Romania we were ambassadors of the United States. I aim to please.

Dana places her reading glasses low on her nose, reaches for a pen. "Shall we begin?" In addition to being a good friend and colleague at the high school where I work, Dana has taken it upon herself to serve as my language tutor. Our friendship disappears from the moment she opens her apartment door; it is as if I become one of the ninth formers that attend her classes. If I am late or fail to do my homework, I am reprimanded. If I speak out of turn it's not inconceivable she'll rap the kitchen table with a ruler. I never speak out of turn. At least not during our tutoring sessions.

"Have you done your exercises?"

Her choice of vocabulary—*exercises* instead of *homework*—makes me think of the aerobics cassette I dug up from my parents' basement before coming here and play every morning to combat the ill effects of the cheese, salami, and bread that have become staples of my diet. I shake dust loose with my stomping and jumping, raining it down onto the kitchen table of my bored, clever neighbor below, a young mother who invites me to coffee from time to time so that she might persuade me to help her with her quest to get to the United States. She does not believe me when I tell her what I have learned from my own immigrant family: Life in America is overrated.

You work until you die there, I say. What I don't tell her is that this is precisely what happened to my grandfather, who recently suffered a fatal heart attack at his fifth and final job as a Walmart greeter.

I love work! says my neighbor. And I've done my time. The world owes me.

The world doesn't owe you anything. I don't say it, but that's what my grandfather would have said had he heard her. For a long time I'd thought it was his way of putting me in my place. Only half in jest, he referred to my sister and me as *spoiled brats* long after we'd disproved the moniker with our own hard work. Lately I've begun to suspect that he was just trying to teach me something—to save me, even—from living a life that might otherwise be filled with disappointment, a lesson in keeping expectations in check.

Dana gives me a pointed look. "You *did* remember to bring your exercises with you?"

"Of course." I pull my notebook from my book bag, slap it open on the table. "I spent an entire hour on them last night."

"There's no A for effort," says Dana. Another of my grandfather's expressions, something she has heard me say to my students at the school, though it is for the most part lost on them: they are graded on a scale of 1 to 10.

While Dana runs red through my homework, I wrap and unwrap the unraveling fringe of my sweater around an index finger, making the tip go blue so that when I touch it I hardly feel the pressure. The numbness soothes, helps me focus on a more direct sensation than the ones I've been experiencing recently. In only a few months my time here will be over, my lovingly combative visits to Dana's apartment abruptly terminated. I will return to a home made unfamiliar by a gaping hole my grandfather had occupied. I give the string an extra jerk before releasing it. The blood rushes back into my veins, feeling returning to my fingertip, a thousand prickling pins bringing water to my eyes.

Eventually Dana sits back, removes her glasses from her face, and rubs her eyes with the heels of her hands. "Only one sentence entirely correct. One out of ten." She frowns at me in a way that is both disapproving and unsurprised, an expression that makes me want to laugh and cry all at once; it reminds me so much of my grandfather.

The world doesn't owe you anything. It has never been truer than in this place.

For the record, Dana is not mean, unkind, or unfeeling. She is simply Romanian. This is, of course, my misrepresentation of a diverse population, what serves, to my mind, as a survival skill. Stereotypes exist for a reason. That's another thing my grandfather used to say. One of his favorite pastimes was telling inappropriate jokes about Jews, the Irish, and Italians, among others. He said he'd earned the right after all the prejudice he'd endured, but growing up I don't think I ever heard a single joke about Romanians. Once, when I had corrected him for using the word oriental in reference to a Chinese coworker, he'd said political correctness oughta be lanced like the boil on society it is.

My grandfather would feel vindicated to know I have lanced many a proverbial boil here. Since the things my grandfather had told me about this place appear not to have held up over time, it is all I can do to make sense of the world in which I find myself. I seek repetition, collecting it like control group data for some cross-cultural experiment. It reminds me of something my mother once said about marriage, how she got through the first year (and the subsequent twenty-five) by counting the number of times my father might say and do the same thing (or *not* say and *not* do the same thing) over and over again. In this way, she said, she learned him. So: I am learning Romanians.

I have only myself to blame. I overlooked the fact that my grandfather was barely a toddler when his parents decided to leave Romania, so much of what he told me in the months preceding my arrival here were his memories of his parents' memories. The information he gave me changed depending on the weather or his mood, the day of the week, the time of day. He said his family fled because of the war, but he was always vague about *which* war exactly. On other occasions, he said it was ethnic discrimination, but his family wasn't ethnically German or Roma, Jewish or Hungarian. At still other times, usually after we'd had some heated political debate, he'd say they left because of communism.

All these contradictions infuriated me. *How could you not know for sure?* I once exclaimed. *Didn't you ask questions?*

Of course! He boomed, then softer: *Sometimes.* He shrugged. *Not always. My parents didn't like to talk about it.*

You know, he said later, *you don't realize this because you're young. But as you get older, it's hard to remember things, exactly.*

Not because of age, mind you—he shook his finger—*but because the more you live, the more there is to remember.*

Now, thinking about what I hold in my mind about my grandfather, I'm far more sympathetic. He was widowed around the time that I turned two; I grew up with him in our home and had always taken for granted that one day all my questions, not only about his life but about him as a person, would be answered. The maddening and sobering fact of this is overshadowed by a much more painful realization: Already I am finding it hard to recall the tenor of his voice, the line of his jaw.

While it's true that what my grandfather shared with me never added up, it's true what he said. It wasn't an aging mind that created his confusion. It was just that he had been trying to remember the truth in things that had only ever been part of his imagination. And imagination, like memory or love, is a slippery, elusive thing.

There is, however, one detail about Romania I desperately wish my grandfather had gotten right: the name of the town where he said our family was from. He'd even written it down on the back of a receipt I folded up in my wallet and have carried with me for the past two years. I'd be willing to bet my life on it, he'd said as he wrote the name down. Now I wonder if maybe he did just that and lost.

As hard as I've tried, the place cannot be found. Whenever I ask, people assume I've confused it with a similarly sounding village. *Perhaps it is________?* they say. *Perhaps your grandfather meant________?* The names ring a familiar note but don't strike the exact chord. And now I will never know for sure which place here *is* our home, for that's how I've come to think of that village he wrote down for me. Our home, my grandfather's and mine.

Dana taps her pen on my notebook. "You understand what's wrong here, yes?"

It is a statement, not a question, intended to release Dana from the responsibilities of teaching. Even though we have barely begun, she is telling me she is in no mood. But then, neither am I.

It isn't that Dana is lazy; she's just tired. We've been working on past conditional for well over a month with no movement forward. If anyone is lazy, it's me. Early on I got to a stage in language acquisition where I could get by, my inaccuracies mattering less and less. This is the privilege of learning a language no one outside the country speaks: no matter how badly, people are pleased you speak it at all. I imagine it is nothing like what my great-grandparents had to endure when they first arrived to the States. In Romania, I can carry on at parties and the school and on the telephone. I have made a small, loyal handful of friends who forgive me my linguistic trespasses. I don't need to read the language all that much, and I certainly don't need to write in it. There is no doubt that I will leave it behind me when I board the plane for home. It will fade in my memory just as Dana's face, the cramped kitchen, the view out the window will, and sooner than I could ever have imagined possible.

I lean over my notebook, reviewing her corrections. "Ohhhhh," I say, slapping my forehead. "Yes. Of course." I don't have a clue what is wrong with my sentences.

"Good," says Dana, offering me her first smile of the afternoon. She rises, ferrets around in the kitchen cupboard, takes a bottle of Coke from the fridge. "Nescafé?"

It seems I have paid sufficient penance.

When I told my grandfather I was going to be a teacher in Romania, I thought he'd be pleased. I thought he'd give me a mason jar and ask me to bring back a handful of dirt from his homeland. I thought he'd tell me to take a photo of the village he'd told me was his place of birth. I imagined doing those things for him, weeping on the threshold of some thatched-roof cottage I'd have arrived at by cart and donkey. I imagined the letters I'd compose about the experience of seeing his childhood home, the emotions I'd feel, the connections to his—and by extension, my—history. How poetic those letters would be!

Even though I'd grown up in the Chicago suburbs and had known no other place than the home in which I had been raised, I always had this nagging discomfort there like a mild but chronic backache that would allow me to be still only for so long before I'd have to get up and pace the rooms, the town, the region. This nagging sent me to Southern California for college. But I found myself missing snow in February, cold days that were excuses to stay inside. Well! I thought. Chicago *really is* home. But when I returned, it was the sun I missed, the ocean. When the teaching gig presented itself, I became convinced that Romania was my authentic home, even though I'd never been there. I thought it would create a layer to my and my grandfather's understanding of one another, an intimacy that hadn't existed before but that we alone would finally share. Like twins, we'd speak some special language only the two of us understood; we'd wink and gesture at each other in knowing ways.

I hadn't realized that maybe my grandfather didn't want that sort of intimacy with me, or with anyone else for that matter. Maybe that is how you get the older you become, the more experiences you have. Your history grows too long and rich and deep for you to muster the stamina it would take to retell it. So you stop revealing your secrets altogether.

When I told him I was going, my grandfather glanced away from the television long enough to suck in his cheeks as if he'd tasted something bitter. *Now why in the hell would you go and do something like that?* he said.

"May we begin?" Dana's words in English are slow, halting. It is always this way; she needs to warm up, even though her English is impeccable. As is her French, her Hungarian, her German, and her Russian.

"Five foreign languages," I once marveled. "When did you find the time to learn five languages?"

"Look around you." She waved a hand. "Is there anything much else to do around here?"

"Of course, we may begin," I say now, taking a wafer cookie from the plate she has set before me. "What would you like to talk about?"

"For starters," she says—another expression mastered—"What did you do today?"

"Let's see," I say. "*For starters.*" I pause. "I called home."

Instinctively, Dana snatches at my hand, but I have anticipated her response and slide it into my lap before she is able.

"How's your mother?" she asks.

"Holding up." I sip at my Nescafé concoction. Each time I glance at her face I must turn away. Why does she do this? She knows I don't want to talk. But it keeps happening, as if I have the memory of a goldfish. I can't stop looking toward, looking away, looking toward, looking away.

Dana waits.

"I went shopping. I cleaned my apartment."

"You know you can tell me," she says.

"I graded papers."

"You know I understand these things. I understand them *very well.*"

I sip some more, even though there's nothing but the remaining sludge of instant coffee left in my cup.

"My father, *draga.*"

"Yes," I say. "Your father." I tap my spoon against the table top, the saucer, anything that will make noise. "We haven't really talked about him much, have we? Tell me about your father."

"It can't be good to keep it inside," she says.

"You would know, wouldn't you?"

Dana blanches, turns as if to rise. "It's not the way we do things here," she says.

"How do you know it's the way we do things in America?"

"It's not how *Americans* do things. It's how *you* do things." So: Dana has been learning me.

It's my turn to reach for her hand. It is limp, but warm. "I'm sorry."

She glances sideways at me, her expression softening. *"Nici o problema, dragă."* Her fingers spring to life, squeeze my own. She leaps up, presses me close. She's quick to forgive me these days.

When she releases me, I say: "I spoke with Lavinia just now." I don't know why I've said it. I know I am walking into a hornet's nest of my own doing, but I don't care. Something about Dana treating me with kid gloves—I'm not interested in being pitied.

Or maybe it's just that I enjoy getting a rise out of her. Maybe I'm still bruised by the accusations of tardiness; I pride myself on my punctuality. Maybe it's because she's asked after my mother, tried to pry out of me feelings I'm not interested in excavating just yet, and it feels like disrespect. Maybe it's because she's reminded me of the burden of guilt I've felt every day, ever since I learned of my grandfather's death. Maybe I'm just feeling a little bit superior.

Dana's cup hangs suspended, just barely touching her lips. "Lavinia who?" she asks, even though she knows who.

I point with my thumb over my shoulder. "Your neighbor. Lavinia. The one outside."

Dana sets her cup down, her eyes glazing over, and gazes through the window. On the sill sit two pigeons, cooing and murmuring to each other. Each time they shift their position their feathers flash pink and green iridescence despite the gray autumn skies that hang over town. One of them stretches out its wings, laying them flat against the cement sill, eyes closed. The other keeps turning and turning like a dial on a game board until it stops, facing us, taking us in. It cocks its head as if listening to our conversation, raps its beak against the glass. It bobs its sleek head, puffs up its chest. Its tail feathers twitch. Shit like egg whites drips onto the sill.

Dana sneers. "Lavinia is *not* my neighbor."

She's right; technically Lavinia is not her neighbor. And it is also true that I would never have referred to the homeless man my grandfather used to give a dollar to each day as my grandfather's neighbor. But Lavinia isn't your average homeless person. There's something about her that I deeply admire. How she lacks caution but isn't blind to danger, a strange sort of worldliness for a girl who cannot be older than twenty. It also doesn't take much to get past the dusting of urban grime and see the small chin, the full lips, the skin brushed with golden, velvety hairs revealed only when the sun strikes her at the right angle. She does not coerce or heckle people into giving her donations but waits Buddha-like for passersby to drop coins into her open palms, her look direct, her smile exuding confidence, as if she knows the money will happen sooner or later. Most days she's right.

Her legs are her vulnerability, giving her away. I have only glimpsed them once during the summer when, while she was adjusting her position on the ground a breeze rustled her gauzy skirt, revealing knees bent in the opposite direction from which they should.

Dana has told me that sometimes to get around, Lavinia walks on all fours *just like a dog.* I'm not sure why Dana expresses such contempt for Lavinia. I know it's not because she's homeless; I've seen Dana offer kindnesses to far less gracious individuals living on the streets of this city. Also, I have overheard their conversations when I wait for Dana on the steps inside her apartment building (I may come to Dana now, but that doesn't mean she'll be there when I arrive). While Lavinia can be coarse and loud, she is always polite to Dana, sending blessings to her family, asking after her day. Dana isn't rude, but she isn't nice either, and after encounters with Lavinia she'll complain of the riffraff (Grandpa, again) invading the neighborhood.

Sometimes I wonder if Dana's beef with Lavinia can be narrowed down to nothing more than limitations. Lavinia reminds Dana of her own, ones she's not proud of but feels, like we all do about those things we like least in ourselves, incapable of overcoming.

"She's offered to read our palms," I say.

Dana shakes a cigarette out of a pack, strikes a match on the side of my chair. "I'm not going to spend money on palm-reading."

"She said she'd do it for free."

"Bah," says Dana, blowing smoke from the corner of her mouth. "And you believed her?"

"She said she's bored today."

"Bored!"

But I know I've piqued Dana's interest. Hand Dana a newspaper, and she immediately opens it to her horoscope. She blames her illnesses on itinerant breezes or her own greed—that extra egg, that double scoop of ice cream she never should have eaten. When we walk down the street she insists that I always accompany her on her right side for fear we might have a falling out if I switch to the left. Of all her superstitions this is the one I like best.

"Actually," I say, "She offered to read your palm. Not mine."

Lavinia doesn't offer her services to everyone, or at least not to me. The one time I asked her to tell me my fortune she refused. When I pushed back, she said unapologetically: "Come back to me when you're older."

Dana and I exchanged baffled expressions.

"Older?" Dana scoffed. "How much older does she need to be?"

Lavinia shrugged. "I don't believe *domnişoara* is prepared to hear her fortune just yet. You have to be *mature* to handle the truths of the future."

"But what about Mihai?" Dana persisted, referring to her youngest brother. "He's not even sixteen yet. Clearly *domnişoara*"—she gestured at me—"is older than sixteen."

"But Mihai," Lavinia said, "is an old soul."

It was what my grandfather used to call my sister. *Emma is an old soul,* he'd say. I could tell that in the eyes of my grandfather it was a good thing to be. *Am I an old soul?* I'd ask. *Not just yet, sugarplum,* he'd say, shaking his head, stroking my long hair. *But you'll get there one of these days.*

"I suppose you're still not old enough," quips Dana, dropping her cigarette into her unfinished cup. It sizzles, puffs its last gasp of smoke—dies.

"Something like that."

"Maybe if she knew—" Dana stops herself, swats at the air, rises to place our cups in the sink. "I just know how old I got. That sort of thing? It makes you old very fast."

I nod. Nothing like someone you love dying on you to make you feel ancient inside. But it's not as if I didn't know the day would come; I just hadn't anticipated the when and where. That I was away when it happened, unable to fly home in time for my grandfather's funeral; that was hard enough. I'd always believed my grandfather stubborn enough to make the decision for himself, and my first reaction to the news wasn't of grief but betrayal. How could he die when he knew I was gone? The where of it, however, overshadowed all else. Wouldn't it have been better, I'd said to my sister one night on the telephone, if he'd died years ago, when he was still working at the printers or the automobile factory? He'd been proud of his work in those places.

"But who's to say he wasn't proud at Walmart?" she argued. "He'd never once complained about it. And he loved the great deals." Every week she said he brought home cases of toilet paper, baked beans. Who was I to say that he hadn't died exactly when and where he'd preferred?

"Well at least one of us can find out what the future has in store for us," I say. "It may as well be you. Are you with me or what?"

"With you?" repeats Dana, turning around. She puts her hands on her hips. "But of course I am *with* you."

The street on which Dana lives is a quiet, residential place with sidewalks that melt into the asphalt, asphalt that is cracked open like oversized sores, revealing dirtied crimson cobblestone and earth underneath. Old apartment buildings mix with still older homes, all of which have gated courtyards shaded by grapevines in the summertime that house chickens and sometimes even a pig. In both warm and cold weather, children dressed in their school uniforms kick deflated soccer balls around, the more observant ones identifying me for the foreigner I am, following me, whispering: *Sprechen Sie Deutsch? Parlez-vous français?* Two of the houses on this street have their own makeshift shops, their inventory a handful of items—a croissant wrapped in cellophane, a bag of sunflower seeds, a cigarette lighter, a dirtied can of warm soda—displayed on a street-level windowsill. Layers of laundry hang on lines fixed to pulleys that screech and moan whenever clothing is brought inside.

It's not the only laundry aired here: people hang out their windows and shout down to passersby in any sort of weather. I've overheard whole conversations—about an impending divorce, an alcoholic father, a lost job, a romantic jilting—conducted this way, no subject too private. Dana says it's the result of the wire-tapping that occurred under communism, the assumption being that your neighbors have heard it all before anyway, so what's the point in hiding it?

I marvel that Lavinia chooses this particular street on which to beg. She's too far away from the markets that might attract more foot traffic and sees the same people every day, relying on their consistent kindness in order to survive. Dana says it's because she's part of a larger ring run by the Russian Mafia; they dump her and a bunch of others like her off at various locations throughout the city at the beginning of the day and round them up in a paddywagon at the end, collecting donations, giving them nothing but table scraps. I've never bought this idea. Lavinia seems too smart to be used. And I like the idea, the humor and mystery, of her choosing this random spot in the city as her nesting ground.

Lavinia greets us. "*Domnișoarele*." When the wind picks up, tumbling candy wrappers and dried leaves in her direction, she leans forward and gives them a graceful flick with the back of her hand. "Lovely day, no?"

"Something like that," mutters Dana, unwilling to be in total agreement. She hesitates in the open entrance of the apartment building, nearly stopping so that I must bump her gently out into the street.

"It is lovely," I say, reaching into my purse and slipping a bill into Lavinia's hand.

She bows her head and says solemnly: "God bless you and keep you always in his gentle and loving care."

"Thank you." I glance at Dana. "Does the offer you made earlier still stand?"

"Of course."

"Perhaps now is not such a good time," says Dana.

"Nonsense! Do I look like I have better things to do?" Lavinia removes the scarf from her hair, shakes it out, lays it open on the ground beside her. Her fingers beckon. "Come. Sit."

Dana obeys.

Lavinia closes her eyes, and together the two women take a deep breath. For several minutes Lavinia strokes Dana's open hand as if it were a plume of peacock feathers or the fur of a Pomeranian. Finally, her eyes fly open and without looking down, she begins to speak.

"Soon, a person who brings you joy will come for a visit."

Lavinia's voice has dropped several octaves. I disguise my laughter in a cough.

"My cousin is coming," Dana says doubtfully.

"You will receive a promotion at work but it will be in title only, not in money."

Dana frowns.

I shrug. "It's better than nothing."

"You will meet someone new. Someone exciting." Now *that's* something.

"Who?" Dana latches onto Lavinia's wrist. "A man?"

Lavinia wrenches her arm away, fumbles: "Um, yes. Yes! A man!"

"When will I meet him?"

Lavinia composes herself, says: "I cannot say when, precisely. But soon. Very, very soon."

Lavinia is no different than my sister and I as girls, playing the fortune-teller game. We'd wrap silk scarves we'd pilfer from a basket on my mother's bedroom dresser around our heads and because our ears weren't yet pierced, hang her oversized gold hoops over them. We'd paint our lips with the most garish lipstick we could find and with eyeliner give ourselves large beauty marks at the corners of our mouths. We'd play when our parents were occupied with other things, but our grandfather was not.

"He will take you far away, out of the country."

"Where to?"

"Maybe Rome."

He was our sole customer, the only person we ever told fortunes to. We'd pass his palm back and forth, trying to one-up each other with more outlandish fortunes. He'd laugh and egg us on, grow very serious, ask probing questions as Dana does now.

"Only Rome?"

"Yes. Definitely Rome."

"But what I mean is: Will he take me to other places?"

It must have been a surreal experience for my grandfather to be told his fortune by two young girls who hadn't yet lived out their own, to be told his fortune when the time he had left for fortunes was swiftly drying up.

"Yes!" cries Lavinia, hopping in her seat. It seems Dana's enthusiasm is rubbing off on her. "He will take you to other places."

"Where?"

"Well . . . to America, of course!"

For a moment the noise seems to be sucked from the street. I realize I'm holding my breath and look to Dana for some indication, but her expression is indecipherable. It strikes me that my grandfather would not find this to be an honest day's work.

Lavinia rushes forth. "You will—"

"I think that's plenty for today." Dana slides her hand away. "Thank you, Lavinia."

I am waiting for *I told you so*. I am waiting for *See what you get with riffraff?* Instead, Dana reaches for the purse I've been holding for her and fishes out a five thousand lei note, winking at me as she does so. She turns to hand it to Lavinia but holds it just beyond her reach, saying: "Now you will read my friend's palm. *Yes?*"

Lavinia hesitates as if she has her professional integrity to consider. Then she gives us a roguish smile. "Of course, *domnişoara*."

I seat myself in front of Lavinia. Her touch is barely a whisper across the skin of my palm. Down the street a dog barks; cars rattle by. The wind suddenly picks up, sending swirls of dust into the air, shaking the laundry over our heads like dozens of flags in a Memorial Day parade.

"You've lost something recently," Lavinia says. Her tone is washed of pretense, so different than the one she'd used moments before. "Lost something of great value to you."

I sense Dana tense up behind me; her shadow hovers. "I thought you told the future," she says to Lavinia, cautioning. "That's the past."

"They're closer than you might think."

The two of them wait for me to weigh in, but for the first time in a long while I feel no sense of obligation.

"So," Lavinia says. "What do you want to know about?"

I follow her gaze down to my hand, study the topography of all those lines and crevices going every which way, crisscrossing and breaking and curving and sprouting still more lines, more paths. The truth is I don't want to know about my future right now. The questions I want answers to Lavinia is ill-equipped to address. But if she could, I would want to know the difference between knowing you'll no longer see someone because they're dead and knowing you'll no longer see someone because you've left them behind. In this way, will leaving Dana be any less a loss than the death of my grandfather?

Dana and I lie a good game to each other. I tell her I'll invite her to the States and come visit her here; she tells me the same. Is the knowledge that the body of Dana still exists on this earth, that she is still walking and talking and breathing, still living out the length of her days—is *that* what makes it different? Is there truly something more final in a funeral?

But then, I didn't attend my grandfather's funeral, I didn't throw dirt onto his casket. So maybe I can think of them all together—the living that are left behind, the dead I'll never see—on some island in the ocean of my memories, some distant country or planet I can get to by stopping and remembering—or better—imagining.

"I don't have any questions," I say. From behind, Dana's hand reaches out, grasps my shoulder. "Just tell me what you see."

Reading Guide

Raised outside of Buffalo, New York, Lenore Myka has published fiction in such journals as the *Massachusetts Review, Iowa Review,* and the *New England Review.* She has won fiction awards from *Cream City Review* and *Booth Journal,* and her work has been listed as notable from *Best American Short Stories* and *Best American Nonrequired Reading.* A graduate of the University of Rochester, the Fletcher School of Law and Diplomacy at Tufts University, and Warren Wilson College's MFA program, she served in the Peace Corps in Romania. She lives in St. Petersburg, Florida. *King of the Gypsies* is her first book.

King of the Gypsies

LENORE MYKA

Interviewed by Zoë Polando

In King of the Gypsies, *you write about how hard it is for your American protagonists to understand or adapt to Romanian culture. As an American yourself, was it difficult for you to write from a Romanian point of view? What was your biggest struggle with this and how did you get into character? As a Peace Corps volunteer, did you experience the out-of-depth feelings that your American protagonists have when trying to work in a completely new culture?*

I think that for anyone writing fiction, it's a challenge to write from the perspective of a character who is vastly different from yourself. But this is also why I write fiction: I want to imagine lives unlike my own. To be honest, I didn't find the experience dramatically different from any other time I write fiction, though at one point I anticipated critics who might say that my representation was inaccurate. When I was really struggling with this, a mentor of mine told me this was just another version of the internal critic and encouraged me to "kick the bastards out of the room." After that sage advice, I just tried to keep in mind what I knew about my friends' lives there and what I had observed and experienced as a Peace Corps volunteer living at essentially the same standard as my colleagues and friends. I tried to be empathic but also true to what I inherently felt about day-to-day living in a post-communist country.

The first year I lived in Romania I definitely experienced out-of-depth feelings. I was young at the time, I didn't have many life experiences and the knowledge that comes with them. But after that first year I felt much more integrated. I spoke the language well, had friends, and felt defensive of Romania. It's a fascinating and beautiful place and deserves more international attention. And the culture shock I experienced moving there paled in comparison to the culture shock I felt upon my return to the United States!

As far as I can remember, I was never taught anything about Eastern European countries in school. Why do you think it is important for Americans to understand the history and current events in countries like Romania?

You mean besides the fact that many Americans are grossly undereducated about the world we're citizens of and should probably know more than we do?

I believe the more we learn and understand other cultures, the closer we are to living in a happier world. Maybe that sounds naïve, but the alternative—the lack of understanding—hasn't gotten us anywhere as far as I can tell. Romania and its Eastern European cousins are becoming part of the European Union, and they'll have an impact on international markets, which have a direct impact on American ones. They're being integrated into a global economy and, as is the case with Ukraine, used as pawns in larger international disputes. The status of countries like Romania will have an impact on American national security and welfare over the long term.

And outside of these pragmatic reasons, Romanian history and culture is singular. Romania has, over millennia, been betwixt and between—a gateway to the West and the East. This means Ottoman and eastern influence as well as western, not to mention the more recent impact of the Ceaușescu regime. There are still arguments about who owns sections of the country. Studying Romanian history and culture might also just teach us about our own—how we identify borders and states, how we decide what belongs to whom, who stays and who leaves.

What titles would you recommend that would give further insight into Romania's history and culture?

When I was a Peace Corps volunteer, there wasn't a lot, at least not in English. In '94 Romania was still newly emerging from having been one of the most impenetrable communist states; little information got out, or in for that matter. As volunteers we read books like *Balkan Ghosts* and *Red Horizons*; books that paint a pretty dark and not always accurate picture of Romania. Because I was intrigued by the challenges surrounding Romania's Roma population, I read Isabel Fonseca's *Bury Me Standing*, which is a wonderful book.

Today, I actually think the best resources for Romanian society and culture aren't history books at all, but the work of artists. Herta Müller, who won the Nobel Prize in Literature not too long ago, is a wonderful novelist. There's also tremendous film coming out by young directors like Cristian Mungiu (*4 Months, 3 Weeks, 2 Days*) and Cristi Puiu (*The Death of Mr. Lazarescu*). Another RPCV (Returned Peace Corps Volunteer), Sean Cotter, is a translator and academic in Dallas and has been translating Romanian poets; of particular note is Liliana Ursu. And there is Bogdan Suceavă, who wrote a magical novel, *Miruna, a Tale*, that I would highly recommend.

Romanian-born writer Andrei Codrescu should also be mentioned here, his book *The Hole in the Flag* most especially.

You write about such difficult topics as prostitution, homelessness, and, orphaned children, in your stories. How do you, as an author confronting such dark subjects, retain hope that there is some good in the world?

I think there is a misconception that because I write about these dark subjects I must be a dark, depressed, hopeless human being. Once when I was on the telephone with my mother she was talking about my story "Palace Girls" and said, "I did wonder: Are you okay, sweetheart?" Of course, I laughed, what else could I do?

There are two separate people inside me: the human being and the writer. And as a writer I am not really interested in happy endings. It is hard, as a writer of literary fiction in particular, to write a happy ending and still have the story resonate on a deeper and more profound level, not to mention have it be unpredictable. I can really only think of a handful of beloved novels that achieve this and only one that was written after the 19th century. How many movies and books end in weddings? But consider what happens after the wedding! That is the really interesting stuff! Rarely do we experience happiness in life that isn't accompanied with some sort of trade-off or complicating factor. Why should this be any different in fiction?

People tend to forget the human experience behind the darkness, which is what I'm really trying to get at in my stories. Maybe this is a result of being desensitized by the news and the abundance of it. Actually, to process news we cannot think of each individual circumstance; it would be too much for us to take on each individual who has suffered during war or famine. I want to consider the individual circumstance, and that's why I did write about some of these darker experiences.

Ultimately my stories are about resilience, and in resilience there is always hope.

A sense of place is an important part of these stories, not just the actual places where the characters are, but the places they instead long for, dream of, idealize from afar, like Stefan, a Romanian boy transplanted to America, who imagines that everything is better back in Romania. How do you understand the relationship between place—real or imaginary—and character?

I don't believe you can have character without place; environment shapes character, and vice-versa. Because so many of these stories have to do with displacement, it seems inevitable to me that the characters would all have an acute sense of their new surroundings and would struggle to figure out where they fit in. In the case of Stefan, his environment is thrust upon him and he fights against it by romanticizing Romania, a place we can assume was no happier for him since he lived in an orphanage there. I think this is a very human response, especially for children, who tend to be victims of their environments. For the adult characters in the book, this relationship is perhaps more convoluted. The character of Gabriela in "National Cherry Blossom Day" must grapple with conflicting desires—wanting to be with her American husband but not wanting to leave her family and homeland behind. And what happens to your sense of home and the stability it seemingly supplies when external forces impose themselves upon it? I explore this question in "Song of Sleep," when Lucy's world is shaken up by the arrival of her parents.

The relationship between character and place is a hot topic for me. Though I grew up outside of Buffalo, NY and it shaped me in significant ways, I never fully felt a part of the community there. Moving away, I idealized it—and occasionally still do. I've also discovered that I've never fully felt a part of any community in which I've lived. So in this way I'm much like my characters, feet forever planted on different shores. I once heard another author say that this forever living outside is necessary in order to be an astute observer of life, and ultimately a writer, and I find some comfort in this idea.

What is the most important impression of Romania that you would like your readers to come away with?

Alas, I think the most important impression I want readers to come away with about Romania cannot be found in my book! I must say that while the book is thematically linked, I don't necessarily think of it as a collection about Romania. There is a little bit of the muse happening in these stories; they are better representative of my creative process more than anything else. While Romania might have started off as the inspiration, what resulted was something very different than I could have ever predicted.

What people—readers and non-readers alike—should know about Romania is that it is a beautiful and fascinating place. It had much to teach me as an American about the generosity and openness of human beings. I had strangers take me in and feed me, give me a place to sleep, and even one time, protect me from danger. I had friends, but also people who treated me like family there. In Romania, I could just knock on people's doors and have them welcome me in. How often does that happen in the United States? And shouldn't it, quite honestly, happen more?

Discussion Questions

1.) *King of the Gypsies* provides a street-level view into post-communist Romanian society. The stories introduce us to a country still reeling from revolution, where homelessness is rampant, prostitution visible, and child abandonment commonplace. What conceptions or misconceptions did you have about Romania going into this book? How did your misconceptions change? And how do you view Romania now?

2.) Woven through these stories is the indomitable character of Irina. We follow her coming-of-age stories through child prostitution, homelessness, and a later return to prostitution. Yet throughout these incredibly difficult experiences, Irina retains her sense of self. Where do you think she finds this resilience?

3.) In *King of the Gypsies*, some American characters feel out of their depth in their quest to help Romanians, whether students or orphans or their own adopted Romanian children. What might be the best training or preparation for Peace Corps volunteers and others who seek to help the people of a country that has gone through significant traumatic events?

4.) *King of the Gypsies* highlights the deep rifts in Romanian society, from the pervasive racism against the Roma people, to the ingrained sexism that defines the roles of woman. Discuss these rifts and address how Myka's characters either challenge, accept, or subvert them.

5.) Many of Myka's characters are from a younger generation of Romanians, who were only children when communism fell. How do you think their childhood experiences of growing up in adversity, born out of a desire for liberation, will affect Romania's future?